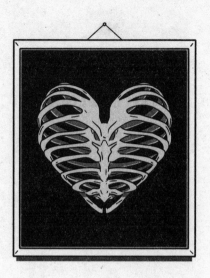

ALSO BY
SAM J. MILLER

DESTROY ALL MONSTERS

The *Art* of Starving

SAM J. MILLER

HARPER TEEN
An Imprint of HarperCollinsPublishers

HarperTeen is an imprint of HarperCollins Publishers.

The Art of Starving
Copyright © 2017 by Sam J. Miller
All rights reserved. Printed in the United States of America.
No part of this book may be used or reproduced in any manner whatsoever
without written permission except in the case of brief quotations embodied
in critical articles and reviews. For information address HarperCollins
Children's Books, a division of HarperCollins Publishers, 195 Broadway,
New York, NY 10007.
www.epicreads.com

Library of Congress Control Number: 2016958596
ISBN 978-0-06-245672-4

Typography by Jenna Stempel
19 20 21 22 23 PC/LSCH 10 9 8 7 6 5 4 3 2 1
❖
First paperback edition, 2019

For Hyman P. Miller, who always knew this would happen,
even if he wouldn't be here to hold it in his hands

Congratulations! You have acquired one human body. This was a poor decision, but it is probably too late for you to do anything about it. Life, alas, has an extremely strict return policy.

Not that I'm some kind of expert or anything, but as an almost-seventeen-year veteran of having a body, I've learned a few basic rules that might save you some of my misery. So I'm writing this Rulebook as a public service. Please note, however, that there are a lot of rules, and some of them are very difficult to follow, and some of them sound crazy, and please don't come crying to me if something terrible happens when you can only follow half of them.

RULE #1

Understand this: your body wants the worst for you. It is a complicated machine built up over billions of years, and it wants only two things—to stay alive and to make more of you. Your body thinks you're still an animal in the jungle, and it wants you to eat ALL the food, and stick your DNA up in anything you can hold down. Lust and hunger will never leave you alone, because your body wants you grotesquely fat and covered in kids.

DAY: 1

TOTAL CALORIES: 3600

Suicidal ideation.

When you say it like that it sounds soft and harmless, like *laissez-faire* or any of the other weird sets of meaningless words they make you memorize in school. The letter from the psychiatrist sounded so calm I had to read it a couple of times before I saw what she was trying to say. She didn't quote me. She didn't tell my mom I said, *Sometimes I think if I killed myself everyone would be a lot better off* or *Five times a week I decide to steal the gun my mom thinks I don't know about and bring it to school and murder tons of people and then myself.*

Instead, the psychiatrist said a lot of scary things in very tame and pleasant language:

Recommend urgent action—

Happy to prescribe—

Facilitate inpatient treatment—

Poor thing. How could she know my mom hides from the mail, with its bills and Notes of Shutdown and FINAL WARNINGS? I didn't want to go see the psychiatrist in the first place, but the school set it up for me because I am evidently an At-Risk Youth. *At risk of what,* I wondered, and then thought, *oh right, everything.* At risk of enough that one or all my teachers filed whatever due-diligence report they're obligated to file on someone who is obviously headed for homicide or suicide, so his or her blood isn't on their hands. And as soon as the psychiatrist's report came, addressed to my mom, I plucked it from the mail pile.

I read it on my walk to school. My mom still thinks I take the bus, but I stopped around the six thousandth time someone called me a faggot and punched me as I walked through the aisle. That kind of thing can really start your day off on the wrong foot. Plus, walking to school makes it easier to get there late, so I'm spared the agony of playing Lord of the Flies while we all stand around outside waiting for the first bell to ring.

The branches were almost entirely bare overhead. Stark and black like skinny fingers clawing at the sky. One crooked tree still had half its leaves. Hunger rumbled in my belly, and I felt like if I reached out hard enough, I could stretch myself taller than any of the trees. Hunger is funny like that.

Anyway. I shredded the letter, let it fall behind me like a trail of breadcrumbs. Lesson learned: Don't tell people you want to kill yourself. Although really I should have known that one already. If high school teaches you nothing else, know this: Never tell anyone anything important.

I slowed down. Savored my last few steps before the hill crested and brought me in sight of the school. Stared up at the trees, and down the garbage-strewn road. Stopped. Breathed. Wondered what would happen if I turned and walked into the woods and never came back. I thought about this a lot. I had plans. I'd hitchhike or ride the rails or follow the river.

Under my bed there was a bag, full of books and hoodies and diet soda from the vending machine behind the ShopRite, and one of these days I would be ready to sling it over my shoulder and run away for real.

But I *wasn't* ready, not yet. As miserable as it made me, I had to go to school. Not because I cared about college or education or a career or any of that pig shit, because anyone who spent five minutes in a Hudson High School classroom would know there was no actual educating happening anywhere in sight. The reason I couldn't kill myself, and I couldn't stop coming to school, was because Maya beat me to it. Because five days ago, my older sister ran away from home. She called the next morning from somewhere on the freeway to assure us she wasn't kidnapped, she was taking a week off ("or whatever") to go to some studio near Providence to record her band's first album, she'd catch up on school when she got back. We shouldn't call the cops. Etc.

She says she's fine. She says nothing happened. But I don't think that's entirely true. I think someone hurt her. And I know who. And I had to keep coming to school because I had to find out what happened, so I could hurt him back.

So I crested the hill and walked down to the squat sprawling one-story building, an ugly heap of aluminum and brick, cursing my abject failure at estimating travel time, for I had arrived too early, and they were there, my peers, my fellow primates, hooting and hollering, pounding chests and grooming each other.

My senses felt like they'd been turned up too high. Maybe it had something to do with skipping breakfast, with the churning engine of my empty stomach generating electricity that danced in my limbs, crackled in my head, but these people stunk. They spoke too loudly.

Their clothes and bags were head-achingly bright. It made every step toward them harder.

And there, at the door, arms folded like the bouncers outside a club in a cop show, they stood. Three of them: Bastien, Tariq, Ott. Hudson High's soccer stars; the shrewd-eyed roosters at the top of our pecking order.

"Pretty," Ott said as one girl approached.

"Not pretty," to the next. Grinning hyena-style at how her face crumpled.

"Pretty."

"Fugly."

"*Thinks* she's pretty."

At this, they cackled. Everyone but Tariq. Tariq, with his perfect stomach and impressive chest and a beard thicker than any high school senior's ever, Tariq of the dimples and broad nose, Tariq who could have stepped out of my computer screen, because he'd fit right in on the sites I spent all night searching when my mom was asleep. Pages packed with boys, beautiful ones—a secret nation to which I would never belong. Tariq, who somehow made me feel fat and scrawny all at once.

Tariq, who saw me and looked away as fast as he could but not fast enough to hide the guilt that soured his face.

We had both been crushed out on Tariq, my big sister and me. He wasn't like the other boys on the soccer team, even if he did spend an awful lot of time with them. He wasn't a bully. He was handsome and smart, and even nice, sometimes.

That's what made him so dangerous. Everybody knows to steer clear of a bully. Maya would never have gone to meet up with Tariq in secret if he had already showed us all he was a brutal thug.

But he seemed . . . human. So she did.

He didn't know that I knew. And, admittedly, I didn't know much. Just that they met up that night. So maybe nothing happened. Maybe he just gave her a ride to Providence, to this recording studio I don't really believe exists, or to where one of her bandmates lived. The fact that he gave her a ride that night wasn't what made me suspicious. What made me suspicious was this: something shifted, in Tariq's body language, after that night. He doesn't look me in the eye anymore. He turns his shoulders away from wherever I am standing.

Like right then, as I approached the front door, where he stood with his best friends, staring at the ground with his perfect lips pressed tight together.

I gnawed my fingernails furiously.

My mom tells me it is a disgusting habit. She tells me to stop. I can't stop.

It hurt, how much I wanted to smash my face against those perfect lips. I wanted it even though I felt pretty sure Tariq did something terrible to my sister. And the wanting got rolled up with the shame and filled me with a sputtering, stupid animal rage. How could it be, that in spite of everything, I still felt lust when I looked at him? Lust, and hate, in equal measure.

That's why I'm writing this Rulebook.

Your body is a treacherous savage thing and it is trying to kill you. I am here to help you win. Together, we are both going to win.

Ott saw me stop and stare daggers at Tariq.

"You want something, Matt?"

That's my name: Matt. I didn't want to tell you, because I hate it.

A matt is something people step on. A matt is full of filth.

I debated lying. Making up something badass or manly, Damien or Colby or Barrett or Bo, something gay-porn-star-y. But honesty is important. I want you to trust me. Because pretty soon I'll be telling you some things you're going to have a very hard time believing.

So, Ott called my name. My whole body twitched with fight-or-flight triggers, but I knew either choice would be disastrous. If I fought, I'd get my ass beat, and if I ran, my limited ability to make Tariq feel uncomfortable, *to apply pressure*, would evaporate.

People were watching. If Tariq hadn't been standing there, I'd have gone about my business, but he was my real audience. Ott didn't matter.

I winced, tasting blood where I bit down too hard on

the cuticle of my ring finger.

In movies and books, all you need to do to stop a bully is to punch them back. Bullies are cowards, the story goes; they can dish out violence, but they can't take it.

This, you should know, if you haven't already found it out the hard way, is bullshit. I tried it, in middle school, and it made things worse. Maybe it'll work for you, if you're stronger than me, or a faster runner, but it earned me a lovely session of puking up blood.

I knew that hitting Ott wouldn't get me anywhere. But I did see something flicker in his eyes, something like fear but not exactly that, something bigger, messier: hate and fear all at once. I took a step closer. I took a deep breath. I *smelled* him.

And don't ask me how, but I knew. I knew from the smell: *I made him nervous. I terrified him. My existence, my gayness, threatened his whole way of understanding the world, what it meant to be the male of the species.*

I'd never understood the word *homophobia* before— people who are homophobic are not afraid of gay people, they just hate them! But in that moment it all made sense. Straight men will insult and assault and beat and kill gay men *because they are terrified*. Because masculinity is the foundation they built their whole worldview on, the set of lies that lets them believe they are inherently better than women, and gay people expose how flimsy

and arbitrary the whole thing is.

I turned to him and said, "No, Ott, I don't want anything. I was just wondering. What about *me*?"

His mouth curled into a snarl. "What *about* you?"

"Which one am I?"

He unfolded his arms with a slowness that revealed his uncertainty. "Which . . . one?"

"Yeah. Am I pretty? Not pretty? I definitely *think* I'm pretty."

A girl giggled. Even Tariq cracked a grin, though he turned his head to hide it from me.

I took another step forward. Ott's lips parted slightly, and I saw muscles tighten in his arms. He was confused and getting angry: he sensed I was humiliating him, but not in any way he could reasonably understand. He was desperate for me to touch him, or explicitly insult him, so he could hurt me. I had planned to tap his chest with one finger when I delivered the finishing line, but that would have made Ott feel justified in a physical response. So why bother.

Seconds ticked away—

"*You* are *Not Pretty*," I told Ott an instant before the first bell rang.

Then I slipped by him and walked inside.

RULE #2

For the student of the Art of Starving, and dear reader, that is what you are, knowledge is the most important weapon. The strongest warrior in the world cannot achieve victory if she does not comprehend with perfect clarity the fight that she's fighting. Here is the most fundamental fact; the most essential rule:

Hunger makes you better. Smarter. Sharper.

I have learned this through practical experimentation.

DAY: 1, CONTINUED . . .

Try it yourself sometime and see. Skip lunch and watch what happens. I'm not talking about sitting in a classroom or a cubicle: go out into the world. Put yourself in challenging situations. Walk a crowded sidewalk, run errands, get in an argument you've been putting off for a while. Your brain, your nose, your eyes are suddenly turned up to eleven. Your skin tingles, newly sensitive. Your muscles thrum with energy. Hunger is your body

working as hard as it can. So all the bullshit gets set aside.

Based on how much I've gone on and on about how hungry I was, you might have gotten the mistaken impression that I'm an impoverished waif, starving from noble poverty. This is not the case. Whatever my mom's money troubles, she keeps the cupboards stocked. We lose cable, sometimes, but never meals. Especially since Maya left. Mom told her closest friends—but not, for some reason, the cops—about Maya's disappearance, and now people show up at our doorstep with all kinds of food, pressing plates of cookies and bowls of pasta salad and baskets of salami into my mom's hands. That won't last forever, though, and I for one am desperate for it to stop. Resisting a fridge full of my mom's friend Shirl's feta kalamata casserole is torture.

No, my hunger has no such dignity. I am that most wretched of creatures, the First World boy who sends his vegetables to the garbage when there are Starving Children in China. Across town there are trailer-park kids who eat three lunches at school because there's no food for them at home, and here I am feeding the trash can.

In my defense, though, I like vegetables. I like *food*, no matter how healthy or unhealthy. I was always an obedient eater, unlike my sister, who, my mother will be the first to tell you, is Picky. She'll say it like that,

too, with a capital letter, like a medical condition or a Deadly Sin.

My sin, my condition, is way worse. I choose not to eat because I am an enormous fat greasy disgusting creature that no one will ever feel attracted to.

Now, you can't see me, but if you could, you'd probably say what everyone else says.

What are you talking about?

You are so skinny!

Here, eat something.

No, really, take my sandwich.

And finally—

Matt, you're crazy.

If you did say one of those things, I'd do what I do with everyone who says one of those things, which is: smile, nod, and silently hate you forever—for you lie.

Thanks to the magic of *Afterschool Specials*, I know that a disconnect between what I see and what others see is a very banal aspect of eating disorders. Here is the thing—what I have is not an eating disorder. I'm pretty sure boys can't even *get* eating disorders. Lord knows there aren't any afterschool specials about it.

My best guess is that a spell has been cast on me, so that everyone else sees me as a scrawny gangly bag full of bones, and I alone see the truth, which is, as I mentioned, that I am an enormous fat greasy disgusting creature.

This whole thing is not easy. It's a fight, most days. Me vs. Food.

Food usually wins. My body, that traitorous thing, makes me cry Uncle. Drags me to the cupboard and makes me frantically scoop peanut butter out of the jar and into my mouth with my finger until I gag on it. But that day, the one that started out with me telling off Ott, I was winning. I was stronger than my hunger.

For once, I was in control of something.

By lunch, I was buzzing, flying, on fire. I watched in horror as boys chewed with their mouths open, spoke with their mouths full, spat flecks of food when they laughed, their voices sounding low and dragged out, like time had slowed down just a little for everyone in the school but me. Everything was going smoothly—

Then lunch fucked it all up.

You probably already know about lunch. High school cafeterias; the stink of scorched taco "meat" and spilled sour milk; hundreds of hormonal mammals heaping abuse on each other and preening for potential mates. If you told me it was a complex sociological experiment or a brutal gladiator-style reality show dreamed up by rich spectators somewhere, I wouldn't be a bit surprised.

I spent fifty cents on a side of tater tots, not intending to eat them.

"Hey, Matt," Ott said, swiveling on his seat. His voice had the high commanding tone that demanded his

fellow barbarians come to attention, that signaled he'd be hurting someone for their benefit and amusement.

I didn't say anything. I picked up a tater tot, dipped it in ketchup, put it back down.

Do your worst, Muggles, I thought. *Sooner or later someone will come along and tell me I'm the Chosen One. And then you can be damn sure I'll punish every one of you who hurt me. Me, and the people I love.*

"Been wondering something."

I turned to look at him. Bastien grinned and leaned forward, the slick, haughty haircut of a filthy rich kid cocked sideways. Tariq stared deep into his phone. Beyond them, dozens of people who don't matter licked their lips or started up text messages and status updates to report the coming fireworks.

"How's Maya? Haven't seen her around in a little while."

An *oooooh* went through the crowd.

"She's fine," I said, and, in a panic, stuffed three tater tots in my mouth.

"I'm really glad," he said. "Because . . . that's not what I heard."

Bastien asked, "What did you hear, Ott?" in the loud, practiced tone of a perpetual accomplice. I hated him more, somehow, than Ott, even though I hated Ott an awful lot.

Ott, at least, was dirt poor, like me, with his mom

working shit-shifts at Wal-Mart and his dad a hog-farm grunt like my mom. They both worked at the same slaughterhouse where Bastien's dad made a cool million a year as a manager, his feet up on a fancy desk all day while she and a couple hundred other grunts swung hammers against the skulls of pigs and used massive knives to tear heavy strips of flesh.

A word, perhaps, will be useful here, on the respective bullying styles of these three. Bullying is an art, too, and their styles say a lot about who they are.

Ott is all physical. Big and dumb and broad-shouldered, he is at his best when he is punching things. There is no finesse to Ott's abuse, no intellect. Thick curly black hair and the pouting lips of Roman busts in our history textbook—he is the thug Caesar of the high school hallways.

Bastien's brutality is all verbal. Emotional abuse is where he excels. As far back as second grade, Bastien was stringing words together to watch people weep. Most of the time those words include *faggot*, or other equivalent snatches of hate speech, but he can be eloquent where eloquence is more effective. Slim-hipped and blond, with the chiseled cheekbones of an underwear model (from hell), Bastien is the kind of smiling psychopath you could very easily imagine becoming president or the villain in a Lifetime original movie.

Tariq's bullying style is more abstract. He watches.

He witnesses. He sees what they do, his friends—he validates them with laughter or silent approval. He never tells them to stop. He is their audience. The one they perform for. He, by the mere fact of his presence, makes whatever they do that much worse.

It goes without saying that I hate them all. What is perhaps less obvious is that I also desire them, desperately. By some cosmic joke, they are all heart-hurtingly beautiful.

Like I said. Nature is a jerk. Your body is a total asshole.

"What did you hear, Ott?" Bastien asked again, rubbing his hands together, leaning forward when Ott went in for the kill.

"I heard she ran off with one of the eight different guys she sleeps with."

I stood up, stepped toward him.

But suddenly, it was gone. Whatever I'd tapped into that morning, when I'd been able to see right to the heart of his trembling cowardice and take him down effortlessly with words, it had vanished.

The tater tots. They stuck like mud in the gears of my body's engine. I sputtered uselessly for five or six seconds that felt like infinity.

I made a noise. Maybe a gasp, maybe a sob. Whatever it was it made people laugh.

"Dude, Ott, chill with that," Tariq muttered, very

deliberately not looking up from his phone, working hard to hide the guilt on his face.

Laughter boomed in the stinking cafeteria as I turned and ran.

RULE #3

Eating slows you down.

This is basic biology. Evolution at work. Animals exert a lot of energy hunting and killing food, and afterward they find a nice place to curl up and doze off. High blood-glucose levels switch off the brain signals for alertness. Blood gets rerouted to the stomach and the intestinal tract to support digestion. Your mind and senses dull.

The diligent student of the Art of Starving will be strong enough to resist both evolution and emotion.

DAY: 1, CONCLUDED

My mother is a magnificent monster. Round and terrifying and able to shout louder than anyone you ever met in your life. When we were little and it got dark out and she called for us to come home for dinner, the echo of it boomed for miles. People made fun of us for it: our mother the foghorn. Muscled-up from a couple decades down at the hog farm, there's probably no one in town

she couldn't pound into submission.

Except, you know, life. Life has got her down for the count, and it's counting slow. The rent, the mice in the walls, the cold, the loneliness, the threat of the slaughterhouse shutting down, they all teamed up on her. And when life couldn't beat her fighting honest: Maya happened. Maya running off might be the death blow. Ever since that, Mom seems to be losing her light.

When I let myself in to the low-ceilinged one-story house we call home, she was passed out on the couch. She was passed out on the couch most days when I came home from school. It was why she still hadn't figured out I was walking home, instead of taking the bus. The air inside was smoky from the woodstove, and the cigarettes she said she'd quit. The television gurgled mindlessly.

"Food in the fridge," she said, when the front door shut behind me. Even in her sleep, the woman doesn't miss a beat.

"Thanks, Mom," I said, and stood over her. She didn't stir. Her hands smelled like blood. The smell never comes out, not all the way, no matter how hard she scrubs. But I like it. It smells like love, to me, and power. Her brow was furrowed, her lips pressed tightly together. Stressed out over something. She doesn't set her burdens down, not even when she's dreaming. I spread a blanket over her, but it was so warm in the

room I took it right off.

And there I was, in the long wide gilded mirror on the opposite wall. Mom had found that ridiculous over-sized thing by the side of the road and single-handedly wrestled it onto her pickup truck, something so big and beautiful it somehow made the rest of our home less shabby. As far back as I could remember, there he was: that boy, in the mirror, happy and laughing, until a couple years back when he started going all Portrait of Dorian Gray on me.

I shrank back from the sight of him now, that boy, that body, stooped and limp-wristed, doomed to never be desired. I envied Dracula, who at least didn't ever have to worry about seeing himself and knowing how gross he looked.

"The power of Christ compels you," I said, making the sign of the cross. My exorcism did not work. Proba-bly because I'm Jewish.

Mom knows. She's got to know I'm gay. Mom knows everything. Hears everything. It's a small town, and she's friends with everyone. I know I'm gossiped about. But until I actually *tell* her, she can convince herself it's untrue. Malicious slander. Small-minded hicks who see a sensitive smart boy and say *faggot*. But to Know, to know for sure, I think, would kill her. Not because she hates gay people. It would kill her because she's spent her whole life worrying about How She Messed

Up Those Kids, and what better proof of her failures as a mother than a son condemned to a miserable life of abuse and loneliness?

Raising us on her own, everybody told her she'd Mess Those Kids Up. *A boy needs a man in his life*, they told her, again and again, like I couldn't hear them, sitting in the shopping cart in the supermarket, building a wall of baked-bean cans. *No telling how he'll turn out otherwise.*

Mom said, *All he needs is love*, every time; *All he needs is me.*

And she was right. But tell that to Hudson's army of backseat-driver moms and men incapable of minding their own business, self-righteous gossips and SUV commandos. All of whom would have the final victory in the moment when I told Mom how damaged I was.

If Maya leaving came damn near breaking her, finding out I'm gay might finish the job.

Knife blades poked and prodded at my stomach. Hunger made me wobble. My stomach never really stopped hurting lately, but by now it was starting to worry me. The three tater tots from lunch hadn't lasted long.

And then I saw it. The photo, stuck to the side of the fridge with a magnet I made in first grade (a crescent moon, made of dried macaroni spray-painted gold). A photo I'd seen a thousand times without truly seeing. Very small, very old; in color but so faded you could barely tell. My mom. My age. Smiling. Skinny.

"Obese" is maybe the wrong word to use to describe my mother now, but it isn't *completely* wrong. How had she gone from super skinny to super . . . not? And did that mean the same metamorphosis was waiting like a genetic time bomb inside of me?

I couldn't say why I noticed it now, when it had been staring me in the face for so long. Something to do with the pain in my stomach and the pleasure it gave me, that small bit of control when Maya's absence made me feel so helpless.

I scurried down the hall, avoiding eye contact with the fridge—but I could still smell tuna fish in the air, smell the lime-juice-and-too-much-mayonnaise mom used, smell the soft challah sliced too thick.

Maya's favorite. The day she left, Mom went out and bought a loaf of challah and made it all into sandwiches, so they'd be ready for her when she got back. Yesterday they were approaching the edge of staleness, so she brought them to work to share with her fellow grunts, and bought new bread, and made new sandwiches, so that when Maya walked in the door her favorite comfort food in the world would be waiting for her.

Even in my room, even with the door shut tight, the tuna smell persisted. I never liked the stuff, but I'd eat it when Maya made me. I always did whatever Maya told me to do.

She was no delicate flower, my sister. When she was

around, no one dared to say a word about me. She cut her hair short at fourteen. She beat up a boy once. She has badass dropout friends. She has metal spikes on her jacket, on bracelets, on collars and boots. Spikes everywhere.

She's had boyfriends, but none of them the assholes who go to our school.

She would have had a dazzling takedown in response to Ott's lunchroom insult, a brilliantly delivered profanity-packed lecture about how boys are allowed to sleep around but girls get punished for feeling desire. And then she'd have punched him in the throat for good measure.

She's in a punk-rock band, plays guitar, sings scary songs. She's her mother's daughter.

That's why I know that whatever Tariq did, it was something terrible. There was no other reason that my sister would be gone, would be this quiet, this long.

Without even thinking about it, my body booted up my computer.

So I want to skip this part, gloss over it and get right to the next day, when my real work began, when my darkest and most horrific fantasies began to really take shape. But what kind of Rulebook would this be, if I left out the ugly parts? I need you to understand what you're up against, when you're dealing with the care and handling of a human body. When you're trying to

master the art of starving.

They were endless, those sixty-or-so seconds while my computer came to life. I spent them looking around my room, shocked to see how small it was, how cluttered, how sad its walls were with their crooked posters that belonged to Ten-Year-Old Matt, Thirteen-Year-Old Matt, Now Matt.

Whales; *The Nightmare Before Christmas*; Venom and Spider-Man grappling; Albert Einstein. I don't even remember how or when *he* got here.

Every night, I sent Maya an email. Sometimes something short about how my day was, sometimes something in-depth and ultra-whiney, throwing a typed temper tantrum because I wanted her to tell me what happened, how I could help, when she'd be coming home.

She rarely wrote back. When she did, it was in single sentences. *Everything's great talk to you soon.*

Bullshit.

I opened my browser.

I always start with video games. Wholesome, childlike pursuits. I do homework. Lurk around social media sites. Look at Maya's Twitter and Facebook to see if she's said anything. Browse fan art sites, look for loving graphic beautifully rendered illustrations of my favorite gay 'ships (Harry/Draco; Zuko/Sokka; Selina Kyle/Harley Quinn). Sometimes I'll go to chat rooms, find like-minded people to talk to. There's a Hudson one,

even, for gay guys in my same small town. Lots of people use these spaces for finding hookup partners, but I don't dare. I know how this really works. They're all faking it, all trying to trick me and any other actual homo, and lure us to a dark place where they can take their long slow painful time murdering us.

And then—somehow—I can never pinpoint when, or how, or figure out what triggers it—*BAM!* My screen is full of naked.

Boys. Men. Men alone, looking moody on beaches or beds, holding themselves lewdly, leering at me, saying *You will never have this; you will never be this.* Men together. Doing unspeakable, marvelous things.

I moaned, out loud, when the first ones shuffled across my screen.

I wish I were strong enough to stop. But really, porn isn't the problem. I only got a hand-me-down computer in my room six months ago, and I was feeling miserable about my hideous self long before that.

Every television commercial, every movie, every photo in every magazine showed me what my body *should* look like. Every walk down the Hudson High halls confirmed I would never be one of those jock boys with the perfect hair and clear skin and jacked stomachs and invincible confidence. I'd never be Bastien, never Ott, or Tariq. But I had this. This this, oh god, *this.*

When it was over, when I looked down at the mess

I had made, when I once again snapped back to reality, terrified that my squeaking chair had made too much noise and awakened my mom and she was standing in the doorway Disappointed In Me, I was almost crying. Because I was so goddamn hungry, because I was breaking my mother's heart, because I was disgusting, because my sister, because my body, because Tariq . . . because life.

I stood up. With Lust momentarily sated, Hunger returned. Black stars bloomed and faded in my peripheral vision. My legs wobbled; the room dimmed.

Finally, I thought. *It's happening. I'm breaking through, escaping the physical world, becoming a ghost, unencumbered by this ugly body.*

I am dying.

But my body was strong. It fought back, held tight to the here and now. Stabbed me in the gut again and again, the stomach pain so sharp this time that I doubled over.

Barely seeing, I stumbled down the hall. Mom had gotten up off the couch and gone to bed at some point. All was darkness. I didn't need light, though. I knew my way in the dark. Ninja-silent, I moved through the house.

When I opened the door, the fridge blinded me. Bright, clean white light. A crinkled landscape of tinfoil-capped casserole pans and cookie tins and deep

glass bowls. So much food, from so many different hands. Food was love. All these people—they loved my mom, loved Maya, and they wanted to help, and the only way they knew how was to make food. I wanted to throw up.

So much food, so many of my favorites, but there was only one thing I wanted. Only one food could make me feel better. The one thing that was irreplaceable.

Sobbing, squatting on the floor before the open refrigerator, I stuffed tuna-fish sandwiches into my face until there were no more.

<u>RULE #4</u>

The warrior well versed in the Art of Starving understands that while the body is the enemy, it is a worthy adversary. It is to be respected and listened to. You are not always on completely different pages. Hunger, you should fight—but fear, you should listen to. Fear is the place where your interests and your body's interests will usually overlap. Fear, you should listen to. Not dying is a goal you both share.

Usually. We'll deal with that later.

DAY: 2

TOTAL CALORIES: 500

The next day, I was sealed up tight inside a straitjacket SCUBA suit made of chewed-up tuna fish.

My edge was blunted. The sandwiches had sealed up my nostrils, caked shut my ears, rubbed Vaseline into my eyes. The dirty high school hallways boxed me in. Also, someone went and filled the halls up with invisible marshmallows, thick billowing clouds of them, and I walked through them in slow motion, sound coming

at me, muffled and stretched out. The trophies in the trophy cases mocked me, laughingly whispering, *This is what normal boys and girls do, they win things, you're only an embarrassment, a source of shame.*

At least my stomach had stopped hurting. My body had won that round and could afford to sit back and gloat.

I thought about puking up all those sandwiches once I saw what I had done, but that's a line I won't cross. If you make yourself puke, you have a problem. Not that I'm above making myself puke—gym class bullying in freshman year of high school made me an expert at the Teacher-I-Don't-Feel-Good-May-I-Go-to-the-Bathroom technique, followed by a precision finger-throat combo, followed by a trip to the nurse's office to get a pass saying I was excused for the period.

Me and the nurse got to be good buddies that way.

But I know myself, and once I start down the road of allowing myself to eat, and then puking it all up, I'm done for. I'll do it at every meal, and I'll be dead in a week.

So when I mess up, I force myself to deal with it.

I am in total control.

See? I told you I don't have an eating disorder.

Due to the tuna incident, the whole day was a slow-motion nightmare. Only dread pierced my walking coma—constant, banal, barely-worth-mentioning dread.

Of the boys outside on the rusty benches before school started, of the boys in the halls, of the boys in my classrooms. The boys I desired; the boys I feared.

In my tuna-befuddled state, I could no longer navigate safely, and at any moment an attack could come. Verbal or physical, there's no real difference. Sticks and stones, etc.—anyone who's ever had a human body knows that's bullshit.

I kind of prefer the physical. The fear of a physical assault is almost worse than the thing itself, so once I've *actually* had my head slammed into a locker or my arm turned into a punching bag, I don't have to worry anymore about whether it'll happen. It's over. And plus, there's something about a verbal assault, even from the crude and inarticulate toad-boys of Hudson High, that echoes for days inside my head. That invades my thoughts in quiet moments. That makes my heart hammer and my brain balk, like, *What is the point of living when I am so clearly less than human?*

Suicidal ideation, folks. Keep moving—nothing to see here.

The day passed at an excruciating pace. I heard every watch tick, felt the massive hands of the ugly 1950s clocks in every single classroom thud through my torpor like distant drumming. My lunch was skim milk, and even that felt so thick and gross. I drank it with tenth-grade biology echoing in my head, *milk is an emulsion of fat globules suspended in a water-based fluid.* Disgusting. So

I threw it away half-full.

By now you are perhaps thinking: wait, Matt, are you really so friendless? Surely you must have *someone*.

And, yes, I do. Or rather, I did. I had Darryl Staffkey. Youngest son of a sprawling trailer-park family down the street from us; fellow comic-book-and-video-game-obsessed nerd. Hopeless as me. We spent every second of every summer together, mostly in my basement, moving between my PlayStation and my laptop. Arguing online, well into the night, over Who Would Win in increasingly absurd fictional character matchups.

And in June, as soon as the school year ended, his father got laid off from the slaughterhouse, and his family packed up and moved to Canajoharie. Which is only an hour and a half away, but might as well be the planet Krypton.

Because Darryl doesn't call; Darryl doesn't write. He doesn't respond to my messages, which are sometimes very long and sometimes very short, beyond the occasional LOL or SMH. Once in a while he'll Like a photo of mine. The bare minimum. He doesn't want to be a *total* jerk who's turned his back on his best friend.

But I see his pictures. I know what's going on. Darryl is different in his new town. He's varsity now. Busy with baseball, parties, beer, girls.

Darryl stopped being, well, him. People do that all the time. I'm not mad at him for abandoning me. More,

I'm mad at him for abandoning himself.

With Darryl gone, I had friends, sort of. I guess you'd call them acquaintances. People, mostly girls, who laugh at my jokes. Who I exchange notes with, in class. Whose jokes I laugh at. For whom I ceased to exist, as soon as we left the building. Which is fine. They ceased to exist for me, too.

Somehow, I made it through the day without a major incident. Donnie Bell punched me in the side in math class; someone else coughed *fairy* behind me in the hall. It barely registered on the Grand Scale of High School Hate. Slowly, dimly, the tuna-fish dullness started to fade as my hunger returned.

Then, late in the afternoon, I heard thunder clapping in the distance, and I knew I was in trouble. Ten minutes later it was a full-on downpour.

Heavy rain meant I couldn't walk home. Which meant the bus. Which meant *waiting* for the bus. Which meant standing in the packed lunchroom, watching buses pull up and depart, waiting thirty or forty minutes for mine to come.

Ott at least did me the favor of not making me wait, sitting and trembling and wondering when the attack would come. As soon as I arrived at the cafeteria he crowed:

"Holy shit, Bastien, did you see that?"

"No, what?"

"Matt was *totally checking out your ass,* dude."

"No way," Bastien gasped, doing his best impression of a scandalized prude. Fear thickened in my stomach.

"For real, dude! Are you going to let him get away with that?"

They let it sink in, let me squirm. Bounced back and forth some pretty standard pieces of macho chest-thumping.

In my mind I was Magneto, reaching out my arms to feel the steel skeleton of the cafeteria, lifting the whole thing into the air, smashing two metal tables together, into Ott, popping him like a pink grape. Or I was Ripley, standing with a machine-gun grenade launcher, staring down the Queen Alien, utterly unafraid.

But really, I *was* afraid. And I stood there, in my fear. Let myself marinate. Felt it ooze through me. Fear cut the last threads of tuna-fish stupor. Fear was good.

I don't know where it came from, the sudden insight that saved me from that moment. My brain cast about blindly for a weapon, any weapon, to use against these boys. And found one.

Hunger, I thought, remembering the almost-supernatural intuition that had helped me insult Ott the morning before.

Focus on the sharp emptiness. Embrace it.

I made eye contact with Ott. I stared. Hunger was an animal, crying out in my gut. It heightened my senses,

and I felt the potential to push it further. I breathed in. I could smell him. Not just the stink of his overapplied deodorant or the reek of his three-days-in-a-row underpants. Him.

He expects me to break, I realized. *To run or to cry.*

If I did nothing, I could unnerve him.

And then, under that, I noticed something else. Something in his eyes that couldn't quite hold contact with mine.

Just like Tariq.

Which led me to Maya. Anger boosted the signal of my hunger, and I took one step closer to him.

"Don't take it personally, Ott," I said. "I'm sure there's somebody out there desperate enough to check out *your* ass."

He punched me. This wasn't like before, when I'd insulted him too intelligently for him to pick up on it right away. This, he knew for the dig that it was. His fist flew out slow, and in the instant before he swung I seemed to see in his face the precise trajectory of the blow.

I could have dodged. That's how sharp the image was. I didn't. Knuckle hit lip, hard, splitting it.

The pain felt right. I laughed.

I tasted blood. I spat it out, aiming right for his shoes. Even my aim was suddenly significantly better. Ott drew back his fist again, and Bastien grabbed it. Held his arm

in place until Ott lowered it.

"Bro," he said, his voice managerial and used to being obeyed. "Let it go."

Throughout it all, Tariq's attention had stayed riveted on his phone. I thought I saw something like a smile cross his face, but whether it was my blood or my insult of Ott that had amused him I couldn't say.

RULE #5

Your body will have weird ways of showing you its hungers. Some are straightforward: food hunger starts in your stomach; sex hunger starts in your groin. Others are spooky, sneaking up on you from strange places. Like my hunger for my father—to know who he is, to meet him, to hear his voice even if it's just on the phone. My hunger for my father starts in my arms.

DAY: 2, CONTINUED . . .

My father is on a lobster boat.

My father, born a Jew, is a Buddhist.

These are the two things I know about him for sure. The things my mother told me. I can infer other things—like, *he is where my bright-red hair comes from,* or *he is not a very good person*—but those two are what I know without a doubt.

The lobster boat thing is what she said when we were little, and we asked why we didn't have a dad. The other thing she told me six months ago, when I found a

copy of *The Dharma Bums* by Jack Kerouac at the bottom of a closet. "That's your father's . . . it's what converted him to Buddhism."

I also found a copy of *The Art of War* by Sun Tzu. Mom didn't know anything about that one.

I know not to ask about him. I know it's a sore subject. I don't know exactly why.

It's one of the many subjects Mom won't talk about, like how she wouldn't let Maya play me any of her punk-rock records because they have curse words. She thinks I'm a child who needs to be protected from the horrors of grown-ups, because she somehow forgot that the world of children has its own horrors. And that the world of teenagers holds the horrors of both.

"Hey, honey," she said, when she came home from work.

"Hey," I said, sitting at the kitchen table, studying the fake wood grain on the dark plastic paneling that covered every surface.

She kissed the top of my head and barreled through to the refrigerator. I smelled the hog blood on her hands. I smelled the cigarettes-and-pig-stink of the slaughterhouse. I shut my eyes and breathed her in, my mom, this towering assassin, massive demon nightmare of every pig in three counties.

The smiley-faced bunny rabbit on her sweater didn't

fool me. She was a terrifying force of nature.

Hunger makes you stronger. Smarter.

It gives you, like, a *power*. You know? An *ability*.

I could see things now. Things I shouldn't be able to. They're dim, like lights through fog, but there. And soon I'd be able to see them clearly.

My mother was good at secrets, but she wouldn't be able to keep them from me for much longer.

"What's happening in your world?" she said, sitting down across from me, her heavy body settling into the chair like a weary king onto the throne.

"Not a whole lot. How was work?"

"Tough," she said. "Quota's up again."

"Do you know something?" I asked, quick before my courage could fail me. "About what happened to Maya? Something she told you but wouldn't tell me?"

Mom sighed, stood up, went to the coffeemaker. Stood there for a little while, wondering maybe whether she had the strength to make a pot. Then she sat back down. "No, honey."

"Why didn't you call the cops? That's what normally happens, on the TV shows, when a teenager runs away. What if . . ." I gulped down air before finishing the terrible, terrifying sentence— "what if she's hurt? What if someone hurt her?"

Mom frowned. "Life's not a TV show. And your sister is going through a really tough patch. Getting the law

involved could hurt her worse. I don't *think* she's doing drugs but, you know, lots of kids experiment. What if the cops catch up to her and end up arresting her? Then she has a record, then she might go to jail. I know too many people who . . ."

She paused, let out a long breath.

"Long as she calls in regular, and I know she's not dead or in a coma, I'm going to give her a chance to figure this out for herself."

"But, why is she in a tough patch? Because of what?" Mom leaned her head back wearily. A sign of defeat, of *stop talking about this*. Before, she'd snap defensively if I implied maybe something terrible could happen to Maya. What did it mean that she wasn't getting angry about it now? Did it mean she was taking the possibility more seriously? Or that she knew something I didn't? I stared at her face, its pattern of lines, its pain, a secret I couldn't unravel, a story in a language I didn't speak. Slowly, wearily, she took her long brown hair out of its ponytail.

I got up and went to the coffeemaker. I didn't quite know what I was doing, but soon it was making a gurgly noise and steam was coming up from it, so I figured I had gotten the gist. Mom must have zoned out or dozed off during this, because when I set a mug of coffee down in front of her, she laughed out loud with surprise.

"Thank you, honey," she said, and grabbed my small

hand with one of her giant ones. Then she grabbed it with the other. And held on.

I looked around the kitchen. It was full of food. Fridge, cabinets, cupboard—all of it calling out to me. But I was stronger now. Strong enough to fight the hunger that made my head hurt. Especially now, when I could sense some kind of breakthrough was coming.

"Your nails," Mom said, holding up my hand, showing the ruined edges of my fingers.

"It's nothing." But I didn't pull my hand away.

After a long time she said, "Dinner'll be ready in a little while," and her voice was different. Shaky. Fragile. I had never noticed anything fragile about my mother before. I kissed her forehead and fled.

I took a tiny secret forbidden sip of her coffee on the way out. It wasn't very good. My next pot would be better.

On the way to my room, I stopped and stood outside Maya's for a little while. Listening.

I used to press my ear to the wall that separated our rooms, trying to hear the secret songs she played on her guitar, the music she wouldn't share with me because it had curse words. The real reason, I knew, was because it was too personal. She always kept her headphones plugged into the amplifier so I couldn't hear anything but the twanging of the struck strings. And now I didn't even hear that.

I opened the door. Went to her desk, pulled out one drawer.

Memories of Maya screaming to *stop spying you little turd* flooded me, and I slammed it shut. My face flushed, and I fled.

I was waiting for myself when I walked into my own room. I stood in the doorway, and also, across from me, I stood in the full-length mirror: eyes huge, chin too big, skin too hideous to describe—a fun-house freak sent to mock me. I opened my window and sat on my floor in front of that mirror. October wind rushed in like a lost dog, curled around my ankles.

My hands gripped the radiator. My arms hurt.

Lobster boat. Men who work lobster boats are strong. Their arms are thick with muscles and hair. Their chests are broad and mighty. They laugh loudly and drink whiskey. They get in fights. They enjoy watching football. My father belongs to that strange and foreign nation, the Country of Men, to which I have no membership.

I draped my jeans over the full-length mirror, then hung a hoodie there, then covered it up with as many clothes as I could add without causing it to collapse.

It had been a long time since I stared out the window and dreamed up elaborate stories starring my father. Watching the road and concentrating all my energy on magically conjuring him up. My knuckles white on the windowsill, my forehead scrunched to high hell with

wanting. Listening for the sound of truck tires on gravel. Praying.

I'm not that desperate stupid kid anymore.

But still.

I've read *The Art of War*. I've taken notes. I've learned a lot about how to fight and win.

I've read *The Dharma Bums* three times. And I've been waiting patiently for the Hudson High School library's lone other book by Jack Kerouac to be returned. *On the Road*, it's called, and that sounds like my father, too.

And I think I might be kind of considering converting—to Buddhism.

RULE #6

Every superhero, every Chosen One, goes through a painful and difficult process of Becoming. On this, all the relevant literature is in agreement. Ask any comic book aficionado, any movie buff. The heroes doubt themselves, even when confronted with irrefutable evidence. They've spent their whole lives listening to weak and powerless people who hate and fear anything that is different, who say that superhuman abilities simply don't exist, and they believe it.

The warrior studying the Art of Starving will pass through a period of pain and confusion. Doubt. Fear. This is normal. You are learning that a different set of rules applies to you.

DAY: 3

TOTAL CALORIES, APPROX.: 500

The walk to school was one thing. Cold morning, no wind—maybe the stink of the slaughterhouse was a little bit worse than normal, but not so bad that I stopped to wonder.

As soon as I stepped foot inside Hudson High, though, I knew something was different.

The place *stunk*. Like: way worse than normal. Mold and rotten meat seemed to fill the lockers; the seats in every classroom stunk of decades of ill-washed ass. Even from across the school I could smell the gym, an inanimate object brought to screaming life by dripping sweat and the grimy festering smell of fear. The cafeteria throbbed with waterlogged broccoli, clots of hamburger meat, dirty hairnets.

First-period math class, I looked around the room in shock, to smell all the stinks these smiling catalog-model boys and girls carried around with them. Boys whose boxer shorts were walking atrocities. Girls reeking of cigarette smoke. I could tell who wore hand-me-downs; how many times they'd been handed down.

A flood of smells everywhere I went, and I felt certain I would drown in it. Between classes, I ran for the bathroom, knowing I was about to puke, but the smell in there was so bad it stopped me at the door. The digested dinners of a hundred sallow boys. The pungent boutique of bottom-grade swamp-rot marijuana.

Stumbling back to class, nose buried in the crook of my elbow, I almost collided with two girls, Regan and Jeanine, best friends since forever, and knew at once that Jeanine had been orally intimate with Regan's boyfriend that very morning.

Fear had me off-balance, made me desperate to know what the hell was going on, frantic for proof that either I was right, or that I was merely going insane. I had to test the validity of what my nose told me was true.

"Oh, hey, Jeanine, didn't see you on the bus this morning."

"No," she said, panic surging through her, panic that had a smell like wet dog, "I got a ride."

"From who?" Regan asked, and that was all I needed to hear. I pretended to get a call on my cell, held it to my ear and said, "Hello?" as I hurried off, wailing inside. In that moment, insanity or delusion would have been so much easier to handle. Was this happening? Was I able to perceive things by . . . smelling them?

"I want this to stop," I whispered out loud.

But no one was listening. No one could help me.

RULE #7

You are your nose.

Smell is the sense most closely associated with memory. It's the most evocative sense—the one that causes your brain to work the hardest. Scientists now believe that the nose can actually distinguish between over a trillion unique odors, making it vastly more sophisticated than any other sense organ.

Every day, you breathe in clouds of unspeakably disgusting stuff. Every single person you pass is surrounded by a floating swamp of grotesque debris—dead skin, fecal flakes, microscopic filth. Your puny human senses keep you blessedly ignorant of these facts. Until you discover you can hone them.

DAY: 3, CONTINUED . . .

Hunger was the answer. It had to be. Hunger had flipped a switch, sent my nose into overdrive.

I skipped class. Went to the library. Ransacked Wikipedia. Learned about the nose, the human sense of smell, how they worked. How they could be controlled.

Kept my nose in my elbow, breathing in my threadbare sweater and the pale flesh beneath. The stink of me was familiar, at least, and unlikely to make me lose my mind. Slowly, painstakingly, I opened myself up. Let myself smell the school beyond. The library at least provided a buffer, the warm calm smell of books, paper, glue, hot computer plastic, cheap copier toner. By the time lunchtime came around, I wasn't ready to risk the cafeteria, but I did have a plan.

Breath held, I sprinted to the boys' locker room. I took hand towels from the laundry bin beside the shower, each one damp with a different boy's sweat.

I went to the side doors where the smokers go, where the alarm is broken, propped it open with the brick strategically left loose in the wall for that purpose. I sat down, outside, gratefully gulping down cold October air. Then I held the first towel to my nose and sniffed.

I smelled cotton and sweat; a flood of body odor that made me gag. The same horrific tidal wave of stink.

I shut my eyes. I let myself settle, rooting myself in the stomach-churn of hunger that radiated out through my entire body. I took ten breaths like that, letting go of a lifetime's learning that hunger was something to be avoided, sated. Hunger was my friend. *Maybe hunger was my friend.* I sniffed again. Sniffed deeper. Let my nose do the work; let it sort through that churning stew of revolting pieces and find . . . find what?

And then I found: something. I wasn't sure what. A shape, a ghost. An outline seemed to glimmer: a person, conjured up by smell.

I breathed deeper. I let go of everything I thought I knew about the sense of smell. About what my nose could do. I let go of my own small-mindedness. My own lack of imagination. My own disbelief that my nose was capable of this thing that was . . . more.

Again, I breathed in. And then again. My brain felt flooded. Not with images, exactly, but impressions. Ghosts. Memories. Things.

"He's poor," I whispered to my pitiful doorway and the empty soccer field beyond. "He's white. I smell his clothes. The T-shirt he wore, before mopping up with this towel. The shirt is old. It was his brother's before it was his."

I breathed it in greedily. There was so much there! How had I never noticed how complicated a smell can be? How much information it carries? How many different pieces it's made of? And how easy it is to disentangle them, to analyze every separate thread and search for its source?

"Will Rutkey," I said finally, louder than I'd meant to.

I clamped a hand over my mouth, but I was still alone. And before I got too cocky, I pointed out to myself that I'd started off with an easy one. Will Rutkey had a pretty strong and distinctive smell.

I went back to the library. I read about how olfaction worked; how odorants are dissolved into the mucus lining the nasal cavity and absorbed by neurons that transmit information to the brain.

I let my hunger lead me.

I went to strange rooms, after school when the buses had mostly left but before the building got locked down. I went to wood shop and the art supply closets. I went in with my eyes closed and turned out the lights and focused on the shape of the space. I breathed it in. I let myself feel it, map it, even in the dark.

The air felt charged, dense with swirling data. I let the smells of the room draw the picture for me. I let go of the sense of sight. And I could feel: the metal and the wood and the overflowing ashtrays; the cinder-block walls and the cold cement floor.

I walked. The hairs on the back of my neck pricked up, electrified. A giddy feeling started in my stomach. Euphoria mixed with fear.

This is wrong, I told myself. *This is so wrong.*

All the Afterschool Specials agreed. Starving yourself is bad.

But it felt so good.

The sense of smell was stronger in women than in men, the internet told me. They had theories from scientists, stuff about choosing a mate and ovulation and nurturing a baby, but I thought of Maya and knew—it

was because the world is more dangerous for a woman. They need to be able to sense predators, because they are most definitely prey.

I walked into a wall. Hard.

I had gotten cocky. I let myself get distracted by what I had learned. The articles and analyses swirling inside my head.

The sharpest senses in the world are useless if your brain keeps getting in the way. And my brain got in the way—a lot. I had a . . . an *ability*. One unlocked by hunger. Concentration and focus were where I needed to work. To develop the ability to tune out all distractions and focus on what my senses were telling me. What my hunger was helping me see.

Or *was it* hunger? What if it was something else? Power can come from lots of places. Superman got his abilities from the absorption of solar energy; Samson's hair made him strong; waterbenders became stronger with the cycles of the moon.

I went to the cafeteria. Empty now, except for the janitor cleaning it up after lunch and the glorious clean smell of bleach. I went to the vending machine and bought a Honey Bun, which I hate, but at 500 calories they're the most fattening things you can find in most high school cafeterias.

I ate it.

I waited.

Was it my imagination, or did the smells die down? I breathed in and out, easier, feeling the weight lift slowly from my chest. But maybe that was just the bleach. I couldn't smell anything besides it. I left the cafeteria, walked through the halls, wandering with no direction in mind . . .

And found Regan and Jeanine, post band practice.

Regan was at her locker; Jeanine was standing beside her. Something had changed between them. Anyone could see it. But they smiled, and talked, and whatever epic confrontation they were going to have hadn't happened yet.

"Hey, Regan, hey, Jeanine," I said, stopping beside them.

"Hey," they said, and Jeanine gave me a death stare and then smiled the fakest smile ever.

I stepped closer. Breathed deep. Smiled.

Because other than the Pink perfume that Jeanine wanted everyone in a two-block radius to notice, I could not smell a thing.

RULE #8

Most people don't realize the extent to which their bodies enslave them. They live like hogs in a slaughterhouse pen, obeying their bodies, blissfully ignorant of the treasonous monster they are chained to, how it will hurt them, how it will fail them. Once you realize the true antagonistic nature of your relationship with your body, you will be far superior to most of your peers.

And yet—

one's enemy is the greatest teacher, according to the Dalai Lama. Respect your enemy and you will learn far more than if you declare that only hate and violence can exist between you. The student of the Art of Starving has much to learn from the body they are at war with. They will listen to it. They will understand it. Only by doing so can they force it to achieve its full potential.

DAY: 4

TOTAL CALORIES, APPROX.: 1000

At home, pondering what I'd learned, I realized: I needed a task. An assignment, something to focus on. Homework.

I needed to pick someone, learn their smell, and then follow them. Using only my nose.

I would let them get away from me—see how far away they could go before I lost track of their scent, and then focus on increasing that distance. Focus on picking that one smell out of the entire crowded school full of girls wearing too much perfume and stinking boys and backed-up toilets and dissected frogs and smokers in the stairwell.

And the second I had given myself that assignment, I grinned. I even said, "Excellent," out loud, like a cartoon villain, because I knew precisely who I would be stalking.

Tariq. Soccer star. In the weight room after school every day, with the body to prove it. One recent addition, which jarred with the rest of his clean-cut jock image: a pierced left nostril. Gifted player, passionate, so competitive that many of his own teammates were afraid of him.

Best friends with Bastien and Ott since second grade. An inseparable trio, egging each other on to increasingly alarming acts of cruelty. His aloofness from their petty violence did not make him better than them. And if they could call girls ugly just to watch them cry—in full

public view of others—what other atrocities might they have collaborated on in secret?

Might one of them have involved Maya?

I found Tariq at the end of the day, standing between two banks of puke-green lockers, arms folded over his chest. Watching traffic. An illegible expression on his face. Was he waiting for someone, lamenting a failed test, looking for future victims? No one could tell. He was a statue. A cypher. I stopped nearby and stood there, smelling the air, sucking up everything I could. Trying hard to tune out the angry churn of my empty stomach.

Pine trees. Gasoline. The vanilla air freshener dangling from the rearview mirror of his truck. The toxic cherry hand soap in the bathroom. But under all that—

"Matt," he said, seeing me.

"Oh, hi, Tariq," I said, after a pause that was hopefully just long enough to weird him out.

"How are you doing?"

I shrugged. "Could be worse."

Worse like my sister. After what you did to her.

Whatever it was.

Tariq smiled. Avoided eye contact like he always did with me. Said nothing.

Smelling Tariq, letting my nose break the boy down into his component smells, I found myself significantly less afraid of him. Whatever he was—bully, monster, untouchable jock superstar—he was also very human.

There was no reason to fear him. Especially since I could find out so much more about what happened to Maya by getting closer to him.

"I heard about a party this weekend," I said, thinking fast, stepping closer. "Tomorrow. Down by the Dunes. Are you going?"

"Thinking about it," he said, and smiled the slightest bit. "You?"

"Yeah."

"Surprised to hear it," he said. "Didn't think it was your thing."

"It's not. I'm actually a narc," I said, deadpanning. "I'm forty years old, infiltrating high school so I can catch teenage drug dealers."

Tariq scoffed. "Then this party is definitely where you want to be." He paused. "I can give you a ride," he said, and his smile widened significantly.

It did things to me, that smile. Those beautiful teeth, those lopsided-yet-perfect dimples. My knees weakened. Revenge is hard when your target is so pretty.

Just remember: he used that smile on Maya.

"Sure. Pick me up down the block from my house, tomorrow around seven," I said, and told him where I lived.

Even though I knew he already knew. Because that's where he picked up my sister the last night any of us saw her.

"You got it," Tariq said.

Pretty brazen, you're probably thinking. A dude would have to be pretty cocky, pretty evil, or pretty stupid to buddy up with the brother of a girl to whom he did something terrible. Or a girl to whom one of his best friends did something terrible.

Of course, it was also pretty cocky and pretty stupid of me to agree to get in the car with him. But I'm both those things.

I needed to know more. I had nothing real to pin on him, so far, except that since my sister disappeared I obviously made him and Ott deeply uncomfortable.

Maya ran with a crowd of tough kids, sure, but those kids were poor like us. Like us, they couldn't afford a car. But Tariq, rumor had it, had a brand-new truck his wealthy father had bought for him. And a clear interest in Maya's company.

I overheard her on the phone with him. That night. I almost asked to tag along, until I heard the urgency in her voice. Urgency and something much darker.

We used to bond over how badly we both wanted him. I freely acknowledged that I had no shot and wholeheartedly cheered her on when he started texting her, then calling, then picking her up to go hang out.

The summer I was fifteen, Maya found me in the living room watching a horror movie Mom wouldn't have let me see if she hadn't been working an extra shift, and

I thought for sure I was busted, because Maya enjoyed being a hard-ass disciplinarian even more than Mom did, but to my great surprise she came with a bowl of microwave popcorn and held it out to me, and when I reached for it she pulled back, so I'd look up at her, and she made eye contact and looked dead into my soul and said, "Just so you know, I know you're gay, and I think that's fucking awesome, because straight guys are *the worst*, and I know you're probably not ready to talk about it with anyone else, and I'll never tell a soul, but I need you to know that you can always come talk to me about anything."

Which made me blow up and scream at her—a classic closet-case defensive overreaction—and go to my room and cry, and not talk to her for two days, and then once all that had blown over go to her and say, "What about [INSERT CRUSH-OF-THE-WEEK NAME HERE]? Do you think I have a chance with him?"

And from that moment on, we were forever gushing over boys together. Reading the *How to Tell if a Boy Likes You* quizzes in *Cosmo* and *Seventeen* together. Digging deep into the Facebook photos of the boys we liked, looking for summer vacation shots where they might be shirtless or sweaty or smiling sexily.

She was the only person on the whole planet who told me to be Me and be proud of it.

Then Tariq befriended her, and got her to let her

guard down, and hurt her—he didn't kill her, didn't cripple her, but whatever it was, the psychological impact was such that she had to get the hell out of Hudson and away from everything she loved.

Now I would do the same to him.

RULE #9

Your body is an animal. Animals always know what to do. They sleep, they hump, they hunt, they eat. They run from danger or they die. Humans are different. They hesitate. They choose to stay in dangerous places—like high school—for a million crazy reasons. So your body will frequently find itself stuck in situations it cannot handle, and it will make you very sorry for putting it there.

DAY: 5

TOTAL CALORIES, APPROX.: 1000

An email from Maya.

> Hey Matt. I'm fine. Tell Mom I'll try to call Monday.

Nothing more. I made a sound, probably a curse word, at the computer, very loudly.

And then I wrote back. I wrote back again and again.

> I miss you
>
> Where are you? I know you said Providence but I don't think I believe you.

In between every email, I hit Refresh a hundred times, desperate for a response.

When are you coming home?

Mom's so pissed at you, for missing school and stuff.

Something happened. Tell me what happened. Did somebody hurt you?

I think someone hurt you. And I think you're probably planning a Bloody Revenge of some kind. I want to help.

I want you to trust me. I want you to tell me what's going on.

Silence was her only response.

Silence was my sister's weapon. When people hurt or angered her, she never got loud like Mom or mean and smart-ass like me. Silence was how she fought back. It wasn't passive, or an act of helplessness: it was a cold cruel withering blade, lasting far longer than my mother's rage or my own antagonism, strong enough to make us practically beg for forgiveness every time.

Except now her weapon had gone haywire, turned on herself, driven her from her home and her support system and into who-knew-what kind of danger.

I taped a note to the phone for Mom. Then I stayed up 'til midnight, when I heard her car pull up. I opened the door and surprised her smoking a cigarette on the front steps.

"Hi, Matt!" she said, hiding it behind her back.

"What are you still doing up?"

"Can I have a cigarette?" I asked.

"No, stupid," she said, as I knew she would, but I knew where she hid them, and anyway smoking was a skill I should pick up sooner or later. Maya and I tried Mom's cigarettes when she was fourteen and I was thirteen. I threw up. She didn't.

Tariq smoked. Smoking might help me worm my way into his life—so I could destroy it.

"It's not your fault," I said, speaking fast before I lost the significant nerve it took to say something like that to my mom. "What happened to Maya isn't your fault."

Mom frowned. She looked at her cigarette, and I thought, here it comes. She's going to destroy me. Instead, her frown deepened. And then dissolved. Into tears.

"It is," she whispered, turning her head away. "In a way, it most surely is."

Something was there. Guilt? Simple sorrow? A secret she was keeping from me?

I flushed with happiness, with pride, and then with shame. *I made my mother cry.* I put my hand on her shoulder.

But I couldn't stop. Because suddenly I had the power to get answers.

"Have you had any conversations with her, without me?"

"Once, maybe twice, she called when you were at

school, and I was sleeping off a night shift."

"What did she tell you that she wouldn't tell me?"

"Nothing important, honey. You know I'd tell you anything you needed to know."

She was lying. I could hear it. Something changed in the pitch of her voice on the word *needed*, something so small that a person without, well, superpowers could never have heard it.

I sank back, sat down on the cold stone of our stoop. "I just don't understand why you aren't more upset," I whispered.

"Christ, kid, you don't think I'm upset?" and the exhaustion I heard in her voice hurt more than the screaming angry fit I'd been fearing. "You don't think I'm *terrified*? You don't think I've been having a hard time sleeping—every night—even when I'm so tired I can't get out of bed to take a sleeping pill?"

I listened. I listened to her words and the spaces between them. I tried to track the ups and downs of her voice. The more I listened, the more I thought I could hear something. A timbre to her words. The specific vibration of particular emotions. My ears felt thick and stupid but also like I was at the edge of a dizzying amount of information. The power to hear what someone was feeling, even when their words tried to hide it. My stomach groaned, and for a split-second I smiled. The hunger was real. Hunger was causing—all of this.

My head spun with happiness, with fear, at this bizarre miraculous thing I could barely believe.

She plopped herself into a plastic lawn chair. Put one hand against her face. Then the other one. Seeing her so in pain magnified my own immeasurably.

"So what are we going to do?" I asked. It hurt even to whisper.

"Be here for her when she gets back."

I didn't want to worry her any worse than she already was. Asking the question I needed to ask might plant bad ideas in her brain. But if she knew something and she wasn't telling me, I had to take a risk. "I'm worried someone hurt her," I said. "That maybe that's what drove her away—what's keeping her away."

Mom lowered her hands. She looked at me a good hard while before she said, "What makes you think that?" And her voice, when she said it, was raw and fragile. My mom wore almost no makeup. I could see the veins through her thin delicate skin, smell the slaughterhouse soap she used to wash up with.

Shame sucker-punched me. I'd let selfishness guide my actions, and now I'd upset my mom. How could I say, *I think Tariq and Ott and maybe Bastien did something? Because Tariq was all interested in Maya, and since she disappeared he can't look at me, and neither can his henchmen.* "Nothing."

She frowned at me. She took a long drag on her

cigarette until there was nothing left of it, all the while holding eye contact. Now it was her turn to not believe me.

"Maya is *hurting*," she said. "I know that much. I don't know how to make it better. But we can't fight someone else's battles for them."

That's bullshit, I thought, but did not say. Power trembled in my hands, in my stomach.

I'll fight Maya's battles.

I'll destroy Maya's enemies.

I'll do it all for her.

When Mom was asleep, I snuck into Maya's room. I shut my eyes until the fear of Maya punching me repeatedly for invading her space evaporated. I breathed in the smell of it. Focused on all the normal notes, the smells of her lip balm and hair products, her dirty clothes and Trident gum. Once I had acclimated myself to *the room*'s smells, I could focus on the smell of *her*. After a while I could almost *see* her with my nose, trace her movements through the room the last time she was in here. I followed that lingering memory—Maya to the bookshelf, and ran my finger along every single book . . . I stopped at *Pretty in Punk: Girls' Gender Resistance in a Boys' Subculture*.

Was it possible? Could it be that I actually knew what my senses told me? Maya had paused here, before she left the room for the last time.

I picked the book up. Maya had held it in her hand, had opened it.

I opened it. And found, stuck between two pages at the back: the SIM card to Maya's cell phone. She would have replaced it if she didn't want to be tracked, but she wanted to still be able to use her smart phone.

And if I put it in my phone, I could send texts and make calls that people would think were coming from her.

My stomach gurgled triumphantly.

I pitied them, all the people I was up against, the ones who had hurt her and the ones who were keeping secrets. All those men and women and boys and girls had puny senses, and the skills of mere mortals.

They hadn't unlocked the power that I had.

RULE #10

Human hearing is a complex mechanical process. Understanding how it works will allow the student of the Art of Starving to expand its power exponentially.

The ear detects vibrations. The outer part of the ear focuses sound waves into the ear canal, where they strike the eardrum and are passed on into the middle ear. There, they pass through a series of complicated pieces that transform mechanical stimuli into neural transduction, ultimately sending information through the auditory nerve and into the brain stem, where it's combined with other signals and filtered through several parts of the brain that enable you to know the difference between a dog barking and a woman singing, and the language you speak from a language you don't.

DAYS: 6–7

AVERAGE DAILY CALORIES, APPROX.: 900

Magneto, supervillain par excellence, archenemy of the X-Men and leader of the evil Brotherhood of Mutants, was a Jew like me. He lost his whole family in a concentration camp, and only survived himself due to his mutant superpower, the ability to control metal. His whole life was about getting back at a world that had hurt him so badly. Professor Xavier, leader of the X-Men, just wanted mutants to be tolerated by an intolerant world, but Magneto wanted to burn that intolerant world to ash.

Darryl and I used to have the Magneto vs. Professor X conversation all the time. Aang vs. Zuko. Donatello vs. Raphael. Darryl was always siding with the pacifists. He even loved Superman, who bores me to tears, because what could be less interesting than someone who is mostly invincible?

The strongest people aren't the ones who are born strong. They're the ones who know what it's like to be weak, and have a reason to get stronger. The ones who've been hurt. Who've had things they love taken from them. The ones with something to fight for.

The ones who want revenge.

I shut my eyes, sat down in the noisy hallway fifteen minutes before the morning bell rang, and listened. I embraced my hunger and tilted my head in one direction and then another. I had studied up, the night before, on

the biology and the physics of hearing.

Sounds are like smells. They carry so much information that most people simply don't know what to listen for.

High school hallways were actually a pretty good laboratory for finding the extra information hidden inside human speech. Teenagers are dramatic; they exaggerate; they try too hard. Turning my head slightly I could shift from someone lying about a fight she almost got into ("And she is so lucky he was there, because I had people with me, and she would not be breathing right now—") to someone spreading false gossip ("His brother got arrested at college because he beat up a black guy—") to someone spreading true gossip ("She told her mom she's pregnant, and her mom agreed to send her to a different school. But she's not really pregnant. Not even a little bit . . .")

Careful listening will tell you precisely where a sound is coming from. Careful listening will let you hear sound waves passing through solid barriers. The sound waves of speech are shaped by the emotions of the speaker, and a listener with abilities can hear those emotions. He can know when someone is lying or sad or about to do something terrible.

Or rather, I can know.

The training montage is a cinematic staple in a whole bunch of film genres—an easy way to say, "A bunch of

time passed, our hero did a lot of really boring stuff over and over again until he or she ceased to be useless." Clips of the main character doing stuff repeatedly, usually getting hit over the head or punched in the face a bunch, usually to weird synthesizer music. You know what I'm talking about. The Bride and Pai Mei. Yoda and Luke in the swamp. Most of *Kung Fu Panda*. Every *X-Men* movie. Etc.

So just imagine a training montage here. Me, researching how hearing works, trying out different methods of auditory perception that are . . . above normal human margins, proceeding with stubborn thick-headed persistence, wrong and wrong and wrong . . .

And then, incredibly, *right*.

Me with my ear to a wall, listening until I could make out the words being said in the next room over and then two rooms away.

Me, moving through the school during the chaos of lunch period, listening for the songs playing in my locker far away and then quizzing myself after—sort of an auditory eye chart.

Me, putting my ear to the cold exposed pipes in the physics room, listening to how effortlessly the metal tubes transmitted sound waves from the other side of the building.

Me, shifting my focus to follow the architecture of the building to selectively listen in on any one of a

dozen different rooms.

Me, clapping in the dark at home, trying—and failing—to use echolocation, listening to how the sound waves bounce off objects and thereby "see" in the total absence of light.

Me, on the internet, looking up the phone numbers for every single recording studio in or near Providence, Rhode Island. Calling every single one. None could confirm or deny whether a band named Destroy All Monsters! was currently recording there.

Me, experimenting with food. Going a whole day and only eating a sandwich, to see how much more clearly I could hear. Me, going a whole day eating only half a sandwich. Feeling the difference.

Movie montages end in success and enlightenment, or at least a grudging smile from the hard-ass master, a tiny acknowledgment that progress has been made. This is not a movie montage. It ends with me, sitting in the woods behind my house at dawn, freezing, scared shitless.

Focus and patience were still where I needed to work. I had to learn to let go of my desires, my needs and wants. I needed to simply *be*. Listen. Hear. Wait. Learn. Absorb as much information as I could from my senses, while turning off the information from my brain.

Hearing meant pulling meaning from chaos. Tuning out the static and taking what I needed. To truly hear

the innumerable sounds of the universe, I needed to quiet my mind.

So I decided to meditate. Focus on erasing my sense of self. Become a vessel for the sounds of the universe. Listen. *Hear.* I went out back and sat down on the ground and shut my eyes.

I'd been to some pages on the internet about it. Buddhist sites and Hindu texts, all about mindful meditation. How to quiet the mind. Except quieting the mind was really really hard. "Mastering the mind is as difficult as controlling the winds," said Arjuna in the *Bhagavad-Gita*, and he had a really good point. Sages and monks spent a lifetime learning to meditate.

So I started with simply breathing. And listening.

I heard my stomach. I heard wind. I heard it shush through the grass, whistle over the roof of my house, sing in the branches of the trees. I followed the sound of the wind into the scattered trailer parks and ramshackle cottages nearby, heard screen doors bang and televisions squawk. I heard dishonest men making promises from a thousand television sets, babies crying, liquor sloshing over ice, and dogs dreaming. . . .

But the wind was moving too fast, speeding through space and taking me with it, spreading me out, turning me into a massive net, sucking up sounds, miles and miles of laughter and tears and plates smashing and doors slamming. It felt like this time when I was a little

kid, swimming in the sea, suddenly realizing I had waded too far, couldn't touch the bottom, and knowing how much deep dark water was waiting to swallow me up.

I gasped, gulped, tried, and flailed.

I heard Ott. I heard his father, his voice thick and hairy and terrifying, the sound of a man made miserable and determined to take it out on the people he had power over—

They're not your friends, you stupid fuck. You'll see—you'll see how they abandon you when you get out in the real world. Live it up now because come graduation you won't have nothing except a shit job, if you're lucky.

Ott only whimpered. I pulled away, desperate not to feel pity for him.

I heard Bastien's dad, my mother's boss, tell her she wasn't making quota for the week, wouldn't qualify for overtime. I heard the soulless calm to his voice, the rational *These are the rules, my hands are tied* tone with which he explained why she might not be able to pay this month's rent, and it made me want to rip the skin from his bones like they did with so many pigs.

Furious, I tore myself away again, losing what little bit of control I still had—

And I heard the cries of the animals at the slaughterhouse. And hearing their cries I instantly, profoundly, felt a fraction of their pain.

I screamed until my throat hurt.

I tried to pull back. Shut my ears. Come back to my body. My mind was a bubble, and in a moment I would pop—

My belly twisted. The pain restored clarity. I was stronger than my body. My hunger was proof.

I breathed. I listened. I let the sounds pass through me. I stopped worrying about what might happen. Let go of the pigs and their pain, their cries, dropped it like a hot coal I'd been clenching in my fist. I focused on erasing—like the books said—my sense of self. I marveled, at how big the universe was. How full of sounds. How cold and solid the earth was. How much power I could tap into. And how easy it would be to let go of the earthly tether that connected me to my body, my troubles, my whole miserable existence. And just cease to be.

It made me shiver. It would be so much easier than actually killing myself. Less pain, less mess to clean up. With practice I could just . . . float away.

I decided to stick with this meditation thing.

<u>RULE #11</u>

No superhero, no Chosen One, no budding witch or demigod or changeling gets better by playing it safe. Sooner or later, you will have to put yourself in a dangerous situation. You will have to test yourself. You will have to risk losing everything, before you can gain anything.

DAY: 8

TOTAL CALORIES, APPROX.: 1000

Two hours before Tariq came to pick me up, while Mom napped, I stole her cell phone from her purse and took it to my room. A simple thing, old and clunky, but that was better, because a smartphone might complicate the kind of shenanigans I needed to pull off.

I switched out Mom's SIM card for Maya's. And sent a text message to Tariq, which would look to him like it came from her:

I'm going to tell.

Almost immediately, Mom's phone vibrated in my

hand. *TARIQ*, it said. I pressed the red button to reject the call.

A text came in.

Please don't.

There were so many things I wanted to say. But I bit my lip and rode out the silence.

A second text from him: It would destroy my life.

At this I smiled, and thought: *Like you destroyed hers?*

A second call. Again I rejected it. And then, five minutes later, he texted: Why would you do that to me? After what we shared?

So. There was *something*. I didn't know *what*, and I needed to be very *very* careful about what I said, because one wrong word would trigger his suspicions that something was up.

People need to know, I wrote.

I know you're mad, came his response. But that doesn't give you the right to hurt me. What's going on? Can we talk? I've been trying to call you at—

Rage made me rip the SIM card from Mom's cell phone. *That doesn't give you the right to hurt me.* He believed *he* could harm *her* with no consequences, but if she tried to fight back she was—what? Violating the Rules?

I stuck the SIM card back in, and looked up Maya's bandmates, and scribbled down their numbers. Then I took it out again, hid it where I kept my porn flash

drives, brought the phone back to Mom's purse, went outside.

Hunger and rage tore and screamed inside me, a whirl of blades that shredded the walls of my stomach. The generator in my gut had been cranked up too far by my anger, and the electricity threatened to split me open.

I had to calm down. My ride would be here in a second or two.

Of course it was a pickup truck. Of course it was brand-new, red, too big for Tariq, detailed with fiery half-circles around the tires. Of course he drove it with a face of grim tight worry, like it was a test of his manhood or a bull that at any moment might buck him. But when he pulled up to a stop and put it in park, his smile was epic.

"Hey, Matt," he said when I climbed up and opened the door. I'd asked him to meet me down the block. Told him it was because I didn't want my mom to know I was leaving, but really it was because I didn't want him to see my house. Its ramshackle frame, its unmowed lawn with fallen leaves piled three inches deep.

When he picked up Maya, it would have been nighttime. He wouldn't have seen, then.

"Hi," I said, trying several unsuccessful times to shut the door once I was in.

"You really gotta slam it," he said, reaching past me to grab the handle and wrench it shut with a manly yank.

The senses kicked in hard. It smelled like *him* in here. Like a well-used pair of soccer shorts had spent several weeks under one of the seats. The intimacy of it was electrifying.

"You got a curfew?" he asked, looking distracted.

He kept glancing at his phone. The texts had shaken him up, no doubt about it.

"Not when no one knows I'm out," I said.

He laughed. Did he ask her the same question when *she* got in? Did *she* have a hard time shutting the passenger-side door? I looked down at my feet. Punk rock flyers and pamphlets littered the floor. SMASH THE SYSTEM, one of them urged, and another said GOD IS A LIE THEY TELL YOU TO MAKE YOU BEHAVE.

"I didn't know you were into punk," I said, thinking of Maya.

"Only pretty recently. I just love it. There's so much . . . anger."

"What do you have to be angry about?" I asked. "Everybody loves you."

Tariq laughed, but it wasn't a funny laugh. "That doesn't mean I have nothing to be pissed about."

It occurred to me to be afraid. If he had hurt Maya, he wouldn't think twice about hurting me. And the texts I sent had made him uneasy, anxious. People, like animals, are at their most dangerous when they're afraid.

So I stepped back from what I'd been about to

say—*Kids whose dads can afford to buy them fancy new pickup trucks don't have a right to be pissed.*—and said nothing at all. He started the car, and we were on our way, the radio filling in the silence.

A few blocks later, he said, "You've never been interested in this kind of party before, so what made you want to come to this one?" He smiled when he said it. A cautious smile.

"Maybe I just wanted to see what all the fuss was about."

"Yeah, well, you're in for a disappointment. I wasn't sure if I was even going to go, until—"

He stopped the sentence, but I think I knew where it was going.

The sad, dirty, trash-strewn roads of my neighborhood were extra pathetic, looking down on them from the cab of that truck. The extra height gave me distance, perspective, but so did knowing how Tariq must have seen them. *This is a place where hard-up people live: workers in the quarry and the zipper factory and the slaughterhouse. People easily taken advantage of. Girls I can hurt with no consequences.*

"Got a cigarette?" I asked, when he came to a stop along a strip of dark road beside a bunch of other cars. Music thumped in the distance. I turned my head in that direction so I could burrow down deeper into the noise of all those people, hear the interwoven strands of so

many conversations.

"Full of surprises tonight, Matt," he said, pulling a pack from his back pants pocket. Then he reached past me to open the glove compartment. Out came a book of matches and the Hudson High School library's copy of *On the Road*.

"You?" I asked. "I was waiting for that book—*you* checked it out?"

Tariq nodded, looked out his window. "Jack Kerouac. I saw you reading that book by him," he said. "It looked interesting."

I read the first sentence of the book, then shivered. The whole thing was just too weird. I put the book back.

He handed me a cigarette, stuck one in his own mouth, lit a match, then lit the cigarette, then held the lit match out to me. In a haze of mesmerized self-hate, I watched his hands fly gracefully through these motions. I lit the cigarette. Then we turned and walked toward the sound of screaming.

"Tariq!" came a booming shout as we drew near a house with pale-blue vinyl siding and expensive landscaping. The whole soccer team was out front, and for a moment I panicked, convinced that Tariq had led me like a lamb to the slaughter. They were waiting to jump me, bash me, break my arms, kick my face to pulp. But one sniff and I knew they were harmless: drunk, jolly, their attention and energy scattered across a dozen

things—getting more beer, banging some chick, a couple of them thinking about a beef they had with someone else that might blossom into violence if that jerk showed up tonight.

Cigarette smoke scraped me raw, scorched my throat, and filled my lungs. This new pain distracted from the pain in my stomach. I grinned, slightly, to myself.

Tariq shared bro-hugs and handshakes and hellos with his fellow teammates. "You all know Matt, yeah?" he said, and some nodded and some looked down and some raised their plastic beer cups in an intoxicated magnanimous show of welcome.

I smelled them. And I listened. And I could go deeper now. Drunk people don't guard their thinking. I focused on my senses, and then, I could hear scraps of words. Phrases that might have been their thoughts.

This faggot. Why's he here?

Does he even go to our school?

I need more beer, but I don't want to go inside.

Could this be real? Could I actually read people's minds?

If I could, I was going to put it to good use. I zeroed in on Bastien and Ott, but both looked away as soon as they saw me. Bastien at least had the sinister intelligence to blink away his discomfort and smile. "What's good, Matt?"

"Not much."

They disliked me, so they were guarded. Their thoughts impenetrable even if they were some combination of drunk and high.

I glanced around.

I had never been to a high school party before. People stopped inviting me around fifth grade. That was also the time people started calling me faggot. I don't know how they knew. I didn't know myself.

At any rate—I'd been wrong to be so afraid of this. I'd always pictured these parties as frenzies of alcohol and weed and sex and violence. And while the first two were certainly in evidence, everyone seemed about as frenzied as an anaesthetized cow. Instead of the hate I always thought lurked beneath every handsome jock's facade, there was mostly apathy. Instead of the violence I always associated with alcohol, there was mostly just a doofy happy lazy buzz. I stood there, smoking, almost belonging.

"Come on inside," Tariq said, "let's get you some food."

In the house, I shut my eyes and smelled, and knew at once that the place belonged to a boy in my grade named Griff. That his parents were not home. Two stuffed moose heads and a taxidermied alligator watched Tariq and me stroll through.

"Hungry?" Tariq said when we got to the kitchen. I almost laughed. Food covered every surface of the place,

great unhealthy heaps of it, oily chips and creamy dips, baked frozen fried breaded appetizer monstrosities, store-bought cookies stacked like coins, sugary sodas, all of it sending broken-glass shivers of agony through my midsection. I smothered the pain with one last long pull on the cigarette and stubbed it out sadly.

"Nah," I said.

He smiled. A lonely smile. Open and trusting. And yet, I couldn't read his mind, either. No doubt, he was an expert at hiding things from the people around him.

But then again, so was I. "Let's go get us some beer," he said.

I followed him outside, down a long, dead, sloping lawn, through flocks and gaggles of boys and girls. I tensed, every muscle anticipating some sort of attack.

I thought of those scenes in *The Birds* when for no reason at all the birds cease to be evil and violent and just stand around harmlessly, apathetic to human beings instead of bent on their destruction. Maybe I was safe . . . for a little while.

Once I no longer feared my own death, I heard everything. Scraps of conversation, words that said almost nothing—while my sense of hearing detected so much more.

"So I went out for the team—"

"All I know is there were rumors—"

"I just stood there, I was so shocked, I couldn't

believe she said that—"

Underneath I heard happiness, fear, insecurity. I looked from person to person in a state of tingly shock. I inhaled. I knew that Tammy Ladonnia was pregnant, and that Pete Shumsky was the father, and I knew that she knew it, and he did not.

I detected things others did not. I saw, heard, and smelled things others could not.

Somehow, I had become Peter fucking Parker.

Somehow, I had—could I even say it? I had *powers*.

I followed Tariq down to a bonfire, blazing tall and bright against the dark. I walked a little bit behind him. His shoulders were so broad, backlit by the fire in front of him. His arms filled out his sweater so nicely. Sad, jangly pop music blasted from a parked Jeep. I let him pour me a beer, but resolved not to drink it. He poured one for himself, and took a sip, and then looked up—

"Pass that bottle," he said, too loudly, seeing glass glint in the firelight, and joy and relief crackled in the air around him. Someone laughed, came closer, dumped tequila into his beer.

"More . . . " he said, laughing, "more . . ." even when it overflowed and soaked his fingers. He took a long, long sip.

I stepped closer and breathed him in. Really breathed. Looked past all the surface smells, the stink of the world he walked through . . . and then past the

smells of him, of the outer shell of his body: sweat and hair and saliva, and found:

Loneliness.

Tariq gave off a crushing, overpowering loneliness. A smell of McDonald's breakfasts eaten alone in parking lots, and long hours standing on the edge of a circle of friends, and the bitter odor of knowing none of his buddies truly knew him. Girlfriends who dated him to piss off their parents but who didn't care about who he was as a person. Random strangers responding with hate and suspicion to his Middle Eastern name or looks.

Loneliness.

The smell was so strong, I wobbled on my feet. For a split second, I faltered. The rage and hate cooled into pity.

He's miserable, I thought.

Then I thought better. *So what,* I told myself. *That doesn't give him the right to hurt people. That doesn't diminish or excuse the hurt he's caused.*

I stepped closer, tapping into some ancestral genetic carnivore. Some feral creature who knew loneliness for what it was: a weakness. Tariq was desperate for a friend. His body had snitched on him.

I could be that friend. I could get close enough to make him feel safe confiding his loneliness. His pain. And something else—

A secret. Something so big and so dark it blotted out

the space between us, turning Tariq into a swirl of night beside me.

Except I already know your secret. Or—almost. And when I learn it, when I know exactly what you did, nothing will save you.

He stood beside Bastien and Ott, both of whom were still trying hard not to look in my direction, and I realized—

Tariq is the weakest link. Whatever happened, he's the one I can get the truth out of. The one who will help me destroy all three of them.

Inside, a small circle of boys and girls played poker. I sat down beside them and watched their faces. Watched the emotions they were feeling, and how they tried to hide them. How they failed.

"Deal me in?" I asked, unsure if that sentence was even a real thing people said.

Here is a helpful hint: even if you've never played poker in your life, even if you don't know the rules, you can be really really good at poker if you can practically read minds. Which is how I earned a hundred dollars in small bills and the respect and semi-frightened awe of a slowly growing circle of soccer players and kids I'd never seen before.

Including Bastien, who clapped me on the back and said, "Damn, son!" at several points, and Ott, who grunted after I won a particularly impressive hand,

which was the nicest noise he'd ever made at me.

"Hungry?" Tariq asked, evidently forgetting what I'd said when he asked me that same question an hour or so ago. Already his eyes were strange and feral, his expression distant and distorted. Alcohol was turning him into something else. Something that made mistakes; something I could manipulate. He stooped to pick up a pan someone was using to cook meat over the fire. The alcohol and the firelight made him look brutal, monstrous.

"Um, sure," I said. If I wanted to gain his confidence, yes was most assuredly better than no. I reached my hand out and grabbed a sausage. Molten-hot hog fat scalded my fingertips, dripped down to pool in my palm. When Tariq wasn't looking I let the sausage fall to the earth, and whispered a tiny prayer of apology to that pig who died for nothing.

Your body is unique. A snowflake. No body is precisely like yours. Over thousands of years, the little differences between bodies add up to genetic drift, the differentiation of species. Evolution. So remember this the next time you curse some knob of fat or funny-shaped thumb, or sexual predilection for something society says you shouldn't predilect: your differences might make you miserable, but they might also make you better.

DAY: 9

TOTAL CALORIES, APPROX.: 1000

My sense of triumph was gone when I woke up. Only sadness was left, and hunger. Sadness over what had happened to my sister and sadness over Tariq's open, desperate smile. Sadness over what I would eventually do to him. Revenge was necessary. He was a monster. But then, he was also a person.

When I came down the hall to find the massive breakfast Mom had made me, I was almost happy.

Bacon, crisp and heaped on a plate, oatmeal bubbling on the stove, a pile of pancakes stacked high, a brand-new box of cereal.

Food was love.

Then I thought, *food is failure.*

I stood in the doorway for a good long minute.

"Can I have some coffee?" I asked, walking in. This made maybe ten years I'd been asking that question, so I was more than shocked when she said, "Sure, I made enough for both of us."

It meant something, something big, as much as if she'd bought me a dirty magazine or box of cigarettes, but not even with my new abilities could I see clear to what exactly it meant.

I sat down. Mom gave me a mug, a spoon, milk, and sugar. I skipped them both. These vile substances are nothing but calories.

"You've had coffee before," she said, when I took a long sip and smiled.

"Of course, Mom. Shouldn't I have?"

Mom shrugged. Then she sighed, sat down across from me. Perhaps she finally saw, that morning, in that moment, that I was a person in the world and could do all sorts of things she told me not to do.

"Eat," she said, pushing plates in my direction. And stared at me, eyes boring into mine.

All of a sudden, my chest hurt.

The bacon, probably made from the sister of the sausage I dropped into the dirt the night before, was pure salty fat, and therefore out of the question. So I slid several pancakes onto my plate, not intending to eat any of them, and added syrup sparingly.

"How is that?" she asked, tapping the well-worn copy of *The Dharma Bums* I took with me everywhere.

"It's good," I said, aware that this, too, meant something. Perhaps as close to a conversation about my father as my mother was capable of having. So I pushed it, just a little. "These dudes just wandering around, seeing the country, no attachments, focusing on living life, you know. Getting down to what's important."

Mom snorted, made a face, looked into the distance.

I sliced off a large strip of pancake, then cut it into smaller ones. "You don't think that sounds good?"

"'No attachments' does not sound good," she said, and I knew she was choosing her words carefully. "Some attachments are beautiful."

Here, she patted my hand. So this *was* about my dad, and his lobster boat—which, from my heightened perspective, I realized was either a lie or a euphemism.

"What's life, if not attachments?" she asked.

I didn't say anything at first. My pancake had been reduced to pieces practically too small to see with the naked eye.

She was watching me.

So far she hadn't said anything. But I had to eat something, as much as it pained me to do so. "I don't know, Mom."

Life was revenge. Life was making bad people hurt. Life was Maya.

"They restricted the runs again," Mom said, rubbing the back of her neck, her voice aching the way it always did when she talked about work. "Another three pickups canceled. That's two more guys laid off."

Here is something you need to know about my mother. She loves her town. She loves the people in it. The ones she works with, the ones she grew up alongside. She loves the rusted wheelless vehicles along its roads and the falling-down houses with the roofs gone. I don't know why. She's a smart lady. She's not small and hateful like so many of them are. And yet she loves the twisted pothole highways and the happy blanket of ignorance everyone wraps themselves up in, the deluded crazy stupid belief that *This is all we need*.

And I realized something, somehow. For myself! Not with my supersenses, but with my mind.

Had I not been born gay, I might have loved it, too. I would have been welcomed into the fold. *One of us*, they would have chanted, like the Freaks in that movie, and I would have lived happily for my whole life in Hudson. I would never have seen the fear and anger and hatred my neighbors and classmates carried around inside

them, aimed at everyone and everything that's different, because I would have shared those fears and hatreds with them. I wouldn't have known how bad it was, kind of like how you can't smell the smell of your own house because it's so familiar.

A ludicrous sentence shivered up my spine and into my brain, shocking me, terrifying me, delighting me, and almost escaping my lips:

Thank God I am gay.

"How is school?" she asked, and didn't look up from her mug.

"Fine," I said, because coffee or no coffee, we hadn't reached the place where I could tell her about how Ott slammed the locker door on my hand last week or Nate Smith threatened to rape me.

"That's good," she said, and got up to pretend to busy herself with something in a drawer. Gracefully, in swift flicks timed to the rhythm of the conversation, I scraped small forkfuls of pancake into the napkin spread in my lap. Then I crushed it in both fists and slipped it into my backpack and went to school with syrup-stinking hands I never once let myself lick.

My mother was worried. I didn't need Starvation Superpowers to see it, smell it, hear it hiding between her words. And I probably wasn't half as slick as I thought I was, disposing of all those uneaten pancake atoms.

But I escaped without having to ingest a crumb. I'd fight my next battle when I came to it.

School passed swiftly, effortlessly. And by evening the worry was still there, but bigger, or maybe by then I was hungry enough to see it for what it really was. Her worry was a knotted swirl, a tapestry woven of a thousand threads. Her fear of the factory shutting down or of losing more friends to layoffs; her fear of getting laid off herself. Her love of the town and her fear of the future. Her worry about me, what I was going through. Her fears about Maya.

Mom and me barely spoke at dinner—and whenever she wasn't looking I tossed food pieces into the Ziploc bag I'd left open in my lap—but I could hear so much even when she wasn't speaking.

For the first time since my powers emerged, I wished I couldn't.

RULE #13

Breath is the tool for uniting the body and the mind.

Chinese traditional medicine calls the energy that circulates in your body chi—which means breath. When you breathe, you're literally sucking in life force, the flow of which sustains all living things. Sophisticated sages can draw great strength and nourishment from the air. And air has no calories. Master martial artists are said to be able to control the flow of chi through their bodies, and even project it out of their bodies to heal or to harm.

DAY: 10

TOTAL CALORIES, APPROX.: 1000

Hunger stretched out time, made me move faster without realizing it, made me seem manic and mad while, inside, I sat patiently in a bubble of calm. Words came out jangly and overflowing; sentences doubled up and intertwined.

The tater tots taught me early on how losing focus

for even a second made my mind waver from its goal, left me defenseless against my body's base and fleshy needs. My mind, it seemed, needed to grow stronger along with my senses.

At school I made myself sit and be still. I ignored my classmates, the words and emotions they disturbed the universe with, the stink of their bodies and their unwashed clothes and their hormones crackling in the air like popping corn. I could see now that I wasn't universally hated, the way I'd imagined I was. Apathy, sweet and dull as gasoline, was the smell that came off most of them. And the hate of the actual homophobes had lost its sting, their coiled violence and cocked fists had ceased to frighten me.

Mostly.

Mostly I felt strong and unstoppable. Better than everyone. Superhuman.

But those moments still came. The ones where I caught someone staring, and shriveled inside. Where I saw my own reflection unexpectedly, and gasped with horror at the ugliness of it. When I felt weak and doomed. *Sub*human.

You're wondering, how is that possible, Matt? How can you be both sub- and superhuman?

That's one of the more infuriating bugs in the human software. You can have two ideas that are total opposites and believe them both completely.

Of course, I ate. I couldn't just starve myself. Not yet, anyway. But I ate very little, and every day I ate less.

When your body has passed a certain hunger threshold, food becomes the only thing you can focus on. The only thing you can think about. Pains pop up in the strangest places. Joints creak and scream, and their screaming sounds like the names of food. Very little is truly frightening, because you have learned the identity of your true worst enemy. And, spoiler alert: it's you.

More than once, I spat out a strip of raw pink bleeding skin I'd unthinkingly torn away from a fingernail. So, another important thing to know about hunger: it can drive you into mild fugue states of self-cannibalism.

I sat, and I listened. I smelled. Did people know, looking at me, that I was transforming from a helpless sissy into something unspeakably powerful? I could barely see them, my peers, the people whose respect I once craved, the people whose hate I once dreaded.

At home, I kept researching.

Online I read about food developed by cultures with severely limited resources, and found tsampa. Tibetan roasted barley flour. Mountain food. Sherpas and yak herders take it with them on long journeys. Maximum nutrition, minimum space. Eat ten tablespoons a day—about 800 calories—and you should be able to keep your hunger in check. Keep the body alive. I found a

place that shipped to Hudson, and put two ten pound bags on my mom's debit card.

I clicked from Wikipedia to pornography. I watched superhuman torsos writhe and flail and grapple. Chiseled manly faces clenched in pain and pleasure. My stomach, angry at being ignored, clenched so tight I gasped. Black stars flashed in the air all around me, spiral galaxies of brain cells dying.

I stood up and collapsed.

I don't think I was out for very long. If I was out at all.

The human body can go for up to thirty days without eating, I told myself over and over.

I was fine.

I was fine.

RULE #14

Should you ever need a reminder of what a savage animal your body is—should you ever start to doubt that you are chained to a wild creature—just hurt someone. Hurt them bad. And see how your body feels after.

DAY: 11

TOTAL CALORIES, APPROX.: 800

I invented a thing.

Food masturbation, I called it. In as much explicit detail as possible, I imagined a hot and heavy scene of mouth intercourse with cheeseburgers or pizza or the seafood *fra diavolo* at La Concha D'Oro in Catskill.

All fantasy, of course.

It is significantly less messy than actual masturbation. But afterward, I feel just as dirty.

I double-fisted french fries, shoveling them into my mouth so fresh from the fryer that they burned my fingers and my tongue. Salt fell off in slow-motion snow showers. I scooped handfuls of fast-food pickles into

my mouth, squirted mustard all over my face in hot wet splurts. I sucked ice cream direct from the Dairy Queen nozzle. I bought an entire pizza from Pizza Pit, on Lower Warren Street, and ate only the cheese, because I don't know what kind of cheese they use or what they do to it, but the cheese from Pizza Pit is a thing of beauty.

I bought more pizzas. I ate them. My food depravity knew no bounds. I rolled a whole pizza up into a tight tube and ate it in five superhuman bites, barely chewing, until—

A hard blow to the stomach snapped me back to reality. Gym class. Dodgeball. Boys snickered at the sight of me struggling not to throw up.

"Lay off him, asshole," Tariq said to whoever threw the ball. Hudson High is a small school; lucky me, I shared gym class with Tariq and eight members of the soccer team. He squatted at the sidelines, having already been hit.

Loss of concentration is a common symptom of eating disorders. The internet says so.

Not that I have an eating disorder, but I'm not eating, so a lot of the same principles apply.

Concentration is a human process. Concentration means trying to keep a lot of things straight in your head. When your body is starving, it doesn't have any patience for complicated mental maneuvers. It just wants you to fucking kill and eat something.

Aggression. My mind came alive. Different parts lit up, clicked together. Things that had never made sense before suddenly fell into focus. Physics, sports, human society—the awakened mind could master them all.

Effortlessly, I scooped the ball out of the air.

"Nice catch," someone on my team said, shock in his voice. I held the ball in my hand for a moment, felt its weight, turned it over to analyze every imperfection on its well-worn surface.

"Come on," the coach called. They stared at me, all of these brutal boys, these bloodthirsty hairless primates, these bullies, these animals. These weak spindly towers of delicate sinew, these fragile heaps of dying cells.

I shifted the muscles in my arms, my legs. I swiveled my hips and knees and shoulders. I was a magnificent machine. I knew the logic of my own body, and I knew the logic of the bodies of my enemies. How had I not seen this before? I could do anything with this machine.

Someone laughed.

Ott's mouth made the word *faggot*, but all sound had dropped out.

I could see how to hurt him.

With a swift punching motion, bringing one arm forward as I brought the other back, I threw the ball at Ott. It hit him in his gut so swift and hard he didn't have time to block or dodge—

—and, quick as lightning, the ball bounced off his

belly and returned directly to my hands.

Physics. Simple.

Ott roared in pain.

"No shit," Bastien said. I took one small step forward to add momentum and repeated the trick on him. His scream when the ball hit his solar plexus was high and deeply satisfying.

Throw—hit—bounce back into my hands.

Another boy curled in on himself, holding his stomach.

Physics was not some complicated theoretical science: it was real and rough and practical. Simple logic; the unshakable cold equations of gravity and weight and surface angles. The body knows physics in a way the mind never will.

I felt like goddamn Magneto.

I knew this day would come, I thought. *A reckoning is at hand.*

Hunger was helping me become the kind of monster that can make it in this world.

With six swift throws, I incapacitated the entire other team. Changing it up some, aiming for the knees or crotch or head when I could see their reflexes were sharp enough to block a shot. One of them ended up on the ground. Crying.

And, just for the joy of causing pain to these boys who had caused so much pain to others—or would *one*

day cause pain to others—I took out everyone on my team, too.

And yes, reader, you're right, perhaps I was going too far. Maybe not *everyone* was a bully. But knocking them down just felt too . . . *good*.

The coach blew his whistle, a long angry shocked screech. Before the sound was finished, I had hit the whistle with the dodgeball, knocked it into his mouth and halfway down his throat. He coughed it up, spat it out. Everyone stared.

I smiled to myself, all the way to the principal's office. I felt proud.

I had never been suspended before.

RULE #15

Sun Tzu said: "Engage people with what they expect; it is what they are able to discern and confirms their projections. It settles them into predictable patterns of response, occupying their minds while you wait for the extraordinary moment—that which they cannot anticipate."

It's astonishing, how many aspects of fifth-century-BC Chinese military strategy are applicable in twenty-first-century American high schools.

DAY: 12

TOTAL CALORIES, APPROX.: 800

It stayed with me, the adrenaline euphoria of hurting those boys. The moment played itself over and over in my mind, sending a fresh rush of pleasure through my veins every time. I could never in a million years have repeated it—I had somehow switched on to autopilot and accessed strength and knowledge I, under normal circumstances, totally lacked. But it had happened, and there were witnesses, and that's what's important.

My epic dodgeball victory came on a Friday, which meant my two-day suspension would start the following Monday. Which meant a four-day weekend. It occurred to me that getting in trouble was pretty awesome.

Saturday morning my phone rang.

"Hey, Matt," Tariq said. "Got plans?"

You may be wondering, Dear Reader: why did Tariq suddenly want to be my friend? Why, when he was so popular and I was so *not*? And why, when I was a useless faggot and he was a ladies-man sports star, did he call me on the weekend to see what I was up to?

I have many theories. Here are my favorites:

1. Tariq's busy throbbing social life left him feeling unfulfilled. There were plenty of ugly words I could use to describe Tariq, but stupid wasn't one of them. Tariq was a smart boy with lots of stupid friends. His soccer teammates and the people they hung out with weren't down for discussions of literature or politics or current events. The best he could do was Bastien, whose intellect lacked imagination, who shunned art and culture and anything else that might involve emotion. Perhaps Tariq wanted a friend who was his intellectual equal. So he turned to me. Which isn't to say that *I* was very smart, but he wouldn't be the first person to mistakenly assume that someone was intelligent because they were unpopular.

2. Tariq liked books. I liked books. No one else in our school liked books. So.

3. Tariq felt guilty. Movies and books are forever saying how criminals feel compelled to confess, how thieves and murderers who got away scot-free are nevertheless hounded by their consciences into doing penance, often in ways that lead to their capture. So even if Tariq didn't explicitly say to himself, *I did something terrible to Maya, maybe I can set my karma straight by being buddies with her poor, ugly, misshapen brother,* maybe he felt some impulse pushing him in my direction, telling him to take pity on me, trying to feel better about the hurt he put on her.

4. Tariq was the helpless victim of the expert manipulation skills that my super-sharpened senses gave me.

5. Tariq was an even bigger sociopath monster than I thought he was, and having destroyed my sister by getting her to drop her guard he had turned his sights on me.

6. None of the above.

7. Several of the above, in a gruesome messy complex combination not even Tariq truly understood.

So I smiled and said, "No weekend plans," and paused for just a second, and said, "Why?"

"Thinking of heading down to the city to see a punk

show," he said, and I could hear in the tone of his voice and the echo of the wind that he was sitting in his truck, alone. "Wanna come?"

"Absolutely," I said without pausing, without thinking, without wondering whether Mom would give me permission, because nothing else mattered but this opportunity to be alone with my enemy. I grinned gleefully.

Poor little lonely Tariq, the lamb leading himself to my slaughter.

I remembered how his eyes lit up when he had a beer in his hand. No more so than most high school jocks, I imagined, but still, it was a weakness. Something I could exploit. I sniffed around the whole house until I found a bottle of scotch—so well hidden it made me stop and think—

I had never seen my mother drink a drop of alcohol.

I wondered why—and put the bottle in my book bag.

RULE #16

Life is suffering. Embrace it, endure it, and you will be stronger than everyone around you. Because everyone else struggles against the suffering, and you have learned to float on its current.

DAY: 13

TOTAL CALORIES, APPROX.: 800

These rules aren't mine, mostly. I stole lots of them. Others I adapted, amended, updated.

Several rules ago, I said I thought I might be a Buddhist, but I don't think I really know what that means. There is a lot of stuff on the internet about Buddhism, but it's hard to make sense of. *It's not so much a religion as it is a philosophy or a way of life. It's about not being materialistic. It's about finding inner peace and enlightenment.* So nothing like any of the really good stories I loved in the Old Testament. The kind where there's fire and plague and smiting of the wicked.

And while I know that in Buddhism there are Four Noble Truths, I really only cared about the First one:

Life is suffering.

That, right there, was enough to make me a Buddhist. Or make me want to be one. Because that much I already knew was true.

It was especially true that Saturday, sitting, waiting, walking around the house, wondering when Tariq would pull up. Listening for the sound of his truck tires crunching on the dirt drive.

Because I'd made up my mind. On this trip, I'd start to question him. Nothing direct. Not at first. Just enough to feel him out, smell whether he had anything to offer on the subject of Bastien and Ott and Maya.

I opened my bedroom window and stuck my head out and shut my eyes so I could simply *hear*. Let my mind drift with the wind, focused on the sound of every passing vehicle, noticed for the first time how every single one had its own unique rhythm, a sound that belonged solely to it, made up of a million diverse pieces—engines, pistons, brakes, shocks, parts made of metal and plastic and rubber, none of which I knew the name of.

By then I had listened a couple dozen times to a CD Tariq had made for me. Punk rock was scary, its noise and its anger, but it was fascinating, too, the way horror movies had mesmerized me when I was a child, and for the same reason: because I believed that if I could survive the experience, I'd emerge stronger. These songs were raw rage, naked emotion, howls that combined the

shriek of frightened infants with the bellowing of angry adults. They scared me, but they also made sense.

Rage, I understood.

I felt rage, even if I also feared it.

I couldn't have told you what any of the songs were about. Incomprehensible lyrics with the occasional stray scrap that made sense, lines about love and rejection and The Man and long-defeated municipal legislative agendas—tough terse band names intended to intimidate, with words like Dead, Chain, Sex, Clash, Toxic.

Five tracks in, I felt close to crying. It was like I had never really heard a song before. Never really listened. Was it the power my hunger gave me, or was this what songs felt like to everyone? I shut my eyes, and I was there, inside the singer's head, inside the echoing snare drum. I felt what they felt even without understanding a single word.

Music was magic. It could make you feel someone else's emotions.

These were the songs Maya used to listen to. The ones she guarded so jealously, relishing her job as Older Sibling, enforcing Mom's rules about no movies or music with cursing in it. Listening to them now, I felt like I could feel her. Like we were connected. And it made me so happy.

I heard the music before I felt the truck, a windborne squall of churning chords, and I shut my eyes and felt it

swell inside me as he came closer.

"Hey, Matt."

"Hey," I said, getting in. "Thanks for taking me along. What's the occasion?"

He smiled. "I figured your multiple assassination deserves celebrating. You are now a legend."

"Legend?" I said, and fought a war within myself over whether to believe him.

"Yup. Everybody is talking about it. It was pretty impressive to start with, but by the time the rumor mill got through with it, you had broken every window in the gym and caused concussions and forced the physical education department to ban dodgeball from Hudson High forever."

"Wow," I said, and then wondered whether I could trust my own memory of what happened. After all, given my *abilities* . . . "But for real—were any of those guys seriously injured?"

"Nah. Only their pride."

I was surprisingly relieved. "They're probably pretty mad at me," I said.

"Actually, they're impressed. Nobody thought you had it in you."

Again the pleasure rush. I could see the peril in that feeling. I could see why bullies bullied.

"Anyway," Tariq said. "You excited about our road trip?"

"I am," I said. "I've never been to New York City before."

"For real? How is that possible? It's so close!"

I shrugged, decided not to say any of the real reasons. *Because my mother never had enough time off from work to take us anywhere fun. Because we never had any money. Because, unlike you, my parents couldn't afford to buy me a truck and give me the gas money to go wherever I wanted to go whenever I wanted to go there.*

Saturday, late afternoon, the sky darkening already. I paused a second before shutting the door behind me, smelling the air, feeling the cold of the coming twilight. Rain felt likely. Mom was at work. She couldn't stop me from getting in the car with a boy I had sworn to destroy. She couldn't make me leave the bottle of scotch behind. She couldn't make me eat.

I was invincible.

We drove south on a punk rock carpet of sound, intricate melodies overlapping inarticulate guitar distortion. He wore all black, strong and graceful as a ninja.

"We're driving to Poughkeepsie, then taking the train into the city. Then we'll take the subway to the club. Okay?"

"Sure," I said.

The music made my heart beat faster. Where had it been all my life, this sound, these noises, all the profanity and bare unashamed feeling that they'd never in

a million years play on the radio or in the supermarket or any of the other places people play music? How big it was, this ocean of music, and here I was standing in water that was up to my ankles. Maya was out there, knee-deep in the same sea.

"You don't say much," Tariq said. "I thought it was just you didn't want to talk to all those assholes at school."

"That's certainly true," I said, watching the world darken before my eyes. "*You* seem to find plenty to say to them."

He nodded. "It's complicated. I've known most of those guys since we were little kids, you know? They weren't always such jerks."

"But they're jerks now."

Again, Tariq nodded. "Some of them, anyway. Sometimes." I took him in: his profile, the slope of his wide nose, the smell of the dinner his mother cooked, spices I couldn't name, meat so rich I could feel it on my tongue.

"Like Bastien and Ott," I said.

He laughed. "They're not so bad. They have their moments. They can be assholes, but it's mostly harmless stuff."

Both my eyebrows skyrocketed. There were a dozen things I could have said, but I decided to be strategic—and neutral. "Just because you don't feel the harm doesn't mean it's harmless."

"That's true."

"And anyway, I wonder. People say sticks and stones, words will never hurt me, all that bullshit, but the first thing you find out in kindergarten is that words *can* hurt. And if someone's capable of hurting someone else with words, aren't they also capable of hurting someone physically?"

Tariq shrugged. I breathed deep, but his guard was up. He didn't like talking about his best friends.

I gave it a second, and then pressed the point. "You don't think so?"

"No. I think so."

Already the streetlights were stuttering on. "And would they? Hurt someone?"

Silence. Stalemate—he wouldn't say anything else on the subject, not for the moment anyway. I'd have to sneak up on it another way. The scotch would help.

Many miles passed before he said, "In a way I envy you, you know? You don't need to be disconnected from all these people. You don't feel this *pressure*, to be some person they expect you to be instead of yourself." I smelled something on him, then: the rush of yearning, the hunger for release. Bingo. I reached into my bag and my hand closed on the neck of the scotch bottle—but then something stopped me from pulling it out.

That smell.

The smell of wanting to be drunk. Of *desperation* for booze.

I'd been smelling it all my life. A knowing settled in my stomach, half eerie suspicion and half gut certainty. *My mother is an alcoholic.* She had kept it in check for longer than I'd been alive. She went weeks sometimes without thinking about it. It was why she went to synagogue so often, when I was pretty sure she didn't believe a word of it. But it was still there, below the surface. Just like this bottle, hidden away. Forgotten sometimes. But *there.* How had I missed it?

"This song is so good," I said, cranking up the stereo.

He smiled and sang along, and so did I. By Poughkeepsie my whole body was singing. We stood on the platform and waited for a southbound train. We stood so close I could feel his heat against the cold of the night. Lights glimmered and flashed on a bridge. The river was a wide rush of wind and water, cold and alive, the weight of the night so heavy it could crack me open. My empty aching belly gurgled out a song, every cramp and spasm an affirmation, a lyric: *I am alive, I am an adult, I control my life, I can do anything.*

RULE #17

Pattern recognition is an innate ability of all animals. Birds and jellyfish and people all learn the same way: by finding familiar things in the chaos of reality. And the human mind's capacity for pattern recognition is the most impressive on the planet. Properly attuned, it can find the signal in an ocean of static.

Only the strongest, purest mind can control the body. But some truths can only be taught by the body. The warrior schooling herself in the Art of Starving will learn to let the body take the reins.

DAY: 13, CONTINUED . . .

This was a terrible horrible no-good very bad idea. I knew it the second I stepped onto the platform at Grand Central Terminal. New York City was the wrong place for a novice in the art of controlling his senses. Overwhelming stinks, deafening sounds. The crushing pressure of a half-dozen million people choking on their own anger and sadness. Like that first day back in high school, before I learned what my powers were, except

cranked up ten thousand times.

"Stay close," he said, leading me through the bustling chaos of the terminal.

"You know the city pretty well," I said, although he didn't hear me. I could barely hear myself.

If his plan was to hurt me, this handsome monster, he wouldn't need to lift a finger. He could slip away from me easily enough in the crowd and abandon me to my fate in this terrifying city. Five minutes on my own and I was sure I'd be knocked out and dragged into an alley and tortured to death, my organs subsequently sold off for spare parts. I glimpsed streetlights, taxicabs; smelled bus exhaust and tar—but Tariq took me in the opposite direction, down a sloping hallway, burrowing underground, boarding an escalator, descending to the subway.

"This is so complicated," I said, staring at the tangled transit lines on a map.

"Nothing to it," he said, stabbing the map with two fine fingers. "Don't think about the big picture. Focus on where you are and where you need to go." He paused. "That's good life advice, actually. Free of charge, brother. Anyway. This is where we are. See?"

I saw: Grand Central Terminal. A green line crossed a purple and a gray one.

"And this is where we're going."

He stabbed a different spot: Bedford Avenue in Brooklyn.

"Okay," I said, stepping closer to the map. "So . . ."

"How do we get there?"

"I have no idea," I said.

"The green line," he said, tracing it with his finger.

"To the L train!" I said, seeing where the lines crossed at Union Square.

"Good!" he said, and clapped me on the shoulder and held on. "We transfer there. You're practically a New Yorker already."

He let me lead us. I got us to the right platform; I got us on the right train. Saturday night and the car was packed, dressed up men and women, drunk kids, and people on drugs. Someone played an accordion. I felt inches away from drowning. Happiness oozed out of him, and I clung to it, wrapped myself up in it. Let it anchor me.

"Here," I said, discreetly inserting the bottle under his arm.

"Matt!" he said, laughing. "You're my new favorite." He drank from it shamelessly, openly.

"Be careful with that!" I hissed.

"Don't be a narc, Matt."

Someone sitting down laughed. We stood together, alone among millions. He handed me back the bottle and I put it to my mouth, lips pressed tightly shut as I tilted it back so I didn't swallow a drop.

By Bedford Avenue the booze had begun to kick in

for him. We had a ways to walk, and I could see Tariq wobbling a little already. I sniffed. Three people had puked on the sidewalk in the past hour, just within a four-block radius of where we stood. Three stories up, in a squalid weed-stinking apartment, I heard two men grappling and punching in a firestorm of hate and anger.

This city would destroy me.

"This place is the best to see shows," he said. "But they just lost their lease. It's the last night. Gonna be a great show. All the good spots in the city are gone, seems like."

"My sister had a crush on you," I said, more out of desperation than Evil Genius Expert Timing.

Tariq stopped walking. "Your sister is awesome," he said after weighing his words for a while. "I was so sorry when I heard about what had happened to her."

We kept walking. The booze was making him less careful, less skilled at hiding his thoughts and feelings. *Precisely as I had planned.* "What did you hear?" I asked.

He shrugged. "You know. Stuff. I heard she ran away."

"But you said *I heard about what happened to her.* That's not the same thing as running away."

"People run away for a reason, don't they?"

I decided not to press the point. I had to be patient. Let him do the work for me.

I felt him start and stop a dozen times, trying to say

something. "I wanted to ask how she was doing, but I figured you wouldn't want to talk about it."

"Why would you assume that?"

"If it was me, I wouldn't want to talk about it. But you're not me. I shouldn't assume other people think like me."

"No," I said, my voice icy. "You shouldn't."

"Sorry I brought it up," he said.

"You didn't. I did."

He laughed. "Then I'm sorry *you* brought it up."

I stopped walking. I couldn't risk driving him off, losing all the work I'd put into bonding with him. So I started to laugh.

"I'm messing with you, man," I said, just like that. *Man*, like I was one of the guys, like this language came naturally to me.

"Consider me messed."

That's how I made it to the club. Faking it. Focusing on my mission. On Tariq. Being what he wanted me to be. Being the smart friend he was so hungry for.

Tariq tried to pay our ten-dollar door fee, but I pulled out my poker winnings and paid for both of us myself. We were whisked down a flight of stairs to a low-ceilinged, basement-smelling, overcrowded room, walls covered in decades of densely layered graffiti, where angry guitars galloped alongside frantic drums, and a wandering bassline struggled to keep up.

"What do you think?" he said, his eyes shining in the dim light, alcohol glee already making him grin like a tiger.

"This is amazing," I said.

It *was* amazing. It was also terrifying. It was anarchy; it was liberation. Dancing in a frenzy, all fists and elbows, screaming out songs of rage. Every few minutes a subway rumbled through an underground tunnel beside our basement, and we felt it in our bones.

They are angry at the same world I am angry at, I thought. *They accept me. I am one of them. All I have to do is step forward and claim it—*

Five or six times I tried to enter the mosh pit. Fear got the better of me, the first two times—made me stop, made me turn back. After that it was simple clumsiness, the inept stumblings of a boy bad at gym class and afraid of all physical activity. Again and again I got pummeled, and barely made it out.

The basement helped; the thick stone walls and the echo of all that music shielded me somewhat from the city. But I still felt raw, naked, open to the suffering of the world. I still felt sick, alone, lost.

And suddenly, hungry. So hungry. What was wrong with me? Right then, I could feel there was *something* wrong with me. I shut my eyes and tried to focus on something safe, and all I could think about was my mother.

"Mommy," I whispered without wanting to. It was the helpless cry of a child having nightmares. And somehow, as it had when I was tiny, just saying it made me feel better.

My cell phone said 11:04 p.m. How much longer would this thrashing go on?

"Come on, Matt!" Tariq called, periodically, whenever the surge and ebb of the pit brought him close to me.

"In a minute!" I said.

I really was content to sit back and watch. I was one of them, even from the sidelines. I watched them punch the air, pound the floor, smash into each other in a haze of testosterone. Sweaty limbs wrapped around sweaty torsos.

One of them caught me staring. And stared back. And smiled. A handsome mess of floppy black hair and pale acne'd skin, his smile said, *We are the same*. His smile started a tingly feeling, so warm and good I knew not to trust it. He took a step in my direction, and I panicked, leaped back into the fray.

Panic made my mind back off, and my body took the reins. I moved with the crowd, a leaf in the wind, effortlessly swinging in a profane, sacred circle. Like a pagan ritual, breathing in and breathing out, feeling life energy course through me, rolling with the crowd of flailing arms and kicking legs.

A hard, ugly truth: *Sometimes you have to let the body take the lead*.

After the show, walking back toward the subway, I knew that nothing would overwhelm me now. The body was the key: making peace with it, letting it find its way. Letting it separate the avalanche of useless information from what I truly needed.

We passed a huge tenement building. Hundreds of apartments. A couple argued out front—her rage singed my nostrils—two floors down an old woman was pouring hot water over a tea bag she'd already used three times—

And I breathed in. Focused on my breathing. Turned my metaphorical back on all those stimuli. Focused on the one I needed. The one I was here for.

"Hold up a second," I said.

Tariq stopped.

"Cigarette?" I asked.

He lit one for me. And one for himself.

"You okay?"

"Yeah," I said. "Never been better. Just wanted to take a minute to appreciate what a nice night it is."

Tariq smiled. I could have walked all the way home, that's how clear and calm the map of the world was, now that I could control the tornado of sense impressions that had threatened to destroy me.

Even the memory of the boy who'd smiled in my direction made me feel strong, powerful, a member of a secret tribe instead of a lonely freak. *My people are out there. Someday, I will be ready to join them.*

"Give me some more of that," Tariq said, drunkenly pawing me in search of the bottle, while we waited at Bedford Avenue for the L train. He had been sweating a lot, down in that basement. He was drinking the scotch like it was water. He couldn't see my smile when I handed it over.

It would be so easy to end him, I realized. *The slightest of motions, and I could pivot his body onto the tracks as the train pulled in.*

But I still needed answers. I needed to know what happened. What he did, or *they* did. Then I'd be able to take the vengeance that was rightfully mine.

And I was still so intoxicated by the moment, by my discovery—I wanted to savor that moment. And I wanted to be clear of distractions when the time came to savor his destruction. . . .

RULE #18

Your body doesn't know the difference between its hungers. It responds the same way to hate as to love. This is why Lex can't get enough of Superman. Why Batman just won't quit The Joker.

This is why every great revenge story is indistinguishable from a love story.

DAY: 13, CONCLUDED

. . . and maybe I wouldn't have to wait too long before his destruction came along.

"Why's it so coooooold," Tariq said—or something like that—back in Poughkeepsie. He was trying and failing to unlock his truck, and I saw for the first time how drunk he was, and how long a drive we had, an hour of winding roads and twisted turns, and Tariq too drunk to say words let alone get us home alive.

Once he had the car unlocked, I didn't get in right away. The smart thing to do was to snatch his keys, make him sleep it off in a hotel room or the bed of his pickup, because to get in the car with him was way too

likely to result in both our deaths.

But so what if I did die? Taking Tariq out would give my sister healing, maybe bring her home. My own death was just icing on the cake, sparing my mother the shame I'd bring her one way or the other.

Suicidal ideation, the words flitted through my brain. It is a persistent little sonofabitch. And quite the opportunist.

"Matt, you're a good guy," he said, hands and forehead resting on the wheel. "I wish everyone wasn't so mean to you all the time."

"They won't be," I said, and he chuckled, either missing the malevolence in my voice or amused by it. "Not anymore."

"No more scotch?" he asked, starting the truck.

"Couple drops," I said, handing the bottle over.

He sucked it dry, then threw it out the window. "Tariq, you shouldn't litter," he said in a deep accented voice—his father's voice—and then burst out laughing.

He picked our way through Poughkeepsie's silent streets with an excessive, paranoid caution. Once he made it to Route 9, however, he floored it. The truck groaned and lurched as it hurried us north. Hunger had me gnawing at the inside of my cheek, and pretty soon I tasted blood.

"I'm drunk," he said. "I shouldn't be driving."

"You'll be fine," I said. "You're an excellent driver."

He saluted. "Thank you, sir. You are an excellent passenger."

He rolled down his window, maybe hoping that the cold might sober him up.

His father was in the car with us, summoned by Tariq's lighthearted impression. I could hear him, echoing in the air, in Tariq's mind. His presence was dark and terrible. Maybe I could use it.

"Tell me about your father," I said, my voice a howl above the roar of cold wind from the open window. "What does he do for a living?"

"Runs a Christmas tree farm," he said. "Jutkowski's, out on Spook Rock Road?"

"I've gone by there a million times!" I said. "But your name isn't Jutkowski."

"No, he was the one who founded the farm. My father worked for him, for years. When old man Jutkowski retired, he sold the place to my dad. Figured changing the name to Murat's might weird people out."

We took a turn too fast. My stomach swung in zero gravity for a second, and I liked it. The fear. The freedom of letting go of that fear. Of embracing what might happen next. "There's no . . . religious problem, with doing what you guys do?"

"No. Just don't tell Allah."

"Look at you," I said, "a wealthy Arab whose money comes from selling Christmas trees to infidels."

Tariq laughed, but his laugh was sad, and I had no idea what piece of my sentence had saddened him. I had a whole line of further Father Questions, intended to shake him, but now I didn't have the heart to ask any of them. He had crested the wave of happy intoxication, and was crashing down hard into depression. I savored the taste of blood in my mouth, and was about to swallow it when I wondered whether even that minimal nourishment might take a tiny edge off my hunger.

How many calories are in blood?

I spat it out, into the night. And then, swift as a snake strike, I asked: "What was up with Ott and Bastien and my sister?"

"What was . . . up?" he asked, his voice slurring nervously.

"Yeah." My instinct was to spin stories, dazzle him with words, trick him into letting something slip, but silence was far more tantalizing. People will tell all kinds of secrets just to fill an uncomfortable silence.

Tariq looked genuinely confused.

"I don't know. I don't think anything was."

The road wobbled underneath us. It never felt like all four of his tires were touching the earth at once. His headlights showed us sheer rock faces, diners shut down for the night. At least it was late, the roads were empty, we'd probably hurt no one but ourselves when we crashed.

Was he lying?

Drunk, tired, disoriented—seeing through him should have been easy. But I couldn't. Did that mean he really didn't know about Ott's and Bastien's part in whatever happened? Or did it mean that there wasn't anything there? That *he* was the only one involved?

"We stink," he said.

"Speak for yourself," I countered. "You moshed for, like, hours. I only did it a little."

He took a deep breath through his nose. "Nope. You stink, too. And I think maybe we're going to die," he said and giggled, after he swerved to avoid hitting a deer that turned out to be a low-hanging tree branch.

"Everybody does," I said.

A sudden, sharp pain distracted me from the prolonged ache in my stomach. My fingertips, bleeding again. I'd been gnawing them without realizing it.

And yet, this here is the weirdest part of the whole weird thing.

Hunger, revenge, anger aside, it felt good, being in that truck. Being Tariq's "friend." Careening toward death together.

I did not want the ride to end. I didn't want to get home, get out of that truck, crawl alone into the lonely cavern of my bed. I wanted to press my warm body against his and fall asleep.

Realizing this made the black stars bloom in the air

around me. Cursing, breathing, trying hard not to panic, I pressed the tips of my fingers to the glass and shut my eyes. Felt energy move through me; felt my lungs suck in chi from the cold dark endless curve of space. Focused the scream of self-hate that was trying to howl out of my throat and forced it out through my fingertips instead.

I opened my eyes, pulled back my hand.

Where my fingers had been pressed, tinted red where I'd been bleeding, were five tiny star-shaped cracks in his window.

RULE #19

Your body is eternally bonded to the bodies of the people you love, and those bonds will assert themselves in terrifying and unpredictable ways.

DAY: 14

TOTAL CALORIES, APPROX.: 1500

Coffee. Pancakes. Anger.

The smells woke me up, dragged me out of bed.

Somehow we had survived. Protected by Allah or Yahweh or whatever other god looks out for undeserving, drunken teenagers, we made it back to Hudson without dying. Now it was morning, and my mother was downstairs, sitting at the kitchen table and waiting for me.

Oh crap, I thought, hopping into my pants, *she knows. Knows I snuck out of the house, went to the city, almost got trampled in a basement mosh pit, and finally got in a car with a drunk driver going ninety miles an hour down Route 9 at two in the morning.*

Or maybe she just knows I got suspended from school?

I brushed my teeth, running through a litany of excuses, knowing she'd see through every one.

And then the trusty refrain of my broken stomach set in, the pain that blotted out everything else, and I marched bravely to the kitchen, to the food I could not let myself touch. Before I rounded the corner, I saw it. On the side of the fridge, still. The photo of my skinny mom. The young woman, probably not much older than I am now. My mom, before she lost control. Before terrible things happened to her, to transform her into the sphere before me.

It didn't matter. Whatever it was, it wouldn't happen to me. And I *would* control that. And I wouldn't lose it, now that I knew about my powers.

"Morning," I said. She sat at the table, pressing her hands to her face. Her wild brown hair still held the shape of her hairnet, which meant she'd only gotten in from work a little while ago, hadn't changed, hadn't showered. Pancakes were stacked ominously high on a plate before the place where I normally sat. I grabbed a mug of coffee.

"Why do you take it black?"

I shrugged. "Tastes better that way."

"You've tried it with half-and-half?"

"No," I said, "but—"

"Try it," she said and handed me the jug.

I stared at it, watched thick creamy fat slosh in the

little jug. "No, thanks."

"I thought so," she said. "Sit."

I sat. Sipped. Waited.

Her face was red and lined and had never looked so old before. "I'm worried about you, Matt. Why aren't you eating?"

I gulped, audibly, idiotically. I had not anticipated *this*. "I'm eating."

"Good. Then eat," she said, and stabbed my pancake heap with a fork. "Eat them all."

"But, there . . . there must be ten pancakes here," I whispered helplessly.

"Then you'd better get started."

"Mom? Where is this coming from? I don't—"

"You look sick. Can you even see yourself? Have you looked in a mirror lately?"

"Of course I ha—"

Up came Prop #3, following the pancakes and the half-and-half: a mirror.

Oh, no. This was an intervention.

My mother had obviously put a lot of thought into it. So the least I could do was look. I saw a chubby face and a fleshy neck staring back at me in that mirror. I saw a nose so large no one would ever love me. I saw a head too big for its body. More than that, I saw the ghost of Christmas future.

The way my cheeks would swell up, my chin triple,

like Mom's had. The way I would have to lumber through the world to get around. It sent a cyclone of broken glass shards spinning in my stomach, but I stared at him, that future failure, and at her, and I smiled, even though I felt like crying. I did it to make my mother feel better. Because pain was booming and crackling like thunder inside of her, and only I could hear it. Only I could see how close she was to breaking.

"I'm sorry, Mom," I said, and put the fork down. "I didn't realize."

She stood, and I saw her lower leg was encased in a plastic boot.

"What the hell?" I yelped. "What happened to you?"

"Last night, at work, I had a . . . a moment. I was swinging the hammer—"

The hammer is how they knock the hogs out. Before they kill them.

"—and I got distracted. And I missed. And hit my leg. The plant doctor said there's a slight chance of a stress fracture." She laughed, although it was not the kind of thing you laugh at. The hammer could kill a person as easily as a hog or shatter every bone in her leg.

"You're such a pro, Ma," I said. "What distracted you?"

Here she turned, eyed me hard. "It was the strangest thing. I thought I heard you calling for me. Like when you were little, and you had a nightmare. Clear as if

you'd been standing right there in the slaughterhouse with me."

I shivered, turned cold inside. "You heard me calling you. Last night. When?"

"Just after eleven p.m.," she said. "I know it sounds crazy, but I really did hear it. Mind playing tricks on me, probably—telling me I needed to get some damn sleep. But then, a mother just knows things."

Had I called my mother with my mind? And had she heard me a hundred and twenty-five miles away?

Tear-blind, I stumbled out of my chair and swamped her in a hug.

"Shhh," she said, because by then I was sobbing. Her hair smelled like pig blood, and it smelled wonderful.

"It's—"

I said it several times, and each time I was weeping too hard to make any other words beyond it. She held me, and even though I was taller than her now, even though I was not that little nightmare-haunted boy anymore, my mother was a mountain of a woman who could keep me safe forever.

"It's Maya," I said, finally, when I felt sure I could say things without breaking.

"I know, honey."

"I want to do something," I said. "I want to help her."

"So do I, Matt. All we can do is be there for—"

"No!" I said sharply, pushing her back. "No, that's bullshit! I won't accept that."

"Matt," she said, the mom-voice, the you-know-you're-being-ridiculous tone made me madder.

"You *know* something," I said. "I know you do."

"No, honey," she said, but she was exhausted from her long shift, and she was thinking, and her thoughts were raw and chaotic and overloaded with emotion.

"You're not telling me something," I said, and she turned her head away, wondering, trying to get her memory online, trying to figure out what she'd told me and what she hadn't, what was true and what wasn't.

"Your sister's fine, Matt," Mom said finally.

"She's not! Why are you not doing anything to—"

"And why are *you* so eager to believe that something terrible happened to her?"

"I—"

"Why do you refuse to accept the possibility that maybe she's actually okay?"

"Because she *left*!" I said, my voice cracking. I couldn't see so well, so I sat back down. "Because she left you. And me. And went away. And she wouldn't do that unless . . ."

I stopped myself, barely. Had my mother really convinced herself that everything was fine?

"There's got to be something we can do," I said. "We need to go get her. Bring her back. Call the cops. Find

out what happened. *Someone* did something. They need to pay for it."

"Life doesn't always work like that, Matt," she said, and in the heartbreaking clarity of her sadness in that moment I knew she was telling the truth. Her truth. But this truth was slippery, elusive. In an instant it had escaped my grasp.

Mom was letting go of Maya. Relinquishing control.

She'd done it before. Let my father go, let herself go.

I'd placate her, but I wouldn't follow her path.

Not ever. I rolled up a pancake and ate it with my bare fingers, and then did the same for three more. By the end I had stopped crying, and she had started.

And I wondered for the first time, if maybe it wasn't Maya who was breaking her heart.

RULE #20

Skin is the largest sense organ. Every centimeter of it is packed with sensory receptors, though sensitive parts have much more than others—your fingertips, for example, have one hundred times as many receptors per square inch as your back does. Scientists don't use the phrase "sense of touch" anymore. They say it's too simplistic. "Somatosensory system" is the new thing. Because what we think of as "touch" is actually a complicated network of different ways of acquiring information from the environment. Touch is the most complicated sense, the hardest to master, and the one with the most potential to cause great harm.

DAY: 14, CONTINUED . . .

I experimented in secret. In the cafeteria at lunch, eyes closed, I slipped off my shoes and pressed my feet to the floor.

I *saw*, through the soles of my feet. I saw the shape of the room, the hallway beyond it, the whole school. I

saw the crowds of kids moving past. I felt the heavy kids and the slim ones, the plodding confidence of the jocks and the delicate steps of shy girls.

I went to the restroom and grasped a metal pipe with bare hands. I felt with my fingertips, as sounds traveled through the pipes. The vibrations were sound waves, and my skin could decode them as well as my ear could. From one end of the school to the other, from top to bottom, murmurs in classrooms and gossip in the girls' room and the thuds and whirs of massive machines.

I pushed it further, letting my body take the lead, surrendering to the sounds. My awareness extended along the pipes, into the ground, past the school, under the fields and into the houses beyond, the muted voices of televisions and arguments, my neighbors, their words incomprehensible, but already I could feel them getting clearer, the entire town a party line for me to spy on anytime I wanted, thanks to the plumbing that connects every building.

I stood in the hallway, feeling people move through the world around me. I charted the infinitesimal changes in air pressure as people came, went, stopped, stayed. My skin sucked up all that information, basking in the feel. I felt the vibrations in my hair. I felt like the whole world was part of me.

I drifted off. I lost interest in my own exercises halfway through. I thought about food or schoolwork,

both of which were sources of much self-abuse. More and more my concentration would falter; I'd lose the thread of classroom conversation or forget how to use a Scantron form in the middle of a test. At home I'd read a hundred pages of *Jane Eyre*, only to realize I didn't remember a word of it.

I was terrified. Of myself. Of the thing I was becoming. Of what I could not stop.

I took myself on a tour of my own body. Stripped down to a T-shirt, I pressed my fingers to different spots. Studied acupuncture charts, YouTube videos. Once you understand how the body works together, you can manipulate pressure points in yourself and others. To heal and to hurt.

But pressure point manipulation is the kind of thing people spend a lifetime learning, and you can mess yourself up pretty bad if you're not skilled. Never mind the Five-Point-Palm Exploding-Heart Technique; there's plenty of mundane tricks that can go horrifically wrong. And while eventually I mastered the moves to make my hand temporarily incapable of feeling pain while still remaining fully functional—testing it by holding a lighter flame to my thumb and feeling nothing—there were a lot of mistakes along the way.

I spent a long time around the neck. The throat chakra deals with truth, after all, and maybe the right acupressure points could render someone incapable of

speaking lies. Like Wonder Woman's magic lasso. Maybe I could pinch a nerve and make Tariq tell me everything.

It didn't work. All I achieved was paralysis in my vocal cords, which went on for so long I was convinced it was permanent, and I screamed myself to sleep, silently.

I spent a long time staring at myself in the mirror. Standing there naked, forcing myself to endure the wretched sight, as I poked and pulled and tapped out little tunes on the keyboard of my body. I thought about how easy it would be to tap the right sequence and stop my breath, arrest the flow of blood, burst the brain, make my muscles melt.

I felt the blood move through my own veins, the organs pumping and tightening, the muscles dragging my bones.

And I puked. More than once. Because the body is a pretty gross place. Astonishing, the complex systems of blood and guts and waste required to keep us alive for even one second. Overwhelming, the number of things that can go wrong. Knowing too much can be dangerous.

RULE #21

Caffeine is a central nervous system stimulant, and the most widely consumed psychoactive substance in the world. It blocks the action of adenosine, a hormone that causes drowsiness. Most importantly for our purposes, however: it kick-starts the human metabolism by triggering lipolysis, the breakdown of fat into energy. Everyone responds differently to caffeine, however, so the student of the Art of Starving should experiment with different amounts to figure out how much leads to heart palpitations and anxiety . . . and stop just short of there.

When your body wants something, that's when it's weakest. If someone knows what you want, they can hurt you in all sorts of ways.

DAY: 15

TOTAL CALORIES, APPROX.: 800

Monday was the first day of my suspension. At noon, my phone pinged. An email.

An email from Maya.

I clicked it open, my heart already pounding, imagining the long, detailed replies she could have sent to my million messages, my two-word ones, and the ones that went forever, all my endless questions finally answered, and found: one small line, and one small link.

Hey Matt here's some music you might like.

The link took me to a cloud storage site and downloaded a folder full of songs.

"Really?" I muttered, miserable.

While I watched the songs download, I typed and then deleted a dozen angry sentences. I cursed her out, called her selfish, demanded she return, begged her to explain what (or who) had driven her away. But of course I couldn't send any of it.

The songs were punk-rock classics, old stuff from the Clash and the Dead Kennedys, and if there were secrets and clues buried inside of them they'd been dug in too deep for me to find. Only the last track mattered: "Black Coffee" by Destroy All Monsters!, Maya's band.

And the song was good. Her voice was harsh and unyielding, the melody line intricate, the drums punishing. The production professional but raw, attesting to at least some level of actual studio activity. So maybe that much wasn't a complete and utter lie. The chorus: chilling, chanted and then screamed, accusatory, and overwhelming.

The truth burns

Like black coffee
Bitter strong and cheap

"God damn," I said to the empty room. "My sister's gonna be a rock star."

It wasn't much. But it was something. Her anger fed me, filled me up. Gave weight and heft to my own.

My doorbell rang on my fiftieth listen. Mom was at work already.

Jehovah's Witnesses, I thought, since they're pretty much the only folks who ever knock on our door outside of election season, and I leaped down the hall excited about the possibilities for Messing With Them.

Do you guys like Jews?

What is your church's stance on homosexuality?

Would it be a good place for me to meet a man?

You may have noticed by now that I was getting a little cocky.

Alas, no earnest shepherds waited on my doorstep to usher me into their flock. Just Tariq, looking a little nervous.

"Hey," I said, opening the door.

The day was cold. I wanted to invite him in. The friendly thing to do would have been to invite him in. But then he would see the place, its tiny size and its clutter, smell its scorched-dinner stink.

"Hey, Matt."

"Why aren't you in school?" I asked. "I'm suspended,

but what's your excuse?"

"Decided to play hooky today," he said. "Can you believe I've never done that before?"

"I *don't* believe it, actually," I said. "Aren't you the senior class bad boy?"

"People only say that because I'm not white," he said.

"And the nose piercing. And the general attitude of *Screw your rules, society!*"

He chuckled. "All of the above. So what do you want to do with this day of hard-earned freedom?" Tariq asked. "Whatever you want, we'll do it. When's your birthday?"

"February," I said.

"Then consider this a belated birthday present from me," he said.

"Coffee," I said. "I want to start with coffee."

Dunkin' Donuts; Tariq ordered us two large black coffees, each with two shots of espresso added.

Espresso, it turns out, should be strictly regulated by the government, because that shit is the very definition of a mind-altering substance.

"Now where to?" Tariq said, leaning back in the driver's seat. He needed a shave. Stubble caught the sunlight, made him radiant. "We could break windows in the old zipper factory, go to Albany and get some records from Last Vestige . . ."

I stared down the road in both directions, imagined

all the adventures that awaited us either way. It had been so long since I'd had someone to go and do things with. And it felt good. And it made me angry that it felt good, because my friend was also my enemy. All that road, all the people who lived and worked and suffered and played and died just past my field of vision. All the paths we could take. I felt like a sieve, a funnel that all the joy and suffering in the world passed through. I wanted to cry.

In the long silence of my distraction, Tariq reached across and took something out of the glove compartment.

"Check this out," he said, and read to me, "'*All I wanted to do was sneak out into the night and disappear somewhere, and go and find out what everybody was doing all over the country.*' Do you ever feel like that?"

He held up the cover of *On the Road*, and I thought of my dad, who snuck out into the night, and disappeared somewhere, and found out what everybody was doing all over the country. . . .

"I'm not Kerouac. I don't want to see any people. I want to go to your Christmas tree farm," I said. "I want to disappear in a forest of Jesus trees."

"The Jew and the Muslim in Christmas Land," he said.

I nodded, so we drove.

"So you like Jack Kerouac?" I asked.

"Love him. Like, how he writes is how I feel. How he sees the world. How much beauty there is, and sadness, and how much other people hold us back from experiencing what life really has to offer. You know?"

I did know. But I didn't say anything.

Tariq's Serious-Driver face broke into a brief smile at something remembered or imagined. I shut my eyes and breathed deep, trying to smell or hear his thoughts, but got almost nothing. He had so many walls up. A secret stood between us, something that scared him so bad that it overpowered everything else.

I came close to killing him in New York City. I didn't, though, and now I know the reason why. I needed him to confess what he did. I needed the details, no matter how ugly they turned out to be, no matter how much it hurt, so I could help Maya heal.

Staying silent was tough, with two espressos hiding inside a large coffee inside my belly, but I managed. I could feel his discomfort, his confusion. We pulled off the road, down a dirt drive, came to a stop in an empty parking lot. "Jesus Tree Land," he said.

We got out of the truck.

Below us a hill sloped down into a wide shallow valley, where pine trees grew in straight lines like marching soldiers. Before my eyes they grew from tiny saplings to mighty trees. Like a flipbook of the tree-maturation process. I stood there, in awe, my hunger-addled brain

forgetting everything other than this simple moment. I shut my eyes, and I was a deer, a wolf, a bear standing in a forest, feeling winter come, feeling the earth beneath my feet, knowing I was part of everything that lives and dies.

"For every one we cut down in winter, we plant another in spring," Tariq said. "Those tiny ones, we just planted them this year. Those down there—they're older than us. Some of them are older than my dad. It's kinda beautiful."

"It is," I said.

"Cigarette?"

"Yes, please."

He lit mine for me after I fumbled several attempts with his Zippo.

"I never knew my dad," I said, breathing in that first sweet bitter mouthful of death and ash.

He looked away sharply. I wondered if Maya had told him about our dad. About the lobster boat. I wondered what they had talked about, when they were together, while he was biding his time, before he hurt her or brought her to Ott and Bastien to be hurt.

"Maybe that's not the worst thing in the world," he said.

"No?"

"No," he said. "At least there's nobody trying to make you into someone you're not."

Nobody but me, I thought.

"Does he ever hit you?" I asked. Tariq frowned. Opened his mouth. Shut it.

"I'm sorry," I said, and I was. "That's a terrible question to ask. It's none of my business."

Tariq laughed. "You know what, though? That much, I don't mind. And anyway, he mostly stopped, around about the time I got to be taller than him. When I started spending so much time in the weight room that I look like whatever stupid soldier man he was, back in Syria, when he was my age. But that's the worst part—it's like he's already won. He's already made me into what he wants me to be. He's in my head. I don't even know how much of me is me and how much of me is him."

"I wonder what fucks you up more," I said. "Having no dad or having an asshole dad?"

He laughed. "If only there was some test you could take to see how fucked up you are. Then we could both take it and decide who's more fucked up. Then that'd answer your question."

I cut my laughter short. Back to business. The business of breaking him. "It's my sister who really got the raw deal here. They say when girls grow up without a father figure, it messes up their whole love life from there. They never learn how to tell the difference between a guy you can trust and a guy you can't. That's

what all the talk show assholes say, anyway."

"Maybe that's true for some people," Tariq said, "but not for everyone."

"But I think in her case, it is," I said.

Tariq's eyes widened just the slightest bit.

"She . . . told you?"

I shrugged. Looked at the ground, at my feet. Shuffled through the deck in my head, wondering if there was another card I could play. "Sort of."

He nodded. "Follow me."

We walked into the trees, which grew taller around us as we went, like something in a fairy tale. We walked for a while, talking, smoking, breathing, being alive. Soon the orderly rows of planted trees broke down, and we were in real forest, primeval growth that stretched probably all the way up to Canada, and through Canada, to the line no trees grow north of. I ached to take off my shoes, dig my toes into the dirt, feel the roots and bedrock and staggering raw scope of the earth we walked on.

I picked up a couple pine needles. I shut my eyes and breathed. Felt life energy swirling densely around me, knotted and looping around the pine trees—here was life, here was power, here was the essential energy that the entire universe was built from, and it was mine to see, control, ignite—

I flicked my fingers, like snapping them, pinching

them with precisely enough pressure and speed to create just enough friction—

The pine needles sparked and crackled and burst into flame as they fell away, and burned themselves out before they hit the ground.

"What was that?" Tariq asked.

I stamped out the embers with my feet.

"Just snapping my fingers," I said.

"I hung out with your sister a couple of times," he said, sitting down on a stump.

This was it. The confession. He couldn't have heard how my heart and breath both stopped, so he kept going. "She and I had never been friends, but she came up to me after school and asked if I'd sell her a cigarette."

That was the line she always used to start conversations with people she was interested in. She used to teach me all her tricks. *Someday you'll be in a place where you can actually be who you really are, and you need to know how courtship rituals work,* she told me.

"I gave her one for free, of course. And you know, we just started talking now and then after that. She was the one who got me into punk rock."

"Let me guess," I said. "The nostril piercing."

He laughed. "Her idea. In a weird, Jedi-mind-trick sort of way."

"My sister can be very manipulative," I said. "In a good way."

So can I, I didn't add. *In a bad way.*

I took a long time thinking about what to say, weighing options, trying to be cool, finding I couldn't. "What did you guys talk about?"

"About you, actually. She'd do anything for you."

"I know," I whispered, hideously embarrassed at how swiftly tears sprang to my eyes and overflowed. "At least, I thought I knew."

Tariq reached out, a spontaneous, unplanned action. We are primates, after all, hardwired to respond to the emotions of others, and the sight of my crying triggered some buried mammalian empathy instinct in Tariq. "Matt . . ."

And there it was, clawing its way up from his gut, squirming out his throat, the Secret, the thing he could never share with anyone, the shame and guilt that made his whole life a living hell, the need to confess, just like so many criminals in cop shows and mystery novels. . . .

I could see it emerging.

"Hey!" someone called. A big, dumb someone, stomping through the trees like an elephant, but with an arrogance no elephant could ever match.

"Hey, Ott," I said, when he blundered into the clearing where we stood. Last time I saw him, he had been sitting on the ground with his face six shades of red from a dodgeball strike to the testicles. I turned my head

and wiped the tears from my eyes as sneakily as I could.

"Matt," he said, looking at me as little as possible. Surprised and unhappy to find me there. I stared at him, the broad rough cheekbones and flabby wide neck, and dared him to make eye contact. I couldn't read him, couldn't get a handle on what he was feeling. Anger, yes, but confusion, too—fear and the uncertainty that comes when you find out you were wrong about someone. "Missed you at school today, Tariq."

"Yeah, well." Tariq shrugged, said nothing more. I smelled worry. Maybe shame. And my newly magnificent mind, amped up by the Art of Starving, made the connections.

He is worried about what Ott will think, seeing him hang out with Known Degenerate Matt.

He is worried about what Ott will say to other people. He is worried what other conclusions people will draw.

"The guys always come here," Tariq said to me. "The soccer team. It's a good spot to get drunk, smoke up."

Ott asked, "You smoke, Matt?"

From a hoodie pocket he pulled a plastic baggie, and squatted down on the ground beside me.

"No," I said, my face deadly serious. "I get high on life."

Then I laughed. They laughed. They didn't notice my expression of disgust.

Three tokes in, smiling already, Ott said: "Nice moves in dodgeball the other day. Since when are you a ninja?"

I shrugged.

"A week ago you were throwing like a girl."

"Shut up, Ott," Tariq said.

"What?" he said, wide-eyed, genuinely surprised at Tariq's objection. "It's true! Right, Matt?"

"Pretty true," I said, laughing, because dumbass Ott had just stumbled on my secret. He'd decoded everything. He had sensed my growing powers.

Ott smoked pot, and we smoked cigarettes. And even once the weed had mellowed him out, Ott remained on edge with me. I caught glimmers of hostility aimed in my direction; shards of discomfort. I knew why, of course, but I didn't know how to dig into it. My initial assessment had been correct: Tariq was the one I could get the truth out of. Because he wanted something from me. Friendship? Approval? Forgiveness?

We walked back through the pine forest, Tariq's father's empire, his family fortune. Tariq was desperate to confess. I was so close to convincing him to do just that. And once I had what I needed, it would be so easy to burn this whole place to ash.

RULE #22

The internet is an excellent place for people with eating disorders. Packed with sites and forums with all the tips and tricks you need to cover up your eating disorder until you disappeared from this earth altogether.

Which is to say, the internet is a terrible place for people with eating disorders.

DAYS: 16–18

AVERAGE DAILY CALORIES, APPROX.: 600

My second day of suspension meant something very special: an entire day of Quality Time with my mother. It coincided with that rarest of events, a Whole Day Off for her.

"Word at the plant is that you murdered twenty people and then told the principal to go screw himself," she said when she woke me up that morning.

"Lies and slanders," I said, rubbing my eyes. "I killed at least fifty people."

"Can't believe I raised such a slacker," she said. "Now get dressed."

"What the hell," I mumbled, my mouth filthy with sleep taste. "It's earlier than when I get up for school. And I don't go to school today!"

"It's not a vacation, slugger, it's suspension," she said, pulling wide the blinds. "Get dressed."

Hunger was a fog, a blanket of gray mist that covered everything. Hunger wrapped me up in a snug blanket of cold and quiet, blinded me to the distant dangers and fears that normally kept me in a stressed-out state of high alert. I took my morning ration of two tablespoons of tsampa, just to be on the safe side.

Something was different when I came downstairs. A disturbance in the air. An echo.

Music. Real music, not a recording.

Could I hear the past now?

"Were you playing Maya's guitar?" I asked.

"Christ, kid, you heard that? Thought you were asleep. Plus, I didn't even turn the goddamn amplifier on."

"I didn't know you played the guitar," I said because I couldn't tell which one was more astonishing, the fact that I could maybe *hear the past* or the fact that I'd never known something so important about her.

"There's a lot you don't know about your fat old mother," she said. "I used to have hopes and dreams the same as you two."

"You wanted to be a rock star?"

She showed a thin and rueful smile. "I wrote songs, had crazy ideas about playing them for people." Then she flapped her hand to whisk away these unhelpful, unwelcome memories. "But winter's coming, and it's a Tuesday. Which means half off at the Salvation Army. We're going shopping."

Once we got there, I fingered jackets and pants in an ecstasy of information, glimpsing scraps of every garment's past life. A fight between a boyfriend and girlfriend; the shirt she donated, along with every other article of clothing he owned, while he was at work the next day. The mothball vacuum cleaner smell of the closet where a coat spent a decade; the hard tavern nights of smoke and barstool pleather that a pair of jeans endured. The pajama bottoms an old man died in. A hat a meth-head loved, until she ended up in prison. And through it all I thought of my mother and the lives she didn't get to live.

"Pick out whatever you want," she said. "Call me Mrs. Moneybags, but only on Tuesdays. And only here." The night before, I had spent entirely too much time on an eating-disorder support website. I read it and felt sick and sorry for these poor miserable tormented souls. But I also scribbled down copious notes.

For example: baggy clothes. Buy big bulky items to hide inside. That way no one will remark, as my mother

did, on how thin you are. No one can tell underneath all that fabric. And when I met my mom at the cash register weighted down with oversize sweaters, et cetera, she was overjoyed to see how fully I had thrown myself into the trip, considering that clothes shopping had always been one position higher than "dentist" on the list of Things I Hate.

"These are gigantic," she said, holding up a hoodie that could have housed ten of me.

"It's the style."

"I thought skinny jeans and tight shirts were the style."

"Yeah, *yesterday*'s style," I said. "I'm fashion forward."

"You're ridiculous, is what you are."

I nodded. "Yes. Yes I am."

In the car, she clutched her leg and winced and waited a solid three minutes for the pain to die down.

"I'm sorry," I said. "I feel like that's my fault."

"Shh," she said, waving her hand to dismiss that "crazy" concept.

"I can't believe they won't give you any time off," I said. "A week, at least, so you heal properly."

"They offered," she said, putting the car into drive, wearing her I Do Not Want to Continue This Conversation face. "But there's layoffs coming, and being a woman I got to work harder than the others."

"That's a shitty fact," I said.

"Yeah," she said. "It is. We haven't been bowling in forever. You and your sister loved that. Wanna go to Chatham?"

"You can't bowl with your leg like that," I said.

"I can watch you. Treat you to one of those paper boats of fried chicken fingers you used to love so much."

I thought of the things we used to do, the Mom-and-the-Kids activities she could actually afford when we were little and had the day off from school. McDonald's, the mall, Friendly's. All involved food. Food was how we bonded, how we talked.

"Let's go down to the boat launch," I said. "Feed the ducks."

We bought popcorn at a gas station and parked at the edge of the Hudson, but there were no ducks.

"Too cold," she said, sitting down on a bench. "Too late in the season."

She threw some kernels into the water and ate some. I even had a kernel or two myself. Rains up north had swelled the river, and random debris bobbed and swam with the current. In the sunlight, out in the world, she looked older than I'd ever seen her. Her drab brown hair needed cutting, and her pale skin had lines I'd never noticed. My mom was the terror of every hog in town, the fearless warrior who brought my sister and me into the world and then carried us safely to (relative)

maturity. Yet in the grand scheme of things, she was no different from any piece of flotsam on the river, carried helplessly south. We all were.

"Did you love my father?"

Mom drew in a breath, the standard moment of decision where she usually redirected me to a safer subject. Instead, she startled me.

"I did."

"Good," I said. "That makes me happy."

She sighed. "We weren't a good fit. No one's fault. You can like someone and also really dislike them at the same time."

"Sometimes it's like that," I said, thinking of Tariq.

Mom looked at me, then reached out to hold my shoulder.

I had to work hard not to use my new abilities on my mother. It felt wrong, an invasion of her privacy, an inversion of our natural roles. But in that moment I knew what she was feeling, maybe from the look on her face and maybe from the simple human telepathy of two people who love each other and know each other well. She looked at me, and she saw that I was a person, that I was learning things about pain and heartache and suffering that she did not know, could not know, that I had a whole world inside me that had nothing to do with her.

"Somebody hurt Maya, Mom."

Mom sighed. "Your sister has been going through a

really difficult period. Trust me. I know what she's going through. You can't see it because she's still your big sister and you idolize her, but she's been working through some really difficult stuff."

"That's not true. She was fine . . . and then she was gone."

"Your sister acted like she was a hundred percent in control, but that doesn't mean she was fine. When I was her age—" and here my mother paused, frowned, debated with herself— "when I was around her age, I ran away from home myself."

"What?" I said, staring at her face, but not looking too closely, not sniffing beneath the surface to find out more. "Why?"

"It's complicated. A lot of reasons. That's what I want you to understand. It isn't always just one terrible thing. Sometimes, it's a million little ones.

"I'm telling you all of this now because I need you to know that Maya is going to be all right. Whatever she's going through, no matter how painful, she's going to get through it. Do you believe that?"

I tried to answer. No words came out.

"I turned out okay. Didn't I?"

"The best," I whispered, and lay my head on her shoulder.

"Oh, honey," Mom said, and stroked my hair.

Unlike our last conversation, I wasn't sad. I didn't

want to cry. I wanted to rage and scream and burn things down. I wanted revenge—for more than just Maya now. On a world that could turn my bighearted mother (who used to write songs!) into a shell. On a world that could be so hard on a person that her only escape was running away from everything she knew.

Many a magnificent supervillain was motivated by revenge.

Maybe that's what I was becoming. A supervillain.

"You need a haircut," she said at last.

"*You* need a haircut."

"Fine. Let's go get haircuts."

Which we did. From the same guy who's been cutting my hair since I was five. Except: now I could see clear as day that he was a closet case. Couldn't tell if that was because of my abilities or my fledgling gaydar. Gaydar is a real thing, evidently—a superpower that even the most mortal among us can acquire—and when he was finished, he and my mother smiled at me in the mirror behind me, and it was the same cut I've been getting since puberty. I looked at my reflection in a state of confusion and shock, because this boy was not me, this haircut was projecting the image of some clean and well-mannered normal person who I most certainly was not. A haircut is a costume, a disguise we wear to trick people into thinking we're someone better or more successful or cooler or just different than we really are, and

this insight made me want to scream and shatter the mirror, and I controlled myself only with great difficulty, because my hunger had progressed so far that I was in a more-or-less constant state of war with my body.

All of which brings me to: vision.

Sight is the most limited sense. The one we rely on too much. The easiest one to fool. It's the most human sense, the one that helps us navigate the man-made world of signs and symbols and words and fashion. We're trained to trust our eyes above all our other senses, but that's a lie. Appearances deceive. Sight must be subjugated to the other senses, or you'll be misled.

That evening I flipped through photographs, slow then fast, then quizzed myself on their contents. Simple stuff—*Was the person in photo #10 a man or a woman? How many African Americans were in photo #22?*—then harder, *How many people in that crowd? What word was misspelled in that page full of text?*

Back at school, suspension over, I logged body language cues from the people around me, looking for tells and tics that betrayed when someone was going to lie, evade, escalate, distract. I gave a trophy in the trophy case a quick glance and then recited the names and years on the trophy by memory. I watched people for hours on end, learned the connections between body language and future action, until I could almost sort of predict what someone was going to do—*before they did it.*

I spent as much time as I could in the high school halls with Tariq and Bastien and Ott. By now the latter two had begun to begrudgingly accept me as a member of the human race. I scanned their faces, watched the way their jaws moved and their eyebrows twitched. I could see the shape of the secrets just below the surface and the careful way they looked at me.

But I wasn't good enough to see what the secrets were, not yet.

At every meal, now, Mom said, "You need to eat, Matt."

"I will," I said, but I wouldn't. I was too close.

And every time, the look in Mom's eyes was too familiar. It was the same look that those boys had, during dodgeball, when they realized they should be scared of me.

<u>RULE #23</u>

The dying human brain floods itself with more than a dozen neurochemicals, desperate to stimulate the rest of the body into saving itself. These include dopamine, which makes you feel pleasure, and nor-epinephrine, which makes you more alert. Scientists point to this chemical flood as the explanation for near-death experiences and other vivid imagery reported by people who survive a brush with death, but the sophisticated student of the Art of Starving knows it's the other way around. Those experiences are real. The human mind, on the edge of breaking free of its body, stumbles into other realities, sees impossible things, accomplishes incomprehensible actions. They are the cause of the chemicals, not their consequence . . .

DAY: 19

TOTAL CALORIES: 0

Hunger was a pack of wolves, starving and mad, running through my bloodstream, gaunt ribs showing

through mangy scabbed fur, fangs bared at every shadow.

Hunger pulled me out of bed after midnight, twisting my stomach like wringing out a wet towel, sinking savage talons into my skin and marionetting me: clothes on, socks off, down the hall, out the door, into the night.

"Whoa," I might have said out loud. Black flowers shimmered in the air around me, swelled into storm clouds, threatened to blind me altogether. My hold on this world felt flimsy, tenuous, like at any moment I might pass out, fall away from my body.

But the answers were out there. The knowledge I needed was out in the night, and hunger goaded me on in pursuit of it. Mid-November by now, the ground frozen beneath my bare feet—*bare feet what the hell is wrong with me, oh right, the common sense center of my brain is pinned to the mat beneath a great big brute named Hunger*—the air so cold and clear that I felt like I was gulping down drugs, breathing in performance-enhancing steroids, sucking up the raw power of the universe. The night throbbed inside me. I was breaking the rules, no one could stop me. No rules bound me. The rules were made by people too afraid of their own power to ever claim it, who wanted to keep everyone else powerless. The police, my teachers, God, the president.

This town is dying.

I could smell it now, like a dead mouse rotting behind a bookshelf. I was shocked no one else could. Shuttered

factories stunk like sewage pits; the empty strip malls smelled like rotten fruit. How did any of these people go about their days, living inside a rotting corpse?

I saw everything, the complex chains of cause and effect, the webs we were all caught in, the dry months and the hard harvest, the corporate trends five states over and the wars a half a world away.

The slaughterhouse will close. Within the next two weeks. Hundreds will lose their jobs.

I shivered to see the pieces come together. To feel this weird new insight spreading out like goose bumps across my body.

I saw the Main Street mom-and-pops shutting down one after another. I dug my heels into the dirt and felt the buildings that would be built in their places. Giant boxes, giant graves.

I ran. The wind ran with me, picking up, tugging at the trees, making a moaning sound that got louder as I ran faster and faster.

I howled. Tilted my head back and howled as loud as I could. Down the block, a dog barked back.

I howled again.

Silently, lightly, snow began to fall.

"Coincidence, that's all," I whispered, even as I sang-thought, *I can make it snow, I can snuff the stars out one by one, I can control the very fabric of time and space!*

But no. Power like this wasn't sustainable. It might

not even be survivable.

I might have run for hours. I might have stood beneath every window in Hudson, listening, smelling, seeing the patterns, understanding how truly helpless everyone was. Snow fell faster and faster. My feet burned. I felt like at any moment I would step up into the air and fly.

And then, all at once it was gone.

"Please," I said, but the world did not care. Hunger was a pack of wolves, turning on one of their own, clawing and tearing at my stomach. Hunger made the world spin.

"Maya," I whispered, into the jagged swirling snow, but flakes filled my mouth, pecked at my face. The wind howled laughter.

Somehow, I staggered home. Somehow, I ended up in our kitchen. I stared at the food on the shelves and in the fridge, and knew that even if I could eat it, it wouldn't be enough. Hunger had progressed too far; the pain in my belly had become too sharp.

"Mom," I whispered, standing over where she slept on the couch.

"Matt? What's the matter, honey?" The black flowers blossomed all over my field of vision, until there was nothing more to see.

RULE #24
The body's truth is not the only truth.

DAY: ∞; A BRIEF PAUSE, SOMEWHERE OUTSIDE
OF TIME AND SPACE

"You're being selfish," Maya said, taking a Marlboro from a pack bent into the shape of a boy's back pants pocket.

"No I'm not," I said, and then looked around. "Where are we?"

We sat on a long bent piece of driftwood, on a beach, barefoot, cold surf crashing around our feet, thick fog obscuring the distance in every direction.

"Is this Providence?"

Maya shrugged. "Sort of."

"When did we—how did we . . ." I looked at my hands in frustration, inspected my clothes, found no clues. "I don't remember coming here."

"You don't *come* here. You just . . . end up here."

"Oh," I said, remembering everything—running barefoot, starving, through the streets, waking Mom

up, seeing the terror and worry in her eyes, riding to the hospital . . . "It's a dream."

Maya shrugged. "Probably. But that doesn't mean it isn't real."

"Of course it does," I said, feeling sadness seize my throat and moisten my eyes. "I was so happy to be talking to you. To have you back with us. But you're not my sister. You're just a part of my subconscious."

She made a face. "That's rude."

The face was so perfectly Maya that I faltered, wondered: *What if this* is *her? Really her?*

She stared at the horizon. She didn't look at me. Her hair was loose and wind-tossed. She wore what she wore the night she went to meet Tariq. Thin olive cardigan. Butch patched jeans. The T-shirt she made that said *Destroy All Monsters!* and had a drawing of a punk rock Mothra. The waves were getting higher, soaking us up to our knees by now. "What would you say to me if I *was* your sister?" she asked.

"I would ask you what happened."

"And if I said I didn't want to tell you? Or that it doesn't have anything to do with you? Or that I'm fine? What would you actually *say* to me?"

"I don't know," I said after a while.

"Maybe that's part of the problem."

I picked up a rock, threw it into the water. The rules of physics seemed to behave pretty well in this particular

dream. "Okay. Tell me more about the problem."

"What does it matter what I say? I'm just a part of your subconscious."

A wave crested higher, soaked me to my belly, the water bitter and cold, salt scouring me.

"You're trying to win someone else's fight for them," she said, and shivered and hugged her knees to her chest. "But you'll never even truly understand how they feel, or the way they're hurting, so how can you hope to succeed?"

"I have to try," I said. "I have to do something."

"You need to understand who *you* are," she said, and turned to me, and don't ask me how but somehow I looked into those eyes and knew it was her, really truly her, Maya, somehow, her spirit or her soul or *her* sub-conscious. She took a final drag on her cigarette, then flicked it into the sea. "Try to fight someone else's war, and you will end up one of the casualties. Believe me. I should know."

"What do you mean?" I asked. She didn't answer. I asked it again, louder, screaming now, but a wave was coming in, higher than the rest, crashing down over both of us, dragging us down and away.

RULE #25

If you don't take care of your body, someone else
might.

DAY: 20

TOTAL CALORIES, APPROX.: 2000

Scenes from a small-town emergency room at 3 a.m.:

Man with pitchfork in arm.

A prisoner from the correctional facility, wheeled in
unconscious and bleeding, strapped down, under armed
guard.

Developmentally disabled man brought in an am-
bulance, wailing loudly about the pains in his leg,
apologizing when his mother urges him to keep his
voice down, wailing some more, making sounds mid-
way between words and shrieks.

Boy with entire roll of paper towels wrapped around
profusely bleeding thumb.

Teen boy and girl with shifty twitchy eyes and grubby
hands, waiting for their friend to get assessed for a con-
cussion, sneaking into the men's room together when

no one—but me—is looking, emerging one hundred and ninety seconds later with smiles so big only sex or drugs could have caused them.

Funny-looking boy, very unconscious, presenting with significant malnutrition, hooked up to a feeding tube.

I had woken up enough on the ride over to tell the triage lady that I thought I had food poisoning; had been vomiting since sharing a chicken sandwich with a friend at school and that she'd been feeling sick, too. Wasn't alert enough to assess whether she—or my mother—bought a word of that utter horseshit; thanked all the gods that I was too out of it to give my lies away with nervousness. Sat down in the waiting area with my mother. Kept flickering in and out of awareness, although I never went back to the dream-beach where I'd met Maya.

"Hey!" the nurse hollered to a different prisoner. "Get your finger out of there! I'm watching you!"

And then I went away for a while.

When I came to I was in a room, sedated, half in and half out of my body.

A tube went down my throat. A machine pumped liquid food into me. I felt my senses dulling, my abilities disappearing as scientifically concocted nutrition-rich sludge bubbled and frothed into my belly. My throat clenched. I coughed. I gagged. I panicked. I wanted to

rip it out but my hands wouldn't cooperate. And then I went away again.

"Matt?" said a lady when I returned. The tube was gone. My gut agony was gone. My supersenses were— gone. I floated on a thick smothering cloud of painkillers and sedatives.

"What time is it?" I asked.

"I'm Dr. Kashtan. Can you tell me a little bit about what brought you here?"

She had rimless glasses, small rectangles over shrewd, kind eyes. Black hair and white hair, trimmed short, warred for dominance of her head, but it seemed like a tie game so far. She looked like a teacher. "Sure," I said, trying to sit but giving up after five seconds. My muscles, always pretty flimsy, had now progressed to full uselessness. "I've been vomiting all day. Food poisoning, probably. I ate a bad chicken sandwich, I think."

"And this is the first such incident?"

I nodded.

She looked like a teacher who is pissed at you.

"Your mom says you haven't experienced any recent illness, haven't been stranded on a desert island for any significant amount of time . . . so why don't you tell me what's really going on?"

"What do you mean?" I asked, all innocence.

"Your whole body is showing signs of malnutrition.

Your mom's worried. She says there's plenty of food in the house, yet you choose not to eat. Why?"

I shrugged. "I'm in training. I want to go out for the track team in the spring."

Amazing, what the brain can come up with, even in the absence of superpowers.

"They don't accept corpses on varsity," she said. She looked like a teacher who is kind but can be unkind when she has to be. From a folder, she produced a stack of photos. "Pick the one that you think is closest to your own body."

The photos showed shirtless men, ranging from Concentration-Camp Skinny to So Fat They Make a Documentary About You.

Smart lady, this doctor.

"This one," I said, settling on something utterly average, neither fat nor skinny, instead of the Ridiculous Blimp picture.

She eyed it, then eyed me. Then she asked me a bunch of other questions, about food and my body. Except, I was on to her. I knew what she was gunning for and wouldn't give her anything that could be used against me. I had learned my lesson with the shrink they sent me to at school, the one who taught me exciting new vocabulary words like *suicidal ideation*.

Do you count calories?

Do you cut your food into small pieces?

Do you avoid completely certain types of food—carbohydrates, fried foods, etc.?

Do you ever experience guilt after a meal?

Do you ever feel that others pressure you to eat?

Do you ever induce vomiting after a meal?

Do you believe that you're less attractive than others in your peer group?

Do you feel a lack of control in your day-to-day life?

No, no, no no no, no no, and no.

And so on. For an hour.

"Are you gay?" she asked finally.

"Can you even ask me that?"

"Many gay and lesbian adolescents have a much harder time at your age than their heterosexual counterparts, especially if there are no opportunities for positive romantic and sexual relationships. They do not experience the emotional fulfillment of being physically desired by someone they in turn desire, and it makes them feel unhappy with their physical appearance. Does that sound at all familiar?"

Yes. Yes. Yes.

"No."

She nodded, put her folder away, sat up straight. She looked like a teacher who had realized she couldn't pierce a particular student's shell of obstinacy and assholery. "I'm concerned that there might be underlying psychological causes to your malnutrition, and I think

you should see a therapist to talk through it. You should know that since you're a minor, we do have the power to force you into a treatment program with your mother's consent, and she's prepared to give that if your behavior and health do not improve. Are we clear?" She stood up, stuck out her hand. We shook. Why did I feel bad about disappointing this lady I just met, and would never see again?

"I gave your mother the information on several therapists. You can call them, ask them questions, assess which ones might be a good fit. They all take your mother's insurance."

I followed her back to the waiting room, where my mother waited with her head in her hands. Her face was red where I could see it. She had never seemed so small before. I stopped, throat clenching as hard as it had with the feeding tube rammed down it, and thought *I worried I would break her heart by being gay. Instead I broke it like this.*

RULE #26

One secret smells the same as any other.

DAY: 21

TOTAL CALORIES, APPROX.: 2000

"Who's Tariq?" my mother asked when I woke up and stumbled into the kitchen late that afternoon.

"What do you mean?" I asked, still groggy, and angry to hear his name in my mother's mouth. *He's not worth the time it takes her to say those syllables,* I thought.

"Someone named Tariq left four voice-mail messages for you," she said. "Sounded very concerned."

"A friend from school," I said.

Every word was an effort. Take the disorientation you feel when you come out of a nap, and multiply it by a hundred. That's how befuddled I was. *Why are the lights out?* I thought, and then *Someone should get up and turn on the lights* and then *I should get up and turn on the lights* and then *But wait, for real, why are the lights turned off?*

"I guess the word is out," she said. "People must be talking. Goddamn small town. One busybody in the

emergency room starts blabbing . . ."

She went to the basement door and stood there for several seconds.

"Why are you still here?" I asked. "I thought you had to work this afternoon."

"Hours cut for the day," she said. "Got the call when we got back from the hospital."

"Oh," I said, and avoided looking at her, afraid of the fear I'd find there, the knowing of what "hours cut" meant.

"We need to talk," she said. "About you. About what they told me at the hospital."

"Okay," I said. "Now?"

"I'll be right back," she said without looking at me, and went down the stairs to the basement.

I made myself some coffee. Sleepiness and satiety had me feeling stupid, stuck in a swamp. I sucked down caffeine as fast as I could, but it would not make a dent. Below me, Mom cursed and grunted, opened boxes, moved heavy things.

Was she looking for the scotch?

I couldn't blame her for needing a drink. I'd smelled the thirst, the alcoholism she'd kept under control for my whole life. And it didn't take superpowers to figure out that she'd be pretty thirsty right about now.

Sleepy and stuffed, my body was out of commission. My senses were offline. I was alone with my mind.

Which maybe wasn't such a bad thing. Maybe I'd made a mistake, expecting my senses to save me. Expecting hunger to solve my problems.

"Sorry, honey, I need to go," she said, emerging. "Shift starts in an hour, and I gotta run some errands first. We'll talk later."

"What errands?"

"Grocery store, pharmacy," she said, exaggeratedly nonchalant, a tell for potential lies that I knew very well, since I used it often. That's how badly she needed relief; that's how deep the hurt I had caused her ran. "You need anything?"

"Nope. Love you."

"Love you, Matt."

I sat in darkness. I thought about my mission, about Maya, about Tariq. What the Maybe-Dream-and-Maybe-Actual Maya said. *You're trying to win someone else's fight for them.*

All this deviousness—befriending him, manipulating him, trying to force a confession out of him—none of that would help my sister. What Maya needed was justice, swift and brutal. She couldn't wait for the days it would take my powers to build up again.

I called Tariq.

"Matt?" he said, his voice bright and happy.

"Hey."

"Hey! How are you?"

"I'm okay," I said. "You heard what happened?"

"Ott's cousin was at the ER with his girlfriend, whose brother had a bad reaction to some crystal and fell down some stairs and hit his head pretty bad. He saw you there. Said you were passed out."

Plausible. Ott had a lot of cousins. "What does the rumor mill say was wrong with me?"

"It's not like that. No rumor mill. He told Ott, Ott told me. Were you—are you—?"

"Meet me at the pine forest in half an hour," I said. "Where the trees are tallest. I'll tell you everything."

"Want me to pick you up?"

"I'll ride my bike."

"Christ, Matt, it's going to be dark soon. Why don't—"

"Don't take the Lord's name in vain. It hurts my innocent ears."

"Whatever, Jew."

"Whatever, Muslim."

We hung up. He had been worried about me.

Fuck him.

I picked up saltshakers, refrigerator magnets, piles of mail. Where before I had seen whole endless chains of events, the long history of every object, now my mortal senses just saw . . . things. And there was something comforting about that.

I got on my bike and barreled out to Route 23 and

headed west. On the way, I stopped at a convenience store and bought a half-gallon of gasoline, which I stuffed into my backpack and covered up with old homework assignments.

To hell with waiting for a confession. To hell with tricking him into something. I'd confront him with what I knew. Tell him the truth. Throw his crimes in his face. See whether he had the guts to deny any of it. So what if I couldn't summon fire from the air? I could burn down his father's business just as well with everyday tools.

By the time I got there, afternoon had just started to tip into twilight. The trees were tall black shadows towering over me, monsters mocking my helpless body and the deranged mission I had come here on.

You think you can destroy us? We were here when your grandfather first set foot on this side of the ocean; we will be here when your bones join our roots in the earth.

But that was *me* talking: *my* mind, *my* fear. I let my bike drop into a ditch, sat down under a tree to wait. I thought about dousing the tree trunks with the gasoline, so I'd be ready to drop a match the moment I'd said my piece, but I wanted to have the conversation as equals.

If it came to a fight—and it probably would—I was finished. Brutal assaulters don't like to be confronted, and he was strong and tall, and I was neither of those things. With my senses dulled, I couldn't see a hit coming, couldn't dodge a fist if it came at me in slow motion.

But what did it matter if he beat me, broke my ribs, put me back in the hospital? I'd have won. I'd have gotten the truth and watched him wither, wilt, fade. Unless he murdered me, I was going to burn down his forest sooner or later.

And if he did murder me, I'd be dead. And he'd go to jail.

That right there sounded like a win-win.

"Matt!" he said, his voice ringing out through the deepening gloom. A dark shape moving through darkness.

"I thought for sure you'd get here before me," I called out.

"My dad," he said, stepping into the light. He made a face like there was more to the story and said nothing else. He stopped, looking suddenly embarrassed.

My knees wobbled. My heart beat like a punk-rock drum roll. The moment had come. My destruction of Tariq was at hand. I opened my mouth but couldn't tell what to do next.

"You're okay?" he whispered.

"Of course. I—"

He stepped forward uncertainly. "I was so worried."

And there it was again, so big and heavy I could smell it even with my senses almost completely submerged: the Secret, the thing Tariq lived in fear of me finding out.

So maybe I wouldn't need to confront him, maybe the confession would come on its own, maybe the universe would deliver it up to me as an act of providence, a reward for finally being strong enough to stand up to him. Finally being ready to drop the charade and confront him.

"There's something I need to say to you," I said.

"No," he said. "No."

Tariq took one, two, three steps forward. He pressed both hands to my cheeks and pulled my face toward him and, his lips parted, kissed me on the mouth.

RULE #27

Your worst enemy cannot harm you as much as your own mind.

DAY: 21, CONTINUED . . .

Okay, I straight up stole that rule from the Buddha.

It's one of those things you see on the internet when you're a sheltered small-town idiot who is trying to learn some incredibly complex concepts—one of those glib little meme-ready sayings that sticks in your head without making a lick of sense, lurking there like a land mine, waiting for someone or something to trip it, so the bomb-blast epiphany will blow you to bits.

"I'm sorry," Tariq said, pulling his lips away from mine. And then: "I'm not sorry."

His eyes bored into mine from inches away, alive with the setting sun. Wind whispered in the tree branches, reminding me to breathe.

"Say something," he said, his voice soft and husky.

"I . . ."

I had lots of somethings to say.

I don't understand.

This can't be the Secret.

This? That you're—gay?

No. The Secret is that you're a monster. That you hurt my sister.

It has to be.

I've put so much energy into hating you.

If I have no reason to hate you, what has all of this been for?

"Do you know I've wanted to do that since the eighth grade?"

"What?" I asked.

Tariq frowned. "Kiss you."

At that—inexplicably, irrationally, infuriatingly—I giggled. "Eighth grade? What happened then? You found that stained blue sweatshirt I wore every single day particularly sexy?"

Tariq laughed. "I remember that sweatshirt. But no. It wasn't that."

We stared at each other. I shut my eyes to smell him, to see the image of him as my mind's eye held it. The wide nose, the lustrous black hair swooped up, the dimpled grin—he was too fine, too beautiful for this planet, let alone for me.

"You didn't—you never . . . but you've had girlfriends!"

He shook his head. Shrugged. Looked scrumptiously sad.

"Then . . ."

"You do the things you have to do. My friends? My *father*? I hide it. I have no choice. But you? You are who you are, and you never pretend to be anything else."

I sat down on soft sharp pine needles. Tariq followed.

"I feel like my whole life is me trying to hide who I really am."

"Well, I know who you really are," he whispered.

I shut my eyes. I breathed.

How bright the world was suddenly. How cool and pleasant the night. How light my heart was, once I'd set down the heavy burden of hate.

I'd been such a fool. I'd been so focused on what I wanted to see and learn and smell and feel that I'd missed . . . everything.

I'd seen Tariq's shame, his Secret, but I was blind to its true nature. In my anger I'd turned it into proof of harm, assault, conspiracy. My senses had been sharp, but subject to the dictates of my treasonous, ignorant mind.

All that time I'd believed my body to be the enemy, when it had been my mind all along.

"Say something," he said, and I could see that the euphoria of his confession was wearing off, the relief of sharing his secret was giving way to fear and worry about what I'd say in response.

Once I'd taken pleasure in making Tariq suffer,

making him afraid or uncomfortable or disoriented. Now his fear hurt. It hurt like fire, searing away the Thirst for Bloody Revenge.

I leaned forward. I kissed him. A chaste, closed-lips, fairy-tale kiss on the lips. The kiss that awakens the enchanted princess.

"Don't play with me," he said gravely.

"I would never."

He laughed, and it was a glorious sound. He stretched out on the ground and pulled me to him. We lay there, on our backs, pressed together side to side, on a soft carpet of cold earth and fallen needles, and looked up at where the stars began to glimmer between the black mountain-peak tops of pine trees. The universe was a cold dark place. Tariq's body was the only warm thing in it. But that was enough.

Questions, though. They bubbled up no matter what I did. *Why did my sister meet you, the night she ran away? What do you know about what happened to her? What didn't you want her to tell anyone when I sent that text you thought was from her?*

Tariq had questions, too. "So why *were* you in the hospital?"

"Food poisoning. Bad chicken. I'm fine now."

"You swear?"

"Triple swear."

"Can we just . . . not ever leave here?" he asked.

"I was going to suggest the same thing," I said.

And then, because rage dies hard, another voice hissed from the basement of my brain.

If you didn't hurt my sister, who did?

RULE #28

The heart and mind are such fickle creatures. Strong new emotions for one person can make you forget your feelings for someone else.

DAY: 22

TOTAL CALORIES, APPROX.: 2700

It's shocking, really, how much less horrific high school becomes when you can walk down the halls and the song your heart is singing isn't "Please God Don't Let Me Get Jumped Today" or "I Wish All These People Were Dead." How much better when the song shifts from a minor to a major key, when the lyrics you're silently lip-synching are instead to a heretofore undiscovered track called "A Beautiful Boy Is in Love with Me"?

I didn't see Tariq all day, but he was with me. Every time I blinked, I saw his afterimage, a ghost-outline burned into my retina, and when I licked my lips I could still taste his. Every time my mind wandered away from whatever unspeakably boring nuance of precalculus or the Civil War was being droned at me, I smelled the

musk of his sweater. Every time someone muttered something in my general direction, his hot sweet breath was in my ear whispering, *Forget them. They have no power over us.*

Eighth period he texted me, Ride home from school? Meet me in the parking lot at 3

Yes! I texted back.

And yet: fear was what I felt when I slammed shut the door of his truck and buckled my seat belt and heard him say, "Hey," and felt myself quiver.

"I want to kiss you so bad."

His hand found mine, gripped it hard. "Not where people might see us."

I nodded, even though my lips burned with frustration.

"Shall I take you home?" His thumb pressed into my palm, triggering a secret button that turned me into a drooling fool. "Or shall we . . . not?"

"Not," I whispered.

"I'm hungry," he said. "You?"

And when he asked, I was shocked to see that I *was*, that I *wanted* food, and that I wanted to eat food with him. *Food is love*, I had learned, kneeling before our fridge, looking at all the dishes brought by worried neighbors and friends who loved my mother and my sister.

"McDonald's," I said. "Take me to McDonald's."

"Yes, sir," he said.

"My mother never let us get food from here," I said ten minutes later when we were parked at the back of the Fairview Plaza strip mall lot with our laps full of drive-thru food. "Said she didn't trust meat killed so far away."

"Your mom's a smart lady," he said, scooping fries into his mouth. "This stuff is terrible for you."

"But so, so good."

I ate. I loved eating, and I loved watching Tariq eat. He bit down on three fries so they protruded from his mouth, then leaned across the cab of his truck to stick them in my face.

"You're gross," I said, then bit down on the offered fry stubs. Our teeth clinked together. We chewed, swallowed, laughed, kissed. I touched his face and his stubble tingled, electrified my fingers. He reached out his arm, draped it over my shoulders, pulled me in tighter. By the time he sat up straight and put his hands back on the wheel, I was grateful for the paper sack hiding the significant tenting of my lap.

"So how is this going to work?" he asked, shifting the truck back into drive.

"How is what going to work?" I asked—even though from his hard, distant tone I knew where he was taking this.

"Us. You and me."

"What do you mean?"

Tariq looked at his greasy fingertips. "We can't let anyone know about it. If my dad finds out he'll throw me out of the house so fast and hard . . ." He pulled out of the parking lot, sped up into the gathering dark.

"Of course," I said, because hadn't I known already that it could never be like it was in my fantasy? That the world wasn't ready for us to hold hands in the halls of Hudson High? That Tariq had a lot more to lose than me? "Although if he did throw you out, you could come stay with us."

"I'd be staying in the hospital, actually," he said, and I heard his voice crack. "Because he'll beat me within an inch of my life."

"If anyone tries to hurt you, I'll break them into a million pieces."

Tariq laughed, but I wasn't joking. And I wasn't exaggerating. Tariq had no idea what I was capable of. How I felt—who I was—who he was.

"I know I can't make you understand," he said. "You're different from me. Plus your mom, your sister, they love you for who you are. And fuck everybody else. But I'm not like that."

"Okay," I said, and felt my immense happiness shrink just a little. I'd imagined, stupidly, that being Tariq's boyfriend would validate me in the eyes of my peers. That being with him would help me step out of the shadows of shame. But that was a childish fantasy.

"I'll be your deep, dark secret. Your friends will never suspect."

He nodded. "I'm sorry. I'm just not ready to . . . " He shivered, and I knew that shiver, that fear I'd lived with for so many years, the terror of admitting, even to yourself, that you're gay. How did he know—how had I known—that as soon as you say it, a door closes, and you step into a whole other life that looks nothing like the one you've spent every day up until then expecting?

Tariq headed toward my house. Mom hadn't been home when I came in the night before. According to her schedule for the week, penciled in on the kitchen calendar, her shift should have been over two hours before then. Maybe she'd gone grocery shopping, I'd thought, or maybe she'd gotten assigned an extra shift. But she always texted me when those things happened, so I wouldn't worry.

And it was only here, now, remembering this, wondering *What if she went to a bar*, that I realized: I hadn't thought about Maya once all day.

"Wait. Drive us to the river," I said. "There's something I have to ask you."

RULE #29

God, your mom, me, Muhammad, Cosmopolitan magazine—nobody's rulebook is right for you. No one will have all the answers. Sooner or later you're going to come up against something they can't answer.

When you're a kid, you follow the rules you're given, but growing up means figuring things out on your own.

DAY: 22, CONTINUED . . .

Hudson has beautiful sunsets. Clouds crossing the Catskills, wind sweeping up the river and pollutants in the air all add up to some glorious spectacles in the sky around twilight. By the time we got to the Hudson boat launch, the place looked like a nineteenth-century landscape painting, except for the seagulls fighting over roadkill and the dudes on cheap boats drinking even cheaper beer.

"So what's up?" Tariq asked.

Fear kept the question bottled up tight behind my

lips. Fear that once I asked it, the bubble of this impossible, undeserved happiness would burst.

What happened the night my sister got hurt?

But the words would not come out. I wanted *him* to say them, wanted *him* to bring them up. Wanted *him* to explain why he'd spent so long sitting on a missing piece of the puzzle. I shut my eyes and tilted my face toward his. I thought the words as hard as I could. But he didn't say a word.

A bottle broke on board one of the boats.

"I know my sister went to meet you," I said, quick as I could before doubt could smother the words back into my mouth. "The night she ran away."

Tariq flinched, turned away.

"I'm sorry, Matt. I should have told you."

I didn't say anything. Just waited.

"She asked me to pick her up, near your house."

"Why you?"

"We were friends, and she needed a ride, and I had a vehicle. *No big deal*, she said. A concert your mom wouldn't let her go to. So I said yes."

"She had a crush on you. We both did."

He laughed, abashed. "Yeah, well. As I was taking her where she wanted to go, she asked me out. And I don't know why, but I said I couldn't. Because I was in love with someone else. And she asked who. And even though I never breathed a word of this to anyone before,

I told her it was you."

I said nothing. I shut my eyes, listened to the tiniest of fluctuations in his voice, the slightest of shifts in his smell. But McDonald's was making a mess of me. My abilities had evaporated.

My voice was barely audible. "What'd she say to that?"

He paused. "Actually, she kind of surprised me. I thought she'd be cool with it—it's why I told her—but she actually kinda got mad. Or, maybe not mad, but . . ."

"Silent?"

"Yeah! Exactly."

"Silence is how Maya handles pretty much any negative emotion. It's her defense mechanism. But I don't know why she would have been upset by what you said. She's not homophobic. She helped me come out, basically."

Unless her crush on Tariq was more serious than I thought. Unless she was really, truly, deeply in love with him.

Which would explain his response to my text to him from Maya's number—I'm going to tell.

The secret Maya knew, the thing she could reveal to the world that would ruin his life, wasn't some horrible harm he had caused her. The secret was that he was gay.

But it still didn't add up. Rejection from a crush is not enough to make someone run away from home.

Something was still missing from the story.

"It's weird," he said. "Girls have a sixth sense for that kind of thing. They know, somehow. A couple of the girls I've . . . . dated." His fingers drew air quotes. "They sensed something wasn't right. I mean, they might not actually think *Tariq is gay*. But on some level, they know."

One of the drunk white-trash dudes threw a beer bottle at the seagulls. They flew away, squawking, and the drunks laughed, and the two crowds sounded creepily similar. Of course the ugly birds were unharmed. Seagulls, like lots of disgusting things, are damn near invincible.

"Where was my sister going?" I asked. "It wasn't a concert."

"No," he said. "Once we got out on the thruway, she had me take her to a rest stop, just south of Exit 20."

"Why?"

"She told me to go home. Said she had a ride back, all lined up. And she made me promise not to tell anyone, anything ever. Especially you." Tariq reached across, moved his fingers through my hair. "You gotta believe me when I say I really, really wanted to."

"Okay . . . but?" He grasped my hand, and turned to look at me with enormous wet eyes. "There's something else I need to tell you. About your sister."

"Tell me," I said, my voice on the edge of breaking.

RULE #30

Your body's hungers are simple. It's the mind that
makes things complex, spinning a web of stories and
fantasies and prejudices around something as basic
as love, until we crave the stories more than the love
itself.

DAY: 22, CONTINUED . . .

I have had many fathers, through the years. An imaginary man for every stage of growth. I've created dozens of different mythologies behind the person whose damaged DNA and fire-red hair I carry.

I feel that it's important to tell you this now, here, in this held breath between Before and After.

One of my fathers was a king, reigning over a distant land or possibly in exile, hiding from wicked brothers or viziers or witches who wanted to kill him for his throne and birthright. As heir to incredible riches and with an army at his command, his wise advisers would find six-year-old me and restore me to my place beside his throne.

One of my fathers was a sports star, magically gifted in every game involving a Ball or a Team, and the switch for that magic gift lay somewhere inside me. He would return to take nine-year-old me by the hand and flip the switch. Then he would teach me how to excel in all the activities my peers esteemed.

My father was rich, and would die, and would leave a mountain of money to Mom and Maya and eleven-year-old me.

My father was a villain, a sneering Lex-Luthorian evil genius who stole everything from us—he alone was responsible for our state, and he would return for thirteen-year-old me to defeat in epic battle.

My father was an artist, beautiful and sensitive and gifted, and even if he would never be in my life, his blessings were with me, inside of me, my genetic birthright, and I would pass through pain to access the treasures he hid inside my DNA, and make marvelous things that would give meaning to my life and the life of all who beheld them.

But none of those men were really my father.

RULE #31

As they approach true mastery of the Art of Starving, students will see that eating disorders are merely one part of a broad spectrum of self-harm. Cutting, addiction, suicidal ideation. These are all ways to assert your power. To prove that you're not weak. To show you're strong enough to control your own destiny by destroying yourself.

DAY: 22, CONCLUSION

"What is it?" I asked.

Tariq turned away, held my hand tighter. He wanted to be away from here, away from me and my capacity for feeling pain, away from all the messy jagged things in his life. He wanted to be in the weight room, grappling with something simple, like steel, something he could make himself strong enough to master. He wanted to punch something. He wanted to punch everything.

"I know who she was going to meet."

Words rose and fell in my throat. I turned to look out my own window. I watched the night come rolling

up the river, flooding in from the west, taking everything away from me. It went on forever. I rolled down
the window.

"Matt," he said.

I heard the word inside his head, heard him wanting
not to have to say it.

"She was going to meet your father."

Eyes shut, I tried to breathe in the night. To smell
the wind, to hear the universe. But I couldn't. Tariq's
words made my chest heavy, made my lungs collapse,
made it impossible to take a full breath.

McDonald's had ruined me. I was powerless now
when I needed my abilities more than ever.

"Let me guess," I said eventually, my words ugly in
a way I couldn't help. "She made you promise not to tell
me that, either."

"Now you're mad," he said. "I'm sorry."

"Take me home," I said.

"Okay," he said, and then— "Oh, shit, Matt! Look at
your fingers!"

I'd been gnawing them again. Blood streamed down
both pinkies. "It's nothing," I said.

He gave me a look that said it was most definitely
not nothing.

Tariq drove me home. I got out of the truck. I
slammed the door so hard it sounded like a gunshot.

I shouldered my backpack, and it was light as air. The night was bitter cold, and I did not feel it. I did not feel anything.

"Matt," he called through his open window.

I kept walking.

"Good night," he said.

I managed to turn around, but I didn't manage to smile. Or say a word.

I spent hours, that night, practicing. Researching. Googling Providence punk-rock show lineups. Writing emails to Maya. Trying to feel hunger again. Trying to see the past; trying to smell the future. Listening for echoes. There was nothing.

Long after midnight, a throbbing in my ring finger made me stop. I'd bitten the nail almost halfway away, on that and on several other fingers. Now that I focused on them I could feel it.

I went to the bathroom, sat on the floor, grabbed the pipes. Willed them to show me things I couldn't see. But I couldn't concentrate.

I gnawed on the nail of my ring finger again, tugging and tearing at it like a dog with a bone, like a starving dog trying to tear the last little shred of meat from a dry bone. And then—

—with a ghastly squelching tearing sound, with a pain like from a piranha bite, the entire nail ripped

away. I held it between my teeth for a split second before spitting it away with a scream, and grabbing a towel, stuffed one end into my mouth to silence the shrieks and wrapped the other around the wound to stop the bleeding.

RULE #32

Almost nothing is under your control. Your parents, your school, the government, the awful consequences of karma and history—all of these factors, and a thousand more, are conspiring against you. They tell you what you can do, what you can't do. The true key to the Art of Starving is this: that your body is under your control even when nothing else is.

DAY: 23

TOTAL CALORIES, APPROX.: 1100

I woke up, and for a solid fifteen seconds everything felt fine. I lay in a square of sunlight, on clean sheets, feeling rested. No one had hurt my sister. I had a boyfriend. Home felt different. It was the place my mother had made, had fought like hell to create and hold on to.

And then: I sat up. I looked down. My stomach loomed huge, an epic wave of pale fatty flesh that seemed to crash past my waistline. My fingers still smelled like french fry grease.

I was hungry. But I wasn't hungry enough.

The mirror boy grinned at me while I brushed my teeth. Mocked my flab. Made sure I saw the skin jiggling on the underside of my upper arms. My chicken legs.

Tariq lingered for a little while. I carried him down the hall with me to breakfast, burning on my lips like the curse words I learned at age six and ached to shout in every room I entered. Tariq changed the scale of things, took the edge off the sordid squalid place. I breezed past stacks of mail, garbage bags sorely in need of a run to the dump, other garbage bags doubling as laundry sacks. I followed the weak light to the kitchen, where two of the four bulbs in the ceiling fixture had been burned out for months. Then I saw my mother, and not even Tariq could keep the pain at bay.

"Matt," she said, sitting up from the kitchen table so fast I knew she had been asleep. Her face was red and groggy, and she winced in the sunlight.

"Hi, Mom. Thought you'd be at work."

"Not today."

A smell was in the air.

Scotch. A new bottle, open on the kitchen table. Next to the "Have You Hugged Your Mother Today?" mug that she used to make us chocolate milk in.

The sight of it brought me crashing back down to earth.

I remembered everything.

Tariq, Bastien, Ott—none of them had done anything to Maya. She left.

She left me. She left *us*. She left me. For him.

I stared at the bottle. Two ways to respond to this new development. Ignore it, or don't. Call her out on it, or pretend you don't see the bottle.

Maybe a better son would have done differently. Maybe a stronger person, one who put the needs of others above his own, would have said to himself, *Hey now wait a minute; this is a bad sign and maybe I should see what's going on.*

But, honestly, I can't tell you what a good son would have done, because I'm not one. So instead I went to the sink and started washing the dishes. Asked her how her day was—"Fine." Said "Fine" very sincerely, when she asked me. Finished washing the dishes. Stood there.

"What'd you do for dinner last night?"

"Tariq and I went out for McDonald's."

Saying his name warmed me up inside, hot and rich like french fries.

"That's good," she said, and put her head down on the table. I pulled out the chair beside her and sat.

"Lotta night shifts lately," I said.

"Oh, baby," she said, not lifting her head. "It's going to get worse from here."

"Business bad?"

"I don't know what it is," she said. "Something to do with corporate. Downsizing. Outsourcing. Offshoring. Some crazy thing."

"Is the plant going to close?"

She shrugged. The table trembled. "If this goes on for one more week I'm officially not a full-time worker. If I'm not a full-time worker I lose my—our—health insurance."

I put my hand on her arm. One of hers grabbed mine so swift and hard I could feel the full force of her hurting. Her need. Her hunger. Her sadness.

"You look tired, Mom," I said. "Let's get you to bed."

"In a minute," she said, but let me take her to her room. She stood in the doorway and switched on the light and blinked her eyes and focused, and for a split second she was My Mother again, the Moving Mountain, wild of hair and sharp of eye, and she grabbed my head and pulled it in for a forehead kiss and stumbled to bed.

"Hit the light," she said, already half-asleep.

I sat at the kitchen table for a while after that, staring at the bottle, debating dumping it down the drain, deciding in the end that it wouldn't help. If Mom had a problem, she'd buy more booze, and it'd be a cowardly action made by a boy too weak to have the real, uncomfortable conversation that was needed.

So instead I did what I'd seen my mother do, when one of us was sick or sad or hurting in some other way she couldn't help.

I cooked.

I found flour and sugar and butter and eggs and chocolate chips and did what the chip bag said to do. I whipped and I blended and I spooned onto a lubed-up baking sheet and I popped it into the preheated oven. Just like a real person.

They smelled like love, like heaven, like all good things. I wanted to eat them all.

I didn't need to continue my Mission of Bloody Revenge. I didn't need to track Maya down and rescue her. So why couldn't I bring myself to eat?

Because she was still there, stuck to the side of the fridge: Skinny Mom.

Because there was only one thing in this whole world I could control, and that was my body. Not to mention that if I had any shot at helping our family, I'd need my starvation-charged senses back.

So I packed the cookies tightly in Tupperware and left her a note with hearts on it. Then I drowned in hot water the excess dough, which under normal circumstances I'd have scraped from the sides of the bowl with my fingers and sucked clean, but circumstances weren't normal anymore, and never would be again.

I stared at my hands, still shiny with butter and sugar. So I ran them under the hot water until the deliciousness melted away and my fingers were scalded and red.

RULE #33

Your body's memory for pain is far better than its memory for pleasure.

DAY: 24

TOTAL CALORIES, APPROX.: 800

I woke up choking, gagging, retching, jolted out of bed and onto the floor by the ghost of the tube down my throat. My body was back in the hospital, or so it believed, drugged and helpless and fed against its will.

"You okay, honey?" Mom asked but did not open my bedroom door.

"Fine," I said, coughing up a throatful of warm phlegm onto my hands. "Bad dream."

"Sounds *really* bad," she said but went away.

All day long I carried that ghost tube with me, an uncomfortable itchiness, a dull throb, through the halls and classrooms of Hudson High. I concentrated on controlling the smell my skin gave off, shaping my pheromones to say *Danger, do not approach*, silently furious at everyone.

No bullies cornered me. No teachers called on me. There was a movie about Spartans instead of an actual lecture in history class. At lunch I ate two tablespoons of tsampa. I did not eat a third.

After that I raised my pheromone cloaking shield again, and stayed alone in my bubble until Tariq cornered me at my locker between sixth and seventh periods and smiled so deep my defenses evaporated.

"Hey, mister," he said, looking sporty in his soccer jersey and thick striped socks over his jeans.

"Hey," I croaked.

"Got plans after school?"

"You tell me," I said.

"I've got a game. Up at Albany Academy. I want you to come with us."

"On the varsity team bus?" I said. "I hate most of those guys, you know that. And the feeling is mutual."

"They're my *friends*," Tariq said. "They're not all terrible. You should come. I want you to be one of them."

I wrinkled my nose.

"Is that even allowed, for nonplayers to ride on the bus?"

"Probably not," he said. "We make our own rules, you and me. But no, I checked with Coach. He'll just make you sign a form. Meet us at three in the parking lot."

"I will," I said and marched to class, and got halfway

through it before I noticed my throat no longer hurt.

The invincible feeling lasted until I arrived at the parking lot.

"What's he doing here?" Ott said as I boarded the bus behind Tariq.

"He's here to take pictures for the yearbook," he said, and I swooned with love at how effortlessly he could lie.

"He doesn't have a camera," Bastien said, but clapped me on the back anyway. Bastien loved clapping people on the back.

"He'll use his cell phone, asshole."

The bus had a faint medicinal smell. Spit was dried on the glass. The seats were dark-green plastic, stretched thin and thick with Sharpie'd slogans. I had fantasized about this, the team bus, being one of The Guys. Usually those fantasies became pornographic. "No making out, I take it," I whispered to Tariq when we sat down in the back row.

He punched me. Tenderly.

"This is crazy," I whispered. "You're not scared about these guys . . . suspecting something?"

He elbowed me in the stomach, then kept his elbow there, then tickled me with his free hand.

"I'm petrified," he said finally.

"Want me to stand up right now and make an announcement?"

"You *would* do that, wouldn't you?" He looked at

me in happy disbelief. "But no. I just wanted you here. These are my brothers, even if I spend more time hating them than liking them."

The ride up was terrifying boredom. Asinine jokes. Exaggerated stories. Poorly remembered movie plots. Watching Hudson's autumn desolation scroll by. Listening to bad music from cell phone speakers. Trying hard to tune out the surging stink of eighteen rival pheromonal signatures. I tried to enjoy being near Tariq, to think that maybe I might sort of fit in.

I was doing a pretty good job of it, I thought. And then, somewhere near Schodack, Bastien knocked a Snickers bar out of some boy's hands.

"Your fat ass doesn't need that," he said and picked it up off the floor and pocketed it. "Last match you were so slow you lost the ball two separate times."

After that, I spent the whole ride sucking my gut in.

Near Albany, we passed the exit for Canajoharie. And I thought, for the thousandth time, about Darryl. My friend who'd not just moved away, but abandoned me. For the thousandth time, I wondered why. Wondering made my stomach hurt.

I hate soccer. I will not describe the game. Tariq looked amazing, though. His long muscular legs pumped harder and struck faster than anyone else's. I basically watched his legs for ninety minutes.

Hudson High lost. This surprised no one, except for

maybe half our team, boys who were clearly deluded about the nature of their own abilities and also the world they lived in.

The coach wouldn't let me in the locker room, which is probably just as well. Terrible things would have happened, and I wouldn't have been able to handle the sight of so much skin. Someone would have seen me staring. Or noticed something happening in my pants. And I'd be murdered.

So I paced the halls of that strange, fancy building, with its high ceilings and the eerie absence of stale-tater-tot smell. Everything was made of marble at Albany Academy, even, apparently, the pale well-dressed boys and girls and parents frowning in my direction.

The Academy is a rich prep school, and they knew me for what I was: a poor, grimy student from another town, who only had the privilege of breathing the Academy's sweet air thanks to their generous compliance with intramural athletic regulations.

I ignored them. This was a ninja knack I had long before starvation gave me superpowers, because if there's one survival skill being a gay boy at a backwoods high school gives you, it's the ability to be unbothered by the behavior of assholes.

Eventually Tariq returned, smelling like tea tree shampoo and dressed in a too-large sweatshirt, his black hair luminous, the rest of his team close behind him.

Bastien handed everyone an orange. Even me.

"Where'd you get these?" someone asked.

"Stole them out of a sports bag someone left in the hallway," he said.

Everyone laughed. Everyone ate stolen oranges. The air filled up with the smell of peeled citrus. And while we were standing there, the team of us, waiting for who knows what, the Albany Academy team came through.

"You guys smell like cow shit," someone said from inside the boisterous crowd.

"Cow? Nah, I think that's horse," another voice added.

"No," said a wiry little guy at the head of the pack. "Pig. The hog-rendering plant is in Hudson, isn't it?"

My fists tightened.

"My dad says it's the last thing left," Wiry continued, pushing the glasses up his nose with his middle finger. "Better up your soccer game, boys. Sports is gonna be the only way out for any of you."

In the hooting and bluster that followed, I flashed back to my dodgeball massacre. To the pleasure of hurting people. And I stepped forward impulsively, into Wiry Boy's personal space.

"What's this skinny freak want?" he asked, then looked me in the eye.

I'm not going to lie. *Skinny freak* made me feel good.

I breathed deep, sucked in the smell of him. Memorized it. "Nothing," I said, and reached out to touch his sleeve. "That's a nice shirt." With two pointed fingers I tapped in three different spots on his arm, triggering pressure points.

He yanked his arm away from me. "Get the hell away from me, freak."

"Want an orange?" I asked, and lobbed mine at him. Not hard. His arm flew up to catch it—and then he screamed.

Muscles spasmed in response to the points I'd pressed, the signals from his brain diverted and rerouted, twisting his forearm in one direction and his wrist in the other, a harsh and sudden agony as the ligaments were stretched, stopping just short of a sprain.

"You okay, there, buddy?" I asked.

His friends stepped closer, eager for a rumble.

"Whatever," he said, holding the arm to his body, confused and embarrassed to have no idea what just happened. "We're going home. Have a nice drive back to your shitty homes in your starving, little nothing town." He led his posse away.

Bastien stared at me. "What the hell just happened?" he asked, not unkindly.

"Guy broke his wrist recently," I said. "I could tell by the way he carried it. Figured if I caught him off guard

I could get him to move it in a way that would be pretty painful."

"You're a spooky kid, Matt," Bastien said.

Heads nodded. A couple guys grunted agreement. I felt proud and happy, but weirdly exhausted. My heart was thumping so hard I could barely breathe.

You really need to eat something, a voice said, but I ignored it.

Ignoring the voices is an essential component of the Art of Starving.

"Where's our bus?" someone asked, tapping on the windows, watching the parking lot.

"There's like five buildings to this fancy-ass school," someone else said. "Eight parking lots. Dude is lost."

I turned from boy to boy, following a sweet grassy smell.

"Somebody here has marijuana," I said, then pointed. "Somebody standing over here."

Silence. Funny looks.

"One of you two," I said, pretending to have a very vague sense when in fact I knew exactly who had how much dope and where it was stashed. "I can smell it."

"Damn, son," said a mellow kid named Danny. "You got a hell of a nose. I'm carrying. Why? You want some? I didn't know you smoked."

"I don't," I said. "I want to go put it in *that* guy's

216

locker, and then call the cops."

Silence, then someone whistled. "Hardcore."

"Badass."

Danny grinned, dug deep into his back pocket. "Hell, I'll happily sacrifice to that noble cause."

"How are you going to find his locker?"

"His name is Wilson Horn," Tariq said. "We've played them before."

"The lockers have names on them," I lied, since how could I explain to them that I'd know it by smell? "And they're alphabetical. That's how fancy this school is."

"Matt and I'll be right back," Tariq said.

"It's always the quiet ones who are evil geniuses," Danny said, clapping me on the back as he handed over the three joints.

We sped off into the maze of darkened hallways. I let my nose lead me.

"You're devious," Tariq said, grabbing my hand. We slowed down and walked like that, holding hands, through the dark halls of a strange school, and I felt invincible.

"They don't have names," Tariq said. "How will you—"

I kissed him, hard and abrupt, pushing him back against the lockers. I tapped one of them. "It's this one. I can smell him all over it."

Tariq turned, sniffed, shrugged. "Really? That's some supernatural nose shit, man. You sure you're not a werewolf?"

"I'm only sure of one thing," I said, and kissed him some more.

He spun us around, so my back instead of his was against the metal locker doors. He pressed his whole body close to mine.

Alone, in bed or at my computer, I indulged in the most obscene and elaborate fantasies. Savage brutal couplings to make Nicki Minaj blush. But with Tariq I was scared and timid, frightened of the thing I wanted so badly.

"You're too sexy, you know that?" he said.

"Stop your lies," I mumbled into his neck, and tried to break free. "We have work to do." His body held me tight. He took the joints from my outstretched fingers and slipped them, one after the other, through the vents at the top of Wilson Horn's locker. Pressed his other hand to the seat of my pants.

"Want to?" he whispered.

More than anything, I thought, but said, "Not now."

"Come on," he said, and began to unbuckle his belt with one hand while the other tightened around my wrist.

"No," I said, harder.

"Fine," he said, stepping back, his face tight with sudden anger.

And then, out of nowhere, he punched the locker beside me. I yelped. He winced, held his fist in his other hand, cursed several times.

"What are you doing?" I asked, my voice light but my heart dark and frightened. "Was that supposed to scare me?"

"No," he said, his face a stranger's. "Sorry. You're not what I'm mad at."

"Then don't ever do that again," I whispered.

Tariq nodded, but didn't look at me. He turned his head back in the direction we had come. Where his friends waited. By the bus that would take us back to our lives. Light from that direction lit him up in profile: his long lashes, his proud nose, his parted hungry lips. I breathed him in, and I smelled:

He wants everyone to find out. More than anything else, he wants this charade to be over.

But he's terrified of it.

We walked back slow, holding hands until just before we turned the corner and were greeted with the cheers of our team.

"It's a Friday," Bastien said as we walked out of that horrible building. "We'll call the cops on Sunday, so it won't point back to us so much."

The air was bitter cold and glorious. We stood there joking, laughing, watching our breath billow in the air, waiting for the bus. They were all terrible people, all monsters.

My powers could help me be one of them. And it felt so so good to be one of them.

RULE #34

Happiness is the most treacherous emotion.
When you're happy, all you want to do is stay happy.

DAY: 26

TOTAL CALORIES, APPROX.: 1300

"You would like Gimli best," Bastien said, and Tariq said "Ooooh" like it was a witty insult, and maybe it was, except my knowledge of *Lord of the Rings* characters was woefully limited.

We sat in the bed of Tariq's pickup truck. Bastien's car was parked beside us, engine running, headlights casting two long bright trails across the ragged lines of pine trees. His stereo thumped out classic rock, dumb empty songs, but the rhythm was nice and the mood was mellow and I didn't hate it half as much as I would have hated it a week before.

Bastien took a long hit and then offered me the joint.

"Matt gets high on life," Ott said.

"No shit," Bastien said, handing it to him instead. "How's that working out for you?"

"Pretty great," I said and pointed up at the sky. "Did you guys know about stars? A bunch of bright dots in the sky *for no reason*? That shit is totally trippy."

Everybody laughed.

"Legolas is where it's at," Bastien said. "Legolas kicks just as much ass as Gimli, but he does it with class and wit."

"Trav says Legolas is a fairy," Ott muttered.

"My brother's an idiot," Bastien said. "Everybody knows Legolas is an *elf*."

"That's not what he means."

"Oh."

Silence. Bastien had no comeback to that, bested again by his absent brother. "Then who does *he* like? Galadriel?"

Ott whispered, "Aragorn," reverently, and Bastien nodded.

"Who's Aragorn?" I asked.

"The King," Bastien said. And I remembered from the movie: tall, handsome, brave, strong, perfect, tiresome. Mighty warrior, wise commander, total bore.

Tariq groaned and stood up. "You're all a bunch of ugly little hobbits, and we need to stop talking about that wack-ass movie right now."

I tuned out their halfhearted objections. I focused on my secret boyfriend, his dark hair and mighty scowl in the late twilight and the back-glare of Bastien's

headlights. His charcoal-gray hoodie, the softest object in the known universe. His huge hands, thumbs hooked into his belt loops.

And then I focused my powers on the two boys beside me in the truck. The connections between them, the thick and complex coil of bonds that stretched from Bastien to Ott and back again. Bright feelings and dark ones, some too strange and complicated to decipher, but others stark and simple and raw. Ott's feelings of inadequacy beside his smart and funny friend; Bastien's guilt and pity toward the poor buddy he'd soon abandon for college and the decent life his father's privilege would buy for him.

Tariq plucked a soccer ball from the bed of the truck and proceeded to work it like a hacky sack. Kicking it straight up, keeping it in the air through nimble leaps and leg thrusts and judicious application of shoulders and chest and back. I watched, transfixed, barely seeing the ball.

"You know what I'm looking forward to?" Ott asked. "Like, in life? Bar fights."

"Bar fights?" Tariq asked, palming the ball and pulling a bent cigarette pack from his back pocket.

"Yeah!" Ott said, high and happy and out of his mind. "Don't you think that'll be something? Getting drunk, legally, with a bunch of people, and then when you see something you don't like? Being able to do

something about it."

"I feel like, overall?" Bastien said. "Avoiding getting hit is a pretty good life goal."

"You only say that because you've never been hit," Tariq said, lighting two cigarettes and handing me one. I could taste the wet of his lips when I put it between my own.

"Maybe," Bastien said.

"Wait, what?" Ott's voice was high and shocked.

"What do you mean, what?" Bastien said.

"Oh, here we go," Tariq said. He went back to the soccer ball. The cigarette bounced between his lips as he moved.

"Have you never been in a fight?"

"No," Bastien said. "Am I supposed to be ashamed of that?"

"Never been punched in the face?"

"No."

Ott howled and leaped up to stand beside Tariq. "You're kidding me. You're lying—right? That's a joke?"

"No. What, that's supposed to make me less of a man or something? Because I don't *look forward* to getting in fights?"

Ott stared at his best friend, mouth open, face askew, his grasp of the English language inadequate to express what he was thinking. Seeing, perhaps, just how wide the gulf between them truly was. Reminded again of

how different they were; forced to contemplate the possibility that maybe he simply did not know the person he liked the best in the world.

Or maybe he was just passing gas.

"I'm going to punch you in the face," Ott said.

Bastien laughed. "No, you're not."

"Yeah I am. I have to! You can't go through life without knowing what that's like. I'm doing you a favor."

"Stop playing."

"No one's playing," Ott said, and stepped into a fighter's stance.

"Holy shit," Bastien said. "You're really serious?"

"Stand up."

"I won't."

"Suit yourself," Ott said, and drew his fist back.

Bastien looked to Tariq and me for confirmation that this was crazy, or wanting one of us to step in. I avoided eye contact, and Tariq said, "Good luck with that."

Bastien stood up. "I'm sorry, buddy, but I'm not going to let you punch me in the face."

"You can't stop me either. So, what happens next?"

They stared at each other. I could see the bonds between them flicker and knot in the air, watch the colors shift.

Finally, Bastien smiled. "Do it," he said. And before the sentence had ended, Ott punched him in the mouth. Hard enough to knock Bastien back down to sit-lie on

the bed of the truck.

"Well *that* sucked," he said, after a long silence. He pressed his hand to his mouth. When he took it away his palm was wet with blood.

"Was it good for you, too?" Tariq asked Ott, who frowned down at his fist and said nothing. Tariq spun the soccer ball on his finger, faster and faster, and then, slipping me the tiniest of tiny winks, he tossed it up and tilted his head and caught it on his cheek, where it continued to spin. Because of course it did. Then he tossed it into the bed of the truck and jumped up after it. Ott followed him. When Tariq lay on his back to look up at the sky, I sidled in beside him and did the same. The other two followed suit.

"You're right about stars, Matt," Bastien said, hands behind his head. "They're totally trippy."

We lay there, looking up. The four of us—friends?

Why had I wanted so badly to believe that they'd hurt my sister? Because it hurt my heart less to believe that something terrible had happened to her than to know she abandoned me. Because a Mission of Bloody Revenge had given me a purpose, let me fool myself into believing there was something I could do about it.

"Anybody know any constellations?" Tariq asked.

"The Big Dipper's over there," I said, pointing. "Beyond that I don't know."

"Back in the day we'd know," Tariq said. "We'd have to. In order to be hunters, warriors, in order to navigate . . . The modern world has spoiled us. Filled our heads up with stupid, meaningless knowledge."

"You're only saying that because you're gonna fail your precalc test next week," I said.

"These are unconnected facts," he said, and kicked me.

"Don't the stars make you feel so small?" Bastien said, and there was a slight roughness around his words from where his lip was already swollen.

"People always say that," Ott said. "I don't understand it. The stars make me feel . . ." I could hear the gears turning, the struggle as Ott tried to cram the whole huge tapestry of his thoughts into the meager words of his vocabulary. "They make me feel *big*. A giant cosmic accident. Like—what are the chances that I would even happen? You know? If my parents hadn't met, if the dinosaurs never died out . . . we might not be here. But here we are. And we get to look up at the stars at night. Who would appreciate them if we didn't?"

"Whoa, Ott," Tariq said. "Unlikely Voice of Profundity."

"Profundity means deep thoughts, Ott," Bastien said.

"I knew that," Ott said, and then, after a second,

laughed and said, "I totally didn't know that."

Tariq's fingers found mine. Our hands clasped in the dark, secretly, watching the stars, and Ott was right: I felt strong, I felt lucky, to be here, to be alive, to be able to appreciate what was wonderful in the world, even as I let what was ugly in it tear me apart.

RULE #35

This is the hardest rule. The one I still have to keep repeating. The one I accept, on an intellectual level, but still cannot truly believe.

Your body is just a thing. Whether it's strong or weak or beautiful or ugly is all in your head. In your mind.

DAY: 27

TOTAL CALORIES, APPROX.: 1600

You're too sexy.

After school I went with Tariq to the weight room. A handful of grim-faced boys and one frightening beautiful girl were in there, too. So I stopped myself from jumping him and dragging him off to a cave somewhere when he stepped out of the locker room in an A-shirt and short shorts. His absurd words echoed in my head, threatening to unravel everything.

You're too sexy.

I watched him lift. Veins stood out in his neck. His beard and hair shone with sweat. His abs and pecs

became hard as iron, strong as anything the Spartans wore into battle.

He can't possibly believe that I'm sexy. There's no way he can look at this disgusting useless weak flabby body and feel physical desire. He must be lying. He just wants to get me into bed. Or maybe it's a bet? Like some gay version of all those movies where the jock's friends bet him he can't bed the class weirdo or nerd or telekinetic religious fanatic. He caught me staring, between sets, and he smiled. I smiled. And I knew, beyond the shadow of a doubt, that it was real. *We* were real.

When I was alone, however, the voices went to work. Reminding me what a worthless ugly slug I was, how filthy and sinful, how only treachery and deceit could explain anything remotely good in my life. Tariq took me home. "Here," he said, reaching into his gym bag to hand me an orange. "Last one, from what we stole up at Albany Academy."

"Thanks," I said, and held it to my nose. It smelled like him. And like an orange.

When he was gone, I went up to my room and sat on my bed. Facing the full-length mirror I'd draped in clothes so long ago. Staring at where my face would have been.

You're too sexy.

I decided to put the echo to good use. Quickly, before my mind could intervene, I stood up and stripped

the clothes away from the mirror. And stared at the boy I found there, the one with the giant lopsided eyes and too-big chin. Touched my face, pinched my cheek, thumbed my lips.

Is this what Tariq sees?

And then took off my sweatshirt. And my T-shirt. And my pants. And turned the teddy bear around to join me in judging myself.

I stood there, in socks and underwear, and made myself watch. Made me see myself.

I felt: fine. Not great, but fine. My stomach still felt swollen and immense, my thighs were still all jiggly flab while my calves were chicken-leg-thin, my arms when I tried to flex a bicep actually laughed at me—but looking up at the mirror the boy I saw was . . . not disgusting.

What the hell happened? I wondered.

Tariq is magic, I answered myself.

Figuring I'd quit while I was ahead, I stepped away from the mirror and dressed myself. Turned off the lights, opened the window, knelt there to breathe in the cold bitter wind. And focus.

A crash from down the hall. Something heavy falling. Something breaking. My heart, already overburdened, sputtered and stopped.

"Mom?" I called, opening my bedroom door.

Silence. I said it again, and took two steps into the hallway.

"I'm okay!" she called. "Stay in your room, okay, honey?"

"What happened?"

"I just tripped over something," she said. Her voice muddled from sleep or . . . something. "Everything is okay. Just go back to bed. Okay?"

I stood there. Wondering what I should do. And then, to my great shame, I did what she asked me to do.

I needed to feel my powers at work. I went into the bathroom and sat down on the floor, reached under the sink to grip the pipe with both hands. Shut my eyes, listened for vibrations. Extended my awareness down the pipe, feeling the miles of cold earth it dug through, the knotted junctures where the copper piping of our house's water line connected with the iron of the county water main, branching back down to someone's home, through their basement and into their bathroom, and listening, listening—

But my sense of touch was dull, and all I "heard" were faint droning sounds like distant machines. When I released the pipe I felt as empty as it was.

Happiness had blunted me. I needed to be sharp again.

In the hallway, I stopped to listen, but heard nothing. My mother was dying. Her situation was killing her, just as surely as if she had some kind of disease.

If I couldn't save my sister—if she had no need of

saving—then I needed to keep my powers up for my mother. I just had to be stronger. I could start with sharpening another superpower: use of the internet. I researched the company that owned Mom's slaughterhouse. Global trends in hog production. I learned that Westfield Foods was "jockeying hard" to be acquired by a Chinese meat-processing giant. They'd been trying to "spend down debt" by selling off assets. They were closing plants all over the country.

Useful. High school would work so much better if the things we learned could actually make a difference in our lives.

I felt my mind kick into overdrive, processing all that information. I began to see the patterns in the chaos, make the connections, understand the problems—but I was still so sluggish, smothered in the food I allowed myself to eat. If only I were a little hungrier I'd be able to see clear as day what needed to be done.

<u>RULE #36</u>

Depending on what the body you're born into looks like, you get put in a box marked either Boy or Girl. That box is packed with expectations and requirements, demands and obligations. The box says you can like This, but not That. The box says you can wear This, but not That. The box might fit you perfectly. In that case, everything will be wonderful. Alternately, the box might be so cramped and tight and full of horrible things that you'd rather be dead than spend another minute in it.

There will always be something. Some horrible thing to stress you out, make you miserable, remind you how little control you have. Once you have begun to practice the Art of Starving, there will be a thousand reasons to continue.

DAY: 28

TOTAL CALORIES, APPROX.: 1000

Tariq is a communist.

He told me this nonchalantly, the way you do with a

deep dark secret you want someone to believe is no big deal. We were in his room, his broad and spacious room, with the wide windows and clean lines and dark cherry wood. His well-ordered room full of books and technology and a closet almost as big as my whole bedroom, his room that brought home to me in a whole new way how different we were, how much money he had, and how much something like money changes who you are. Tariq was never ashamed to bring someone home; Tariq never had to wear the same sweater more than once a week. Tariq's mom, who I met when I arrived, who was sweet and thin and quiet and seemingly as in awe of her son as I was, did not have to go to work. Did not have to heave a hammer, murder hogs, drench her forearms in blood every day.

But Tariq was very concerned about injustice, about poverty, about rich corporations and greed, about the exploitation of poor countries by rich ones. He gave me a copy of *The Communist Manifesto*, and something called *What Uncle Sam Really Wants*. We sat on giant beanbag chairs on the floor behind his bed, talking politics and gossip and our hopes and dreams and nightmares, listening to punk rock music, looking up at the gruesome and obscene album covers he'd stuck to his ceiling, kissing and cuddling clandestinely. Every few minutes he'd stop and tilt his head and listen for his mother's footsteps.

I wanted to tell him not to worry. I wanted to tell him she was watching television in the living room, and I'd hear her if she so much as stood up. I wanted desperately to tell him that I had very good hearing—because I was starving myself—because it gave me superpowers.

I didn't tell him any of that. In all honesty I didn't say much of anything. I listened to him. I nodded, agreed or expressed anger when appropriate. I tried to concentrate. I put my hand out to rest on his shirt, pressed tight to feel the muscled stomach beneath. But I couldn't stop thinking about my mom—and my sister—and my father—and my own repulsiveness, especially when compared to Tariq.

"Your hands are so cold," he whispered, holding one up.

"Poor circulation," I said, and did not say *Poor circulation is a symptom of many eating disorders*. Because as I have discussed . . . not my problem.

"And I hate to say it, but your fingernails look gross."

I shrugged. *Fingernail deterioration is a symptom of many eating disorders.*

"Huh."

Tariq was a paradox. He made me feel better and worse, all at once. His interest in me, his desire for me, made me feel almost human for the first time ever. But when I looked at him, when I touched him, I felt my inadequacy more sharply than ever before. *Here is a man,*

I thought. *Strong and beautiful and perfect. Here is what you'll never be.*

Tariq smelled like pine sap. December, by then: the busiest time of year for Christmas tree merchants, and his father was working eighteen-hour days, and Tariq himself was spending every available hour hauling and sawing and being an all-around brutish burly sexy person.

This was homework time, my visit technically a study session. His father believed in education, in bettering oneself, and had Tariq's whole educational career and rise to staggering success in business and industry planned out.

His father believed in the opposite of everything Tariq believed. The rich were rich because they were better. The poor were poor because they were bad, broken, lazy. Men should behave like This, and never like That. Women should simply behave.

"Your mom's coming," I said, scooting my beanbag chair away from his.

He cocked his head and listened. "No, she's not."

"Trust me."

It took her five whole minutes, but she came. Bearing a plate where two strange pastries nestled intimately together.

"Wow, Mom, thanks," he said, and snatched one up. "These are called ma'amoul," he told me. "They're

stuffed with dates. My mom's an amazing baker."

"Thank you," I said, sincerely, touched and moved and terrified all at the same time. They practically sparkled with butter, with empty carbohydrates, with demonic sugar.

"What are you two studying?" she asked, standing in the doorway, almost certainly waiting for me to take a bite and express astonishment, happiness, gratitude. I took the pastry off the plate. My stomach screamed with wanting it.

"History," Tariq said. "American for me. European for Matt."

"You're not in the same class?"

"I'm a senior, he's a junior," Tariq said. "But we've both got tests this week. We're quizzing each other."

"Ah," she said.

Tariq's cookie was almost gone already. His mother waited an extra five seconds, ten, fifteen. Waiting for a response. Expecting me to take a big bite, and tell her how wonderful her pastries were. When none of that happened, she said, "Well, I won't distract you any further."

"Thanks for the pastry, Mrs. Murat!"

She smiled, bowed her head slightly. When the door had shut behind her, Tariq said: "After World War Two, the rise of the labor movement had made manufacturing and other industries too expensive for American corporations to continue making the same obscene profits."

"Fascinating," I said, and set the cookie down as discreetly as I could and scooted my beanbag chair alongside his. Slid my hand under his shirt, watched him flinch from my cold fingers. He giggled, a boyish sound from a body that was so close to being a man's. He shifted, straightened out, spooned his body behind mine. Kissed the back of my neck.

His heat melted me. His touch triggered terrifying things. I wanted him so bad it physically frightened me. The wanting was different, now, from when I lay alone in my room in the dark and mentally superimposed his head over scraps of dirty movies.

Was this how girls felt all the time? Torn between fear and desire? Wanting, but afraid to show it, because they weren't supposed to want?

This was beautiful. This moment was perfect.

But what if we could stand in the sun, walk through the halls, hold hands? The knowledge that Tariq and I were together made me stronger. But if *everybody* knew it—if everyone saw me like that—

"Hey," I said, and poked him in the pectoral.

"Hey yourself."

I poked again.

"What's up?"

"I don't like keeping this secret," I said. "Keeping *us* secret."

"Me either," he said.

"Then let's not."

Tariq sighed. "Where's this coming from?"

"Take it from someone who knows. Coming out is never as bad as you think it's going to be."

"Just because it wasn't as bad as you thought it would be for you, doesn't mean it won't be worse than I think it's going to be for me."

"But you won't be doing it alone," I said. "And you know I'll murder anyone who so much as looks at you cross-eyed."

"Don't be ridiculous," he said, but there was a pause before *ridiculous*, like maybe he'd been going for *stupid*.

I turned around, scooted down to rest my head against his chest, looked up at the sharp stubbled mountain range of his chin, the smooth sheer slope of his neck.

"I'm sorry," I said. "I know. It's a process. You're not there."

"I'm sorry, too."

We lay like that. Everything was perfect, as long as I focused on the moment. The room. But I couldn't go ten seconds without my mind starting to wander out of the room or worry about the future or stress out about the past.

And then—as clearly as if it had happened again—I heard the crash from the night before. My mother, falling. In the morning there'd been no evidence, but I

knew what had happened. My mom was drinking, and I couldn't find a thing to do about it.

Why couldn't I stay in the moment? Why couldn't my mind remain there, cuddling with my beautiful secret boyfriend? I wanted to choose happiness. I really did.

"You didn't eat your cookie," he said, pointing to where it lay on the floor, looking sad.

"Yeah," I said. "I'll take it with me."

He frowned, upset with me. Something was wrong, and he could see it. My heart hurt harder. My head spun.

"We should get you home pretty soon. My dad'll be back."

"So?" I said. "I want to meet him."

"You two would probably get along great, actually," Tariq said, laughing. "He's cool with everyone. Everyone but me."

I shut my eyes, focused on my abilities, and tried to imagine him, this template of what Tariq might become, this ogre whose expectations were a weight threatening to break Tariq's back—

And then, as my head spun faster, as the black stars bloomed and swelled all around me, I *saw* him. Not as he was, but as he appeared to Tariq. A towering monster with massive forearms, all muscle and rage. I saw him lock Tariq out on the back deck no matter how cold or how hot it was, and watch through a window while his

son practiced with the soccer ball, banging on the glass if Tariq stopped for a second.

No wonder he could bounce the ball so well, I thought, *could spin it on his fingers or on his face.* That gorgeous graceful motion ceased to be beautiful and became sad, the tricks of a trained dog.

"Are you crying?" Tariq asked.

I jerked my head away. It broke the spell. "No, just tired," I said.

We were quiet for a while.

"What do you think my sister's doing now?" I whispered.

"Conquering the world," he said.

"Kicking someone's ass," I said.

He kissed my forehead. His lips were very warm and I was very cold. "Don't worry about her," he said. "Your sister's strong."

I shut my eyes, and I could smell her. Maya, just out of reach. I could hear her voice. A strummed acoustic guitar; waves crashing; a seagull shrieking.

I'm so sorry, I thought, reaching out, certain that if I just pushed a little harder I could push my arm through the fabric of space and find her, wherever she was, and seize hold of her, and pull her back to me, and hug her, and everything would be fine—

"You okay?" Tariq said. "You sort of . . . went away.

For a second. I was talking, and it was like you weren't even here."

"Sorry," I said, still reaching, still aching for her. In my mind, I went to the beach. The dream place where I last saw her.

"What've you got there?" Tariq asked, tapping my hand, which hovered in the air holding tight to something.

I opened my folded hand to find a fistful of sand.

"What the hell?" he said, laughing. "Where'd you get that? Have you been carrying it around with you?"

"Sort of," I said, shivering now, so badly the sand began to spill out onto the beanbag between us.

Tariq touched the sand with two fingers, and pulled them back fast. "It's freezing cold. How can that be?"

I said nothing, because what I would have said was *Ha-ha, no big deal, I just opened up a tiny wormhole and grabbed it off a frozen beach somewhere near Providence, that's all.*

Your phone offers dozens of apps that are sup-
posed to help you recover from an eating disorder.
Most are probably used for the opposite of that. My
calorie counter has come in super handy as I obses-
sively track each and every thing I eat, the better to
constantly whittle down my diet to nothing.
DAY: 28, CONTINUED . . .

Mom was at work when I got home. I went right to my
room, did not touch the tsampa my stomach was shrieking for, and opened my window. Stuck my head out.

I could smell the winter air, feel the wind on me. I
tried to unweave the thin garment of scent, separate out
every strand of smell that I detected. I found jet fuel from
miles above me; the lingering smell of a thousand family
dinners; a dumpster full of unwanted popcorn behind
the movie theater. Cigarettes. Deer poop. But the night
was so cold that few scents survived. Molecules stopped
moving. Stinks settled. The air told me little.

He was out there, somewhere. My father. The real

villain. The one who stole my sister away.

I would know his smell when I found it.

I buried my nose deep in *The Dharma Bums*. I sucked in, searching for him. I found myself, I found Tariq. I even found my mother. And something else, the faintest scrap, something mostly dead, a salty smell that might maybe possibly have been him.

I stayed up late. I woke up super early. When she walked in the door at 7 a.m. I was already in the kitchen, coffee percolating for her.

"Jesus, Matt, isn't this a sight for sore eyes," she said, easing her weight into her chair. "Why are you up so early?"

"Don't know," I said. "Woke up with a lot of energy."

I did not say, *Manic bursts of intense energy are a symptom of many eating disorders.* Because, still, that's not my issue.

"You're smiling more than usual," I said. "I know it's not because you think my coffee will be any good."

"No," she said, shaking out her hair with both hands. "I had a good talk with my supervisor."

"Oh yeah?" I asked, wondering what new twist Bastien's father might have added to the equation. "You think there's hope for the plant?"

"For the plant, not so much," she said. "He kept saying, 'We'll see how things shake out,' but I can tell when he's lying. Or when he's only telling me the tip of

the truth." My mom took the mug I offered her, already complete with precisely as much cream as she likes. She pressed both hands against it and lowered her face to breathe in the coffee steam. When she raised her head, she seemed strengthened. "But he's helping me out in a major way. I'm being promoted to 'transition supervisor,' which involves helping coordinate all the moving pieces as they scale back operations. Complicated stuff, looking at inventory and transfer and personnel . . . but it's a management position, so not only will the money be better, it'll mean I'll get training and experience that could help me get a better job if the plant does close."

"That's amazing, Mom!"

"Thanks, honey," she said and sipped my coffee. "You're getting better at this. Still needs to be stronger, though."

"You always say that."

I sat down beside her. We drank our coffee, and she didn't say a word about how I shunned the creamer. *I should say something,* I thought. *About the scotch bottle. About her falling down.* But if I wasn't ready for that conversation, she probably wasn't either.

"Do you have anything of his?" I asked. "My father? Anything other than those books?"

"I do," she said, and if my question hurt her she hid it well. "A baseball cap, I think. Do you want it?"

"Yes." I said. *Why have you never mentioned this before?*

She sipped her coffee. "I'll see if I can find it."

"When do you start the new position?" I asked, to shift her mind back to something happier.

"Next week," she said. "I'm floored, honestly. I never thought he thought much of me. So for him to pick me for this . . ."

"You deserve it, clearly," I said, and wondered whether *I* had anything to do with it. Whether being Bastien's friend, even his fake friend, had helped this happen. Mom always talked about how there were no women in management, and the guys who ran the plant treated girls like secretaries no matter how hard they worked. People as powerful as Bastien's dad could afford to make big decisions based solely on who their son was friends with.

A whisper in my mind, *I wouldn't be Bastien's friend without my powers.*

"Makes me feel guilty, in a way," Mom said. "To be getting a promotion even as other people are getting screwed. And to get a leg up on the competition if the plant does close, and I'm up against a couple hundred of my coworkers for a handful of jobs. But I can't take a stand here. Being principled doesn't do us a lot of good when we're living out of a car."

"Amen to that," I said and clinked my mug against hers.

It was a raw, living thing, my mother's love for this

town. As much as I hated the place, I could still appreciate how much it meant to her. Eyes shut, silently starving, I could see and smell so much more about it now.

Wherever Mom came from, whatever town and family had created her, she never talked about it. And now I thought I knew why. Abusive or repressive or just plain boring, she ran away from it as soon as she could. Mom had the courage to escape from everything that wanted to keep her locked up tight in a box of things she did not want to be. To build a life for herself on her own terms. Some day, could I?

*Mind and body both crave worldly things, but
these attachments tie us down. Slow us up.*

DAY: 29

TOTAL CALORIES, APPROX.: 400

"You don't look so good."

I opened my eyes. Tariq stood before me, hair still
wet from showering. I sat on the fender of his truck.
"Nice to see you, too," I said.

"I wasn't making a fashion judgment," he said. "You
look unhealthy. Were you asleep?"

"No," I said, and didn't offer an alternate explanation, because it would have gone something like this: *I
was trying to meditate my way back to the Spirit World beach
where I met what might have been my sister or might have been a
figment of my imagination.* "And anyway you'd look rough,
too, if you'd been shivering in the cold waiting for your
closeted secret boyfriend to finish up being Mr. Soccer
Star Man."

"No one told you to wait out in the cold," he said,

and unlocked the doors. "Why are you mad at me?"

"I'm not," I said and got in. "I didn't mean to snap at you. You're right—I'm not feeling so hot." The shouts of post-practice locker room boasts echoed on his skin. His gym clothes were in his bag, on the seat between us, rank with the sweet scent of him. My powers were in full force. "I'm sorry."

Irritability is another symptom of eating disorders.

"You want to do this some other time?"

"No," I said sharply, then smiled. "I need this. *We* need this. Right?"

"Yeah," he said and smiled back.

A date. A real live date. Like couples do.

Our destination? A diner, three towns to the south. Where no one would know us.

Tariq put the truck in drive. Once we were out of the parking lot, he took his right hand off the wheel and fumbled for my left one.

Hunger was a river, a surging primal force that had breached its banks and flooded me, making me into one long yelp of pain in which my stomach was merely the deepest spot. The sun was close to setting, and when I looked up I saw a sky full of black stars swelling and throbbing and bursting.

I rolled down the window and gulped cold air, tried that swallowing-the-energy-of-the-universe thing again.

It didn't do much for my pain. When I shut my eyes, the black stars didn't go away.

"Tell me about your day," I managed to croak.

"Practice was ridiculous," he said, clearly relieved, and launched into a story.

That's how we made it all the way to the thruway and south to Exit 20. He spoke, I nodded, attempted to make sounds like I was listening, like I wasn't trying to keep a lid on the jerks and spasms my belly pains brought on.

"We should have picked a more romantic spot," he said after we'd parked and walked into the busy diner, all clean chrome and dirty linoleum, where four glass coffeepots bubbled and steamed on the counter.

"Baby steps," I said.

Every seat at the counter was occupied. All men, mostly middle-aged, frowning at their food. The oldest-looking one turned and watched us for what seemed like maybe a little too long.

A waitress showed us to a table.

"Y'all believe it's dark so early?" she asked. A short, spry, aging thing.

"Crazy, right?" Tariq said.

"Solstice is close. After that, the days'll start getting longer again. I'm a Wiccan, so I pay attention to things like that."

"Two coffees," Tariq said.

"I asked for a table, not your life story," I muttered in her direction after she'd walked away.

Tariq frowned. "You sure you're feeling okay?"

I was sure I *wasn't* feeling okay. And coming *had* been a mistake. The place was full of food. Dead animals glistened and oozed on the plates of the people around us. Starches and fats shined in the fluorescent light. Butter and salt covered everything.

"It's okay," he said, leaning forward, putting one warm hand on my knee. "I'm scared, too."

I *was* scared. I hadn't realized it until he said so. But of what? These men, or the contents of the plates in front of them? Men didn't just up and murder gay boys in diners. Did they?

I took Tariq's hands.

"You're freezing," he said. We were silent a moment. Then Tariq said, "Matt. Please talk to me."

I had to throw him off the trail of *Matt is slowly killing himself in exchange for superpowers.* "I want to find my dad," I said, because Tariq knew something was up, and because maybe, just maybe, talking about it might help.

"What do you know about him?" he asked.

"Not much. Mom never talks about him."

"What do you think happened after Maya connected with him?"

"I don't know. How should I?"

Unfazed by my assholery, Tariq said, "I'm asking what you *think*. You don't have a theory?"

I think they went back to his mansion or lavish Madison Avenue apartment, and she's living the good life while Mom and I are miserable.

I think he kidnapped her.

I think he murdered her.

I think he told her lies and turned her against us.

I think she's never coming home.

"I don't think it was a cheerful family reunion," I said. "Maya's more the angry punishment type. She didn't say anything to you about it?"

"Just that she had to make things right with her father. Why do you think it had to be something bad?"

"Because she abandoned us," I said before thinking could talk me out of it.

Tariq nodded. We sat in silence and chewed on that for a while. Then food appeared in front of me. Where had it come from? Oh, right. Tariq. He had ordered. Time had passed. I looked at him, watched the healthy thoughtless way he put food into himself. His hair askew from the knit hat he'd been wearing.

"You ordered me chicken soup?"

"You said that was fine," he said around a mouthful of pizza fries. "Anyway don't they call it Jewish penicillin? The miracle cure of every Jewish family? You look like you're in need of a miracle."

"How do you know a thing like that?" I asked.

He shrugged. "*Seinfeld* reruns? One of my dad's Jewish friends? I don't know."

"That's racist," I said, aiming a soup spoon at him. How did the spoon get in my hand?

"Whatever, Jew."

"Whatever, Muslim."

Outside, twilight had turned everything a deep dark blue. The tint gave a sad grandeur to the sorry spread of strip malls and trash and rust outside the window. I pressed my fingers to the table beside my water glass and pushed, just a little, with my mind, sending tiny shock waves through the table that made ripples in the water. I pushed harder and the ripples got bigger. Tariq frowned, unsettled without knowing why, looking around like maybe a little earthquake was happening.

"I'm sorry I'm taking you away from the weight room," I said.

"I'm happy to be here," he said. "With you." But was he? I wouldn't blame him if he was desperate to be anywhere else. I was irritable, starving, unpleasant. I stared at his face, wondering what he was feeling. I couldn't penetrate whatever force field surrounded him. I'd have to make my powers stronger. "After this, we should go to a movie and make out," I said. "Or maybe forget the movie part."

He smiled, and a flush of desire forced me to bite back a moan. Black stars bloomed by the dozen. The whole diner spun. "Bastien's having a party. Tomorrow night, at his house. You up for that?"

I wasn't. But then my eyes locked onto Tariq's, and I was. "Yes," I said. "I am super up for that."

I lowered my face to the bowl of soup. I looked up, at the crowd in the diner, at all the crisscrossing lines made by people, the smells and emotions and energy that swirled around them, the traces they left, tiny as molecules sometimes, but still there, right there, right in front of me, a code I couldn't crack, a riddle I couldn't unravel. Because I was weak. Because I chose earthly attachments like Tariq and food over limitless power. I looked up, through fogging eyes, at the connections between people, the way they carried their pasts on their backs and their futures strapped to their chests, the way time itself was a shifting wave like smell or sound, something I could crack or control, if I pushed a little further, if I became a little stronger.

My glass of water broke.

I started to cry.

"Hey," Tariq said, looking bewildered, leaning forward to grab my hands under the table. "Hey, Matt. Don't cry. Everything's . . ."

His voice trailed off. He looked down at his plate, at the carnage of pizza fries. And suddenly I wasn't afraid

of homophobe lunatics with guns or the waitress spitting in our food or someone from the slaughterhouse or his father's tree farm seeing us and snitching. Nothing on earth frightened me as much as the thought that Tariq might leave me.

"Come around the table," I said. "Nobody knows us here. You don't need to be ashamed of me." A sob-hiccup.

He came around. He draped his big strong arm across my shoulders. He stared out at the diner and dared anyone to give us a second glance. No one did.

"What's going on, Matt?" he whispered.

"My mom is going to lose her job. And my sister won't talk to me. And I . . . And I . . ."

I stopped myself. I had been way, way too close to telling Tariq the thing that would make him run screaming out of my life. He'd tolerated so much of my awfulness. Expecting him to be understanding about my self-imposed starvation was absurd.

"Yeah," he said. "Keeping us a secret is hard for me, too." There were lots more things he wanted to say, and he wanted to say them so bad I could hear them. Some of the things were precisely what I needed to hear. But he didn't really say them, so they didn't count.

"I'm sorry," I said, conceding defeat in the who-can-stay-silent-longer contest. "It's the solstice. I'm a Wiccan, so I'm very sensitive to these things."

"Eat the goddamn soup," he said in my ear, then bit it lightly.

I ate two spoonfuls of the soup. I wept because it tasted so good, and because Tariq cared so much for me, and I wept because I was so, so weak.

RULE #39

Separation is an illusion. All living things are one. Trapped in our bodies, chained to dying animals, we forget that each of us is one with all creation. Only the Supreme Master of the Art of Starving can pierce through this illusion.

DAY: 30

TOTAL CALORIES, APPROX.: 200

I am strong, I told the mirror boy. He grinned a Real Boy's smile, something he could turn on and off at will, because no one would ever again say to him, *Why aren't you ever smiling in any photographs?*

I can pass, I said, and he believed me. Dressed in a hoodie and jeans and sturdy boots, I could have blended in with any gathering of average American adolescent males. A knit cap covered my wildfire hair.

We can do this, I said. *We've done this before.* If the mirror boy had any doubts, he kept them to himself.

An hour later I was at Bastien's house, along with every high school A-lister in the county.

"This isn't going to be too miserable for you?" Tariq asked as we approached the front door.

"Your friends aren't *all* awful," I said. Truthfully. "And parties are interesting, from an anthropological perspective. Such a strange ritual . . ."

Tariq laughed. "Let's just hope the natives don't turn out to be cannibals."

"Anyway, if *you* enjoy parties like this, they can't be completely worthless." I touched his arm. He fought the urge to flinch away. "I want to know how to live in your world."

I was being sincere, and he could see it.

"My world sucks," he said, and *he* was being sincere. "But it's nice to just make stupid jokes, to play video games, to feel on the same page with people. You know?"

"Totally," I said. "Wolves get something out of being part of a pack."

"You're so deep," he said, knocking lightly on my forehead. And then Bastien's front door.

And then we were inside. Tariq's house was nice, but Bastien's made it look like mine. *So that's how rich you are if you run a slaughterhouse,* I thought, looking up at the double spiral staircases connecting the front hall to the second floor, the wide windows that let in so much light, the wings branching off in both directions to untold wonders. The potted palm tree, two stories high, *indoors,* standing right in front of us.

"Wow," I said.

"Yup. Everybody always wanted to come play at Bastien's house. The best video game systems, the best snacks . . ."

" . . . the blood of the workers on his hands . . ."

"That, too," my communist boyfriend said.

"I promise to try my hardest not to jump your bones," I whispered.

"I appreciate that."

The party was perfectly banal. It needs no description, deserves no aggrandizement. Parties happen every night. Kids get drunk and loud every night. A thousand parties are happening right now, as you read this, wherever and whenever you are.

What made this one special was *me*. How I felt. *I belonged*. Weeks or months ago, at the party down by the Dunes, I had felt like an impostor. Now I knew I wasn't simply equal to these kids—I was superior to them.

Call it another manic energy burst, a spasm of adrenaline, but I felt fantastic, taller than the indoor palm tree, sturdy as the marble columns. I wasn't slave to my impulses, the way these boys and girls were. I was stronger than my emotions, strong enough to bend and break my body into obedience, strong enough to access powers they could not imagine. I could joke and laugh with them, smile for photographs, but they were not my equals.

An hour in and Tariq and I found ourselves in an upstairs room, massive and purposeless—no bed, no desk, just some comfortable chairs and little tables and a lot of books I'd bet good money had never been touched—just some random room for hanging out with friends, because when you're that rich you can have all kinds of superfluous rooms. Half the soccer team was there. We sat on the floor, at the edge of the flow of conversation. Bottles were passed. Tariq drank from his, long, gasping gulps, then pressed one into my hand.

"I don't want any," I said.

"Come on," he said, drawing out the second word pleadingly. "Get drunk. You'll have more fun."

"I'm having fun now."

"You drank with me when we went to New York City. Why not now?"

I shrugged. *I wasn't really drinking, I was trying to trick you into getting drunk because I wanted to avenge a horrific crime I erroneously believed you committed.* "Maybe the question isn't why I'm *not* drinking, it's why you *are*."

Tariq made a sound like a game-show buzzer when you guessed incorrectly. "Nope. That's not the question at all."

"I know you want to feel like you're one of them," I said.

"I *am* one of them," he said.

"No you're not. You're going to have to accept it sooner or later."

"Everybody's got something that makes them different," he said softly. "Being gay doesn't make us a separate species."

I thought it did, but instead of saying so, I said, "You're so much better than them."

"They're my friends."

"Your friends are—"

"Stop talking now," he said, pressing his finger too hard against my lips and reaching out to intercept the bottle on its way to someone else.

I wanted to get up and walk dramatically away, but I sat and watched the party. We both had our walls up, and I could smell them between us, like burned cookies, something sweet turned noxious.

An hour passed like that, us on the floor, saying little to each other and to the people around us, and the walls eroded bit by bit, and were almost gone when Ott walked in and scanned the room and saw me and stopped smiling.

"Jesus Christ," he said, his voice thick and drunk, "why does this fucking faggot have to be here?"

Conversations stopped, with the record-scratch suddenness of sitcoms. The remark was probably meant to be quiet, a mild complaint to whatever deity waits on dumb drunk kids, but everybody heard it.

I breathed in deep, through my nose, then held my breath. Felt the temperature change in the room. Smelled emotions churning, responses formulating. My skin tingled. How would they respond, these kids, my peers? I felt suspended between two moments, two worlds—the one where everyone thought like Ott and I was subhuman filth, and the one where people like Ott were a backward shrinking minority.

"Not cool, man," someone grumbled.

"I mean it!" Ott cried, defensive and confused. "Where the hell did he come from? Why's he always around all of a sudden?"

"He's my friend," Tariq said, shocking me. He stood up, and stepped forward, shocking Ott. "So be quiet about him."

Ott opened his mouth, and I saw what he was wanting to say. I think Tariq saw it, too, so clearly was it written on the boy's red, sweaty, drunken face. Something impugning Tariq's manhood, implying that something more than friendship was at the root of his relationship with me.

"Get out of here," Tariq said, putting his hand on the drunk boy's shoulder, gently, and then pushing, hard. "Go find another room to bring down."

Ott huffed and puffed and left.

"And *that's* why I don't drink," I said when Tariq returned to sit beside me.

"Not everybody turns into a raging asshole," he said.

"No, but if he pulled that shit and I was drunk, he would not be breathing right now."

Tariq sniff-laughed, but I didn't press the point.

I basked. There is no other word for it. I sat beside the boy I loved and watched a party unfold. I let my stomach shout and wail in agony, and with every twist I felt *proud*. I watched people argue and laugh and joke and gossip. Felt, maybe for the first time, the thing Tariq had been talking about. The bliss of being a pack animal who has found his pack.

A month before, when Tariq took me to our first party, I'd been a prey animal. A sheep with no herd, wandering into a world full of wolves.

Now, thanks to the Art of Starving, I was a wolf.

Herds are for sheep and pigs. Packs are for wolves.

At one point I locked eyes with a girl, looking over at Tariq and me, who smiled apologetically and looked away. *She knows*, I thought. *She sees. What we are. How we feel about each other. How many other people do?*

The thought made me giddy-happy. *Maybe the world has more decent people in it than I thought. Maybe I'm not truly surrounded by homophobic assholes.*

I didn't fight my hunger. I surrendered to it. Settled into a semi-meditation state. Focused on erasing my sense of self. Thought of Maya, briefly—but I had to set

her aside along with every other emotion, every other attachment, every other aspect of myself that stood between me and the raw limitless power of the universe.

I was so close. If I wanted to find Maya, reconnect with her, bring her home, punish our father for taking her away from us, stop the slaughterhouse from shutting down, save my mother's job, keep our dying town alive a little longer, I had to push myself harder.

A door slammed. Someone hollered. Stomped down the hall in our direction. *Ott,* I knew, from the dunce-heavy tread, and Bastien close behind, yelling at him to *calm down, come back, don't, stop.*

"Hey," he said, standing in the doorway, whiskey bottle in hand.

"Don't start more shit, bro," Tariq said without getting up.

"Not here to start shit. Wanted to apologize. To . . . Matt. Can I? Apologize?"

No one stopped him. He stepped in. He hadn't come to apologize. He had come to hurt me. So I stood up and held out my hands, a gesture somewhere between *Well?* and *Come at me, bro.*

"I'm sorry, Matt."

He crossed the room, stopped in front of me. Took a long sip. He telegraphed his actions to me clear as day, trying hard to concentrate in spite of how falling-down drunk he was. I knew what was coming. I could have

stopped him or stepped aside. But I wanted him to do it. I wanted an excuse.

We'd been buddies a couple days before, watching stars in the bed of Tariq's truck. Or, if not buddies, at least he hadn't hated me so much that the very sight of me made him want to murder things. What had changed? Was it just the alcohol? Simple intoxication making him lose control of whatever it was that made him so afraid of me?

"Sorry for what?" I asked—and I could see it now, dimly, the anger he carried inside, the thing he fought against, every day of his life—

"For . . ." A bad ad-libber, Ott had to work on that one for a little while. "Being a jerk."

At this point he skipped to the main event, which was pouring the whole bottle of whiskey over my head.

I let him soak me in expensive booze.

"What the fucking *hell*, dude!" Tariq leaped up, struck the bottle from his hand, drew back a fist.

"Stop," I said, my voice sounding eerie-calm. Tariq stopped as much from fear as anything else.

Time slowed down.

"Ott," I said, and he was an open book, a painting to be read, every hurt and anger spelled out in the pores on his face. I wasn't reading his mind so much as really seeing him, all of him, the scared damaged little boy

inside the bully's body, and somehow I already knew, or suspected, the truth.

Time stopped.

People were statues all around us. Mouths opened midsentence, arms frozen midflail.

"What . . . happened?" Ott asked, his mouth opening and closing.

He could move. I could move. No one else could.

Time had stopped. Because I wanted it to.

"Ott," I said, taking a step closer, "why do you have such a problem with gay people?"

"I . . ." Ott's mind spun open like a scroll. Ott's mind wasn't separate from mine. We were four feet apart, but we were one. Two sundered pieces of the same whole. My starvation-crazed body had broken through the delusion of separation, let go of its ego long enough to see that Ott and I—and everyone—were one.

"What the hell are you?" Ott whispered, and I heard his heart pound, and his mother calling him to supper, and every remembered sound inside his head.

And just like that—I didn't hate him anymore. I understood him, completely. I saw him, all of him, the complex messy angry sad sensitive creature that he was. I saw the true Ott, the pure unsullied part of him, the divine spark, the spirit that was separate from the body with all its blood and shit and needs and flaws, the

innocent child Ott had been before he'd been battered and deformed by this broken horrible world.

My voice softened. "Why do gay people make you so afraid?"

Because I saw it. The secret. I don't know how, but I did, as clearly as if someone whispered it in my ear. I saw it, and Ott saw me see it. Tears flowed from both eyes simultaneously. It would have been so easy to destroy him. To let time start up again, to expose him in front of everyone. But that would only hurt him more. And the more someone is hurting, the more likely it is that they'll hurt others.

"Is that all?" I said, stepping closer. "A little thing like that?"

He hissed, "I don't know what you're talking about," but by now the tears were a torrent.

"You did something naughty with another boy," I said. "You were twelve. He was twelve. Baseball camp."

I'm pretty sure Ott was trying to say *How did you know that,* but the words weren't coming out as words at all. More like wails.

"And you've been miserable about that ever since."

He wiped one eye with a clumsy, shaking hand. And nodded the tiniest of nods.

"Do you know how many straight kids mess around? It's just curiosity. I'm not going to tell anyone," I said.

He flinched. Made eye contact. Looked confused, mistrustful.

"You're fine, Ott."

The world around us sped up. Sound bled back in, slowly. The statues of our fellow partygoers came back to life.

"You fucking asshole," Tariq said to Ott, his fist still drawn back.

"It's okay," I said. "Really. We're cool."

Ott stared at me, mouth open, terrified, confused, but not crying anymore.

"Right, Ott? We're cool?"

Ott nodded.

"I'll get you a change of clothes," Bastien said, as baffled as Tariq was.

RULE #40

Few things are more frightening to the body than getting what it most wants. Because what are you, when you get the thing you've shaped your whole identity around wanting?

DAY: 30, CONTINUED . . .

Two hours later, Tariq took me home. We stayed till the party had mostly wound down, after most of the people had gone home. I hadn't been looking at my watch every thirty seconds either or desperately wishing I was somewhere else.

"Admit it," he said, pulling out of Bastien's long driveway. "You had a good time."

"I had a good time," I said.

"I think you broke Ott's brain, though," he said. "That's the best explanation I can come up with. He tried to pick a fight, wanted an excuse to beat the shit out of you, and you pulled that Gandhi nonviolence turn-the-other-cheek thing, and he just did not know how to handle it."

"You think so?"

"I know so."

And yeah, he was pretty much right. Maybe he didn't know the *whole* story, but he didn't need to. No one did. Ott's problems belonged to no one but him.

Tariq was happy. I was happy. One in the morning, and the town belonged to us. Not even the reek of pig waste on the wind could bring me down.

"And you look sharp in those clothes. Who knew you had some preppy in you?"

"Shut up," I said. "You know I'd never wear any colors this bright."

But they were nice clothes. Way nicer than anything I owned. And I enjoyed the way they were too big on me. Like I was slimmer than even soccer-skinny Bastien.

"Pull over here," I said when he'd turned off the main highway, and onto the narrow road through the woods where I lived. "I don't want to say good night to you just yet."

He unbuckled his seat belt and came across. We kissed in darkness, in silence, moving to the rhythm of the clicking of his hazard lights.

"I really want to get in your pants," he whispered.

"I know," I said.

"So? Why don't we?" He put his hand on my thigh, then pushed it up to grasp me through the fabric of my pants.

"I want to," I said. "I'm just . . ."

"Afraid?"

"Yeah."

"Afraid of what? You want to get tested for STDs together? Planned Parenthood does it. I'll do it for you."

I'm afraid it can't possibly be as good as I've been imagining it will be—

Afraid it will be better—

Afraid that once we do it, I'll be your helpless slave forever—

Afraid you'll see me naked and be disgusted and never speak to me again—

"I don't know."

He kissed my neck, put two warm hands under my shirt.

"Stop," I said, praying he wouldn't.

He slid one hand up, to grab my chest, and the other down, past my waistband, to grab me.

"Stop," I said, pushing him back.

"Fine." He gripped the wheel, hard, with both hands.

"I wish I was ready," I said. "But I'm not."

"Fine."

Tariq's eyes glared into darkness, the whole way to where he left me. And again I kept wanting to say something, and again I kept not knowing what it would be.

Mom was awake, waiting for me at the kitchen table when I came in at two in the morning.

"Didn't hear a car," she said.

"Tariq dropped me off down the block."

"Why?"

"Thought you'd be asleep. Didn't want to wake you."

She looked doubtful. "Sit."

I sat.

"Did you call any of those numbers for therapists the doctor gave you?"

"No," I said.

She flung a tea bag into a mug, poured hot water over it. Then she stopped and sniffed me. "Oh my god. You smell like a—have you been drinking?"

"No, Mom. Some jerk spilled a bottle all over me."

"And these clothes?"

"Bastien loaned me some of his."

"Open your mouth," she said. I did, and she sniffed, and then stared into my eyes like she could spot a lie there.

"I hate drinking," I said.

"Good," she said and sat. "Repeat after me: He thrusts his fists against the posts and still insists he sees the ghosts."

I did so, swiftly and free of any slurring. I could have asked her about her *own* drinking. I did not. We sat in silence and watched our tea steep. This was the mother I remembered from my childhood: huge, unstoppable, a human bullshit detector. There was something comforting about being in its crosshairs. As a little boy, I

had been in awe of those moments where she caught me doing something bad, and enjoyed, on some strange level, the stern punishments she administered. *You will be better when this is over,* they seemed to say, and when it was over, I was.

But the ER doctor's sentence still echoed in my head: *Since you're a minor, we do have the power to force you into a treatment program with your mother's consent.*

"Being a parent is terrifying," she said. "You have no idea. Every day, you live with the possibility that you'll make some terrible mistake that will ruin your kid's life forever. You wonder if you've already made an awful mistake and not even known about it, passing on some gene that'll cause cancer or Alzheimer's or something. There's never a clear answer. No one else can help you because no one else has ever been in the exact same circumstances with the exact same kid. You do too much, you cause a problem. You do too little, you cause a problem."

"You're a great mom," I said.

"I'm an alcoholic," she said, and sipped her tea. Me, I came damn near to choking on mine. I was touched that she'd trust me that much, but disturbed, too. That kind of trust was terrifying. "I've been mostly sober for about seventeen years." *I am almost seventeen.* "Sometimes I falter. Lately, I've been faltering."

"I'm sorry," I said. "I've been causing you—"

"Shush," she said. "That's not why I'm telling you all this. I'm telling you because lots of doctors think alcoholism is genetic, and since I've kept it a secret from you and your sister all these years, you don't know that you have that predisposition. You might start down a road you don't otherwise know to avoid."

"I hate drinking, Mom. I'm not in danger of starting down that road."

"It isn't just alcohol. Addictive personalities are addictive personalities. It means you don't know when to stop. If something makes you feel good, you'll do it until you're sick. Or worse. Like with eating." And here she patted her own ample stomach. "Or not eating."

Or love, I thought, thinking back to Tariq and my terror when he put his hands on me and begged for it.

"That's what I mean when I say being a parent is terrifying. You're always on the lookout for how you've failed. When you were little, I was constantly looking for signs that you'd inherited my problem. Do you remember when you had that ancient cassette player, and I got you that Beyoncé single you liked?"

"Yeah," I said. "'Crazy in Love.' I listened to it over and over again, for hours, every day, until you had to take it away from me."

"And spent weeks worrying about whether I'd made it worse."

"You totally did. I was so mad at you."

She laughed, then got quiet again. "You and your sister were always so different. I only ever had to tell you something once. She used to pester me about the same things all the time. I told you your father was a crab fisherman in Alaska, and that was enough for you. She asked me every other day where he was, why he wasn't with us, how she could get in touch with him."

"Lobster," I said, trembling. My voice was barely audible. "You said Dad was on a lobster boat."

"He was probably on both," she said, rolling her eyes. "Or neither. Anyway, your sister always wanted a relationship with him, and over the past year, as she got more and more unhappy with Hudson and school and her life, I started to realize that I had hurt her by keeping her in the dark. So I gave her his mother's old mailing address, which was the only connection I had."

"Tell me about him," I said.

"Your father." She looked at her hands. Shut her eyes. "Your father was strong and smart and handsome. Confident. The world was his. He was never in doubt about anything. Which is actually an incredibly frustrating trait for someone who is wrong *all the time*. Full of big ideas about how to change the world, but never wanted to do a damn thing to make them happen. Convinced everyone was out to get him. Hated *society*, whatever that means. Wanted to go his own way."

"Am I like him?"

"I don't know," she said. "I see him in you, physically. But I can't be objective about either of you. I'm convinced you're a hundred percent Perfect, and that he's a hundred percent . . . the opposite of that. There's no rulebook for being a parent, Matt. Rulebooks are bullshit."

I looked around the kitchen, at the rabbit-shaped saltshakers and the Salvation Army mugs with faded witty slogans, at the dirty stove and the sink full of dishes, the garbage can so full the lid wouldn't shut, and I realized that for all its smallness and its shortcomings, it was home. It was safe and warm and full of love.

"Everything you've done as a parent has come from a good place, right? And overall I think Maya and I both turned out pretty well."

She looked at me, hard, a look that said, *Really? You think so? You with an eating disorder you think I'm too stupid to see and your sister a runaway?* Or maybe she was just exhausted and had said what she needed to say to me and was out of things to say. I had to work hard not to read her mind or her body language or her pheromones, but I managed.

I checked my phone. Maya's bassist, Ani, had posted a status update that said *Destroy All Monsters! RIP* and my first thought was sadness for my sister's sake, because of how much that band meant to her, and my second thought was hope that maybe this would mean she might come home.

Me and Mom drank our tea. I dropped a spoonful of
honey in. She didn't see me, didn't know what a sacrifice
it was, what a great concession I had made to her.

But it didn't matter. *I* knew it.

<u>RULE #41</u>

A wounded animal can only hide its damage from
others for so long. Sooner or later, someone will see.

DAYS: 32–33

AVERAGE DAILY CALORIES, APPROX.: ~~2100~~ 150

"Got you a present," Tariq said, picking me up to take
me to school Monday morning. His hair, scooped up
into a fauxhawk, still glistened with gel. His truck
smelled like Dunkin' Donuts and gasoline and his sweet
spicy aftershave. He handed me a book-shaped rectangle
wrapped in an Arabic newspaper.

"Can you read this?" I asked.

"I barely know the alphabet," he said. "There's no
place around here that does Arabic education or even
Islamic religious schooling. Mom tried to teach me for a
while, but I hated it. This newspaper is from Syria. My
father subscribes."

He tapped a grainy photo showing tanks in a street.

"News from home is rarely good."

"Holy shit," I said when I unwrapped it and found

the Hudson High School library's copy of *On the Road*. "What are you doing? You can't give this to me. It's not yours!"

"I checked it out, it's under my name," he said. "I will accept the consequences."

"You're ridiculous," I said. I looked at his forehead and wanted to kiss it but didn't. "And anyway, aren't you rich? Couldn't you just buy me a new copy?"

"Sure," he said. "But where's the sentimental value in that? Anyway, it's a great book. I know you've been waiting for me to finish it."

"Did you?"

"Only five times. It's very helpful for planning our Great Escape Road Trip Across the Country."

"Shut up," I said, not daring to hope for such a thing.

"So. Speaking of pride and confidence, I need to tap into some of that. Wednesday is Christmas, and since we don't celebrate it, we have a family tradition of going out for Chinese food. I figured since you guys don't celebrate it either, you might not have plans, so you might be able to . . . come out to dinner with us. The book is not a bribe."

I laughed out loud. "You want me to sit down with your mom and dad and somehow keep from jumping your adorable bones right in front of them?"

"It's asking a lot, I know. And actually I know it sounds perfectly dreadful. But I need you there. Dad's

been coming down hard on me lately. About my soccer performances—*unacceptably weak*—college and my future—*I'm not taking it seriously enough*—what he wants me to be—*him*. But he'll behave himself if there's an outsider present."

"It totally does sound dreadful," I said. "But you know I can't say no to you."

"Yeah, you can," he said. "You say no to me all the time." It was clear, his meaning.

"A pleasure postponed is a pleasure magnified. Or so a fortune cookie told me once." Thinking about fortune cookies woke my stomach up. It was not happy.

"So you'll do it?"

"The dinner, yes. The other thing . . . maybe."

Tariq beamed. He was the sun. "If you did both, it would be the best Christmas present a Jew ever gave a Muslim."

Which is how it happened that my mom dropped me off at the Spring Garden on Christmas and then went to ShopRite to pick up challah and tuna fish. Which is how I took a deep breath and walked inside to a restaurant empty except for a couple of Jewish families and some lone lonely diners for whom Hudson's only halfway classy Chinese restaurant, with its red decor and fading ornate felt wallpaper, was the most festive spot they could find.

I'd been there a billion times before. Everything was

familiar, down to the man behind the bar waving at me when I walked in. But now I was terrified. The giant fish tank was still there, packed with dozens of ageless koi I'd been tapping the glass to annoy since I was five years old. Through it, distorted by the glass and the water, were stretched-out, shrunk, warped fun-house-mirror versions of the boy I loved and the people who gave him life. Being with my mother always made me feel like a child, but seeing Tariq beside his parents I saw that he was an adult.

"Hi!" Tariq said, rising when he saw me, with a joy that made me swoon with happiness but also fear that his parents would know from that one syllable everything that was between us.

Introductions were made. Hands were shaken. Mr. Murat's grip was tight and almost painful. Mrs. Murat's was delicate, ladylike. I sat down knowing exactly what a criminal feels, sitting in the courtroom before the judge and jury who will decide his fate.

"Matt's mom works at the slaughterhouse," Tariq said.

"Ah," his father said. "I know many men who work there. Terrible thing what is happening now. So many people losing jobs. But what can you do. It is the way of business." His voice was terse, tight, controlled, accented. He was a man uncomfortable with language, I realized—not English specifically, as an immigrant, but

language in general. Trees, chainsaws, trucks, business, money, books, and balances—these were where Mr. Murat felt most comfortable.

"But it shouldn't be that way," Tariq said. "Aren't there more important things in life than the bottom line? Doesn't a business have a responsibility to its workers?"

"No one owes anyone anything in this world," he said and smiled apologetically at me. "An ugly truth, perhaps, but one you are better off knowing. We are all on our own. We work hard, or we perish. Look at me. I came here with nothing. I worked hard. And in time I was able to save money, make smart decisions, own my own business." He *was* Tariq. The same height, the same nose, the same overall sense of mingled pride and humility. The same dense lovely beard, though Mr. Murat's was much longer and more grizzled. But where Tariq was strong and handsome his father was fat and frayed, looking like life had hit him hard, and he'd put up a good long fight.

"You got lucky," Tariq said. "Didn't you? Plenty of people come here and work their fingers to the bone and never get a pot to piss in. And anyway, capitalism doesn't actually reward hard work. The guy who picks the tomatoes for Taco Bell makes twenty cents an hour sweating in the hot sun, and he works a hell of a lot harder than the CEO, who sits in an office and makes four million a year—about two thousand dollars an hour. Or am I

wrong about that?"

His father rolled his eyes. They really were the same person. "Matt, do you pick fights with your mother in front of other people?"

"No," I said. "But that's just because we're never around other people."

His father laughed. "Well, if ever you are in such a situation, do not do this. It reflects poorly on the people who raised you."

Tariq's mother intervened, her voice bright and incisive, asking what my favorite subject was—English—what my favorite book we read this year—*Macbeth*—and why—because I liked Lady Macbeth—and had I ever seen a movie of it—I hadn't. Her favorite was the one with Patrick Stewart, though the Roman Polanski one was also good. I got the impression that she spent a lot of time diverting attention and defusing conflict between her husband and her son.

And then something very strange happened. I realized I was having a great time. I was laughing and sitting next to my boyfriend, out with his parents, like grown-ups, and instead of the lonely-sad feeling I always got on Christmas, knowing that everyone else was celebrating something without me, I had found people like me, even if they were also nothing like me.

And then the food came. Pork lo mein, my child-hood favorite. And I didn't even remember ordering,

that's how pleasant the conversation had been. I didn't look at the menu or stress out about how to order something that would be easy to fake eating.

There it was, in front of me, a steaming heap of delicious-smelling fat and starch and salt.

A nest of noodles. Impossible to shred into a pile of "maybe half eaten, but really all there."

I stared at it for a good long while before picking up my chopsticks and poking at it. Conversation subsided as everyone dove into their food, and I prayed for it to start again, for distractions, for time to think about what to do. I could spread my napkin on my lap, plop clods of food into it when no one was looking, fold the napkin up and leave it under my seat . . . but Tariq was sitting too close, he'd see, he'd—

"You're not hungry?" Tariq said, and his eyes were shrewd and narrow.

I panicked. "Sorry," I said, chop-sticking a loop of noodles into my mouth.

They tasted so good it hurt. I chewed twice, swallowed, speared another chunk of food.

My body laughed at me. *You thought you could deny me indefinitely? I will always be here. You are weak. You can't fight me forever.*

Damn you, I thought, drowning in the taste of delicious pork fat. My body began to shut down, slow the rush of adrenaline, draw back its overextended senses.

Before I knew it, I was done. My plate was empty. The battle was lost.

I sat back in a haze of despair, watching the scene I was no longer a part of. The happy conversation. The people eating carelessly, thoughtlessly, enjoying food for what it was, living in balance with their bodies, a balance I lacked. The koi in the tank, blowing mocking kisses at me.

And Tariq. So trim and full of energy. And his father. Fat and sluggish and exhausted. Like Tariq would be one day. Like I would be. My mom, small and happy on our fridge, large and sad at the kitchen table.

Why bother? Why keep breathing when every breath only brings us closer to pain, suffering, old age, sickness, loneliness, death?

"I'll be right back," I said. "I need to call my mom. I'm so sorry."

"Don't be silly," Mrs. Murat said. "Go! Tell your mother you're in good hands."

Hardly anyone was out in the parking lot. The highway beyond was bare. Everyone was at home, celebrating, enjoying the warmth and safety of their beautiful balanced lives. The night was well below freezing, and I had left my jacket inside. I wasn't thinking straight, could barely think at all. Couldn't argue with myself, couldn't explain how This Was a Line I Swore I Would Never Cross, when I staggered out to the middle of the

lot and squatted beside a lamppost and spun my head around six times clockwise and then six times counterclockwise and then stuck my finger down my throat, just like I'd done all those times in junior high gym class so I could get a pass to the nurse's office and escape my bullies for one glorious hour.

It all came up instantly, effortlessly. My shrunken stomach had already been uncomfortable with the heavy load I'd dumped on it. Within seconds my belly was empty and a hot puddle-pile of slimy partially digested pork lo mein lay steaming in the freezing air. I sat there, looking down at it, smelling bile and stomach acid, seeing bean sprouts and chewed water chestnut chunks, feeling the tears come flowing down my face.

So it's true.

You are sick.

You are broken.

Now you know.

I heard the door open, saw Tariq scan the lot and come in my direction, wanted to get up and meet him halfway and hide the evidence of my crime, but I couldn't move.

"Oh, my God," he said, and dropped to his knees beside me. "Matt. Is everything—are you crying?" He leaned forward, embraced me—then saw the puddle of puke and drew back. "Is that—did you . . ."

I nodded.

"Are you sick?"

I nodded.

"What's the matter?" he said.

I shook my head.

"Tell me what hurts."

"I . . ."

I felt it coming. I could have stopped it. I didn't. In that moment, I knew what Tariq felt about coming out—the wanting more than anything to utter one secret forbidden sentence but being more terrified of that sentence than any other, and I knew, in my pain, in my sickness, in my wishing I could snap my fingers and cease to be alive, that I had to say my sentence to keep myself from dying.

"I . . ."

Tariq's eyes were black topaz galaxies, swirling supernovas of love and kindness, boring into me, seeing me, all of me.

"I haven't eaten that much food in weeks," I said.

"Why n—" He stopped. "Oh."

I nodded.

"Do you . . . Are you . . . anorexic?"

"I don't know," I said. "But I . . . I'm something." I took a breath, a deep deep breath, the deepest breath I'd ever taken. "I— I have an eating disorder."

"Oh, baby," he said, and kissed my forehead. He hugged me again, and I realized I had never heard *that*

tenderness in his voice before. I began to sob, and I hugged him back, and we sat on the bitter-cold ground of a mostly empty parking lot, while the whole world celebrated a holiday without us.

"Your parents," I whispered into his ear when the sobbing calmed somewhat. "They could come out."

"Fuck them," he said. "I don't care about that right now."

Eventually the position got uncomfortable for him, and he sat back so his knees were touching mine.

"Come inside," he said. "You're shivering."

I nodded. I was.

RULE #42

The body's truth is beyond beauty, beyond desire.
It is magnificent in ways that have nothing to do with
appearances or any of the other impermanent, shift-
ing things society values. The body's truth is the truth
of the soul shining inside of it.

DAY: 33, CONTINUED . . .

"And here he is!" Mom said, when the door shut behind me, and I knew that tone of voice, and I rushed in without stopping to take off my boots, tracking in dirt, stomping like Frankenstein, because the happiness in her words meant Mom was talking to Maya—

Which she was. But when I burst into the kitchen, arms already raised for a hug, tears already halfway out of my eyes, I found that Maya wasn't there. Only her voice, on the phone, which was better than nothing, but not as good as my sister, my whole entire fearless amazing sister, which is what I wanted, what I needed.

"Hey!" I said, taking the receiver. "Lucky timing!"

"I've been calling every ten minutes waiting for you

to get home, so, no, it wasn't luck, it was stubborn persistence."

"That's good, too," I said. "Happy Christmas, nonbeliever."

"To you, too." Her voice was rough and ragged, like she'd had a cold or been smoking too many cigarettes or screaming or singing too loud. Or all of the above. And there they were again, the waves in the background. She was near the beach. In real life. "Did you and your boyfriend have a nice date?"

"Shhh," I said, looking over at Mom, who was washing dishes with a deep beautiful smile on her face.

"Don't be stupid," she said. "Mom can't hear me. So? Did you? Have a nice date."

"Yeah. How did you . . ."

"Mom said you were with your 'friend' Tariq." She let out a ragged breath. "Listen, brother. I gotta confess, I was kind of a jerk. Tariq told me he liked you. I never passed the word to you, 'cause I was pretty crushed out on him myself. It was stupid. You should forgive me." I had missed this so much: my sister, the bossy older sibling, the one who always made up the rules, still deciding where the conversation went, when I had so many questions I needed to ask her.

My head hurt with questions. *Why did you do this to us? Are you with Dad? What's he like? Can you two come and take me away? When are you coming back? What's up with that*

status update that said your band broke up? How could you abandon me? Instead I said, "How are things going?"

She sighed. "These people are just not serious about music," she said. My supercharged hearing heard waves crashing and wind blustering through the wires. "But I've been able to get a lot of work done. I'm writing some really good songs, I think. Getting away from everything has been so, *so* good for me."

"Well, maybe not so good for your schoolwork and chances of getting into a good college and *entire future.* According to Mom . . ."

"She makes some good points."

"We need to see you," I said, looking over at Mom, too scared to mention Dad as long as she stood there. "I need your number. I need to call you again."

"No," she said, and she said it sadly, but she said it in that Maya way that meant there'd be no arguing about it. The Matt of a month or two ago would have dropped it right there. But I wasn't that Matt anymore.

"Why not?"

"We definitely need to talk. I know that. I want to. But I can't."

Short pause. "Why not?"

I heard her through the phone. The conflicted whispers of her thoughts. Her own pain, almost audible, every bit as real as mine. In the end, she chose silence.

"Fine," I said finally. "But call me. Soon. On my cell."

"Maybe."

"I miss you," I said.

I pictured her, conjured her up as she had been before she left. Brown hair cut pixie short, probably getting shaggy by now, eyebrows arched somewhere between skepticism and amusement. Maya was not beautiful, but not beautiful in the way the Mona Lisa or Virginia Woolf were not beautiful—my sister was beyond beauty, beyond convention. Her ears were multiply pierced. Even seated, she looked tall and strong. She wore a studded jean jacket and corduroys. She wore them with ease and grace, and she was not afraid of anything.

"I miss you, too," she said.

My stomach whimpered. I shut my eyes against the ocean-pull of words I wanted to say. *I'm dying. I need help. I can't stop. I want to stop. But I can't.* Tears sprang to my eyes, and I prayed she could hear them in my voice, that I could project through the phone lines the depth of my fear and my hurt. "I need you. Okay? Please? Come home?"

She took a long time before she said, "Soon, Matt."

Later, when I got out of bed to go to the bathroom, I heard my mom sobbing in her room. I wondered if Maya was crying, too, in that house by the sea near Providence, or wherever she was, and whether it meant anything that we were all three crying together, apart.

RULE #43

You are never alone, no matter how alone you think you are.

DAY: ∞; A BRIEF CIGARETTE BREAK, OUTSIDE THE TIME/SPACE CONTINUUM

I realize I don't know who you are anymore, Reader.

In the beginning, you were me. I started out writing this Rulebook for myself, messages sent into the ether in the hopes that they'd reach a younger dumber version of myself, someone so desperate for guidance that he'd turn to anyone, even someone as messed-up as a marginally less-messed-up version of himself.

Somewhere along the line, I realized I was writing for boys in general, especially the lost lonely isolated ones, the boys with no one in their lives to teach them The Rules, or the boys who had to settle for less-than-perfect guidance from exploitative or predatory men who know hunger when they see it and know how to use your hunger against you.

Then, before I knew it, in my twisted starving mind,

the audience I imagined was everyone, all the millions who don't fit into neat boxes, everybody who got bent or broken on the way to becoming a grown-up, who Ideates Suicidally, who is at war with their own body.

But then I realized I am as flawed as any guide can be. And now I know that anyone looking to me for rules to live by is sort of screwed.

I don't think this is a rulebook at all. It might be what the therapeutic professions call A Cry for Help. It might be a road map to how to get to where you know you need help.

I started out thinking I had so much to offer. But I've got nothing to share but the hope that my pain can be helpful to someone.

RULE #44

Your mommy really can make everything better.

DAY: 34

TOTAL CALORIES, APPROX.: 200

"Did she tell you anything?" I asked my mom the next morning. "When you talked, before I came home? About . . . anything? Why she left, when she's coming back?"

"No, honey," Mom said. And smiled at how strong my coffee was. "Do you think she'll come home soon?" I asked, staring at Maya's shut door, aware of what a ridiculous question I was asking, because of course Mom had no idea, of course I was being a little boy looking to his mommy to make him feel better about something out of everyone's control.

"Of course, honey," Mom said, and believing her felt good. Standing in the hallway felt good.

Back in my room, I turned off the lights and stuck my head out the window, smelling the winter air, feeling

the wind on me, but the cold winter air still told me little.

He was out there, somewhere. My father. I would know his smell when I found it.

I meditated, dug deep down into my freshly emptied stomach. And found: nothing.

Every time I shut my eyes, I saw Tariq. His eyes on me. Not when he learned the truth, there in the Spring Garden parking lot, because in that moment he had exuded only care and concern, but later, when he dropped me off at home. When he'd had some time to think about things. When I got out of the family wagon and they all gave me a rousing good-night, and our eyes met, and he looked away just a little too fast, and I saw the rising fear in his eyes, the realization of just how messed-up I was.

If he broke up with me, I'd die. I knew it. Ever since the moment I learned the truth about who he was and how he felt about me, he'd been the thing propping me up. The thing that took the place of my Mission of Bloody Vengeance. The thing I loved instead of myself.

I took *On the Road* out of my backpack. It still smelled like his house, faintly like him. Pine and cigarettes and his mom's vanilla candles. Underneath that, I smelled the previous borrower—patchouli and chocolate—and beneath that another—beer, summer—a whole shifting

totem pole of people who had borrowed that book.

I read it in one sitting, crouched beneath my freezing window, crying in spots at the wild madcap journey these two men were on, and how much beauty they found, and how much sadness, getting up often to make coffee or get cigarettes, and it was dark when I neared the end, and I felt like I owned the night, and I was my own person, and I was still reading when I heard my mom stir as she got ready for the night shift, but before that, somewhere on Sal and Dean's fourth or fifth crisscross of the country, I made a decision.

RULE #45

*Some sicknesses are so severe they can trump
even the most powerful positive force on the planet.*

DAY: 35

TOTAL CALORIES, APPROX.: 50

Reader, I made love to him.

December 27: no school. I held the book in my hands
and waited until dawn had passed and a reasonable hour
arrived, and then texted him, bantered back and forth
a bit, told him to come get me. I felt it inside me like
a bubble of pure light, this secret: I knew what would
happen today, but he did not.

"Hey!" he said when he met me down the block,
when I was up in his truck, when he smiled and we
kissed. He had no idea what was about to happen. I did.
I had never felt a power like that, not even when I could
make it snow or conjure fire out of the air or smell a
bully's deepest shame and know exactly how to use it to
destroy him.

Was there a new distance between us? Was his happiness at seeing me any less than what it had been before he knew about my sickness? I couldn't tell.

"I stayed up all night," I said. "I read *On the Road* in one sitting."

"And?"

"I loved it," I said.

"Me too!" he said.

"I have to read it again."

"Yeah you do. Where do you want to go today?"

"To the pines," I said. "The deep pine clearing."

"You sure?" he asked, blowing on his hands because his truck was sluggish and the heater slow to come around. "Pretty cold out there."

"We'll sit in the truck," I said. "Our portable home."

"Sounds good," he said and kissed me again and looked at me from the driver's seat, across the wide gulf that separated us, and his eyes scanned me in the light of day looking for signs of my sickness.

"They weren't gay," I said. "Were they? The two guys in *On the Road*?"

"I don't think so," he said. "Best friends, but pretty straight. They sleep with an awful lot of women. And there's gay people in the book, friends of theirs, and they certainly don't let society's expectations limit them, so it's not like they would be too afraid or repressed to act on those impulses if they felt them."

"True," I said.

"That's *our* book," he said. "The gay-guy version of *On the Road* is our story to write. Our wild and crazy adventures when we leave this town and drive to every awesome hidden secret place on this super huge planet."

"That book sounds amazing."

The truck rattled on through empty after-Christmas streets, stopping for Dunkin' Donuts coffee.

"It felt so . . . forbidden, somehow," I said. "Staying up all night. When I was a little kid my mom used to make me take naps, and I hated it, and not sleeping felt like such a rebellious act."

"Yeah," Tariq said—but his mind was elsewhere, on me, on last night, on what he learned about me. "What are you going to do?" he asked. "About . . . that thing?"

For a second I couldn't speak, I was so grateful to him for not saying it. To hear him use the words *eating disorder* would make it too real, too frightening. "I don't know."

"You have to get help."

"I know."

"You'll die if you don't."

"I know."

He turned to me. "So what are you going to do?"

"Eyes on the road," I said, but he did not take them off me. "Eyes on the road!"

"Answer my question."

A car horn blared as his truck inched into the opposite lane.

"Okay," I said. "Okay! The ER doctor gave me some numbers for therapists. I'm going to call them."

His eyes still on me. The truck still drifting.

"I don't have the numbers with me!"

More car horns. Some brakes squeaking.

"Okay!" I said. "As soon as I get home! I'll do it."

"It won't be murder if I drive us into a tree and you die," he said, eyes on the road again, straightening the wheel. "It'll just be hastening the inevitable."

"Such a drama queen," I said.

He parked in the pines, the deep old-growth forest his father never touched, pines that had survived so long they were too big to be chopped down and fit inside any home, had earned the right to live out a natural lifespan without being sacrificed on the altar of Christian ritual.

"How long have you . . . had this?" he asked, putting the car in park.

"I—" and I realized I didn't know. Long before I began to school myself in the Art of Starving, I'd been limiting what I ate. Fasting and then bingeing. Lying to myself. Googling eating disorders to figure out tips. "A while now," I said. "You never guessed?"

"Of course not," he said. And turned up the heat and blew into his hands again.

Because I'm such a disgusting fat greasy hog, I wanted to

say, but not as much as I wanted to say, "I don't want to talk about this anymore," which is what I said.

"You have to confr—"

"I want to talk about your Christmas present," I said. That stopped the flow of words from his mouth, started a slow smile spreading across his face.

"The best Christmas present a Jew ever gave a Muslim was how I think you described it," I said.

Silence. "Shut the eff up," he said. "Don't play with my emotions like that."

"Who's playing? Take off your shirt."

He giggled, a little boy and a man all at once, as he stretched out his long mighty arms and peeled the flannel off. I almost cried at the sight of it, there in the cold air of his poorly heated truck, in bright December daylight, his torso, its smooth lines and curved muscles, its dark dense hair, its perfection, its beauty, my helplessness.

Maybe your first time should not be like this. Maybe it should happen because you're both super excited about it—not because you're terrified you're going to get dumped because your significant other found out just how damaged you are. Not because you're using sex to fill an emptiness inside you. But I *was* super excited about it. We both were. And there were so many reasons, pro and con, so many fears, but in that instant they all fell away.

You don't want the details. Well, maybe you do, but I don't want to share them.

Here are a few things I don't mind sharing with you.

When he saw my own naked torso, he said, "Oh, baby," and his voice was thick with fear and pity, and he touched my rib cage, and for a split second I saw myself as he did, no longer the fat tub of guts I saw when I looked in the mirror but a tormented tortured body starved to the edge of breaking.

And then he pulled me to him, and his heat blocked out every other concern.

And I was, to use the secret language of gay sex, the bottom.

And it hurt.

And it was wonderful.

And we used protection.

And before we started Tariq whispered, "I have no idea what the hell I'm doing," and we both laughed, and I knew from the way my heart beat under his hand, from the perfect mix of fear and fearlessness that I felt, that *here* was true power, here was real magic. Sex was magic. Love was magic. None of the harsh brutal bloody abilities I had figured out for myself were anywhere near as powerful as this.

And "All I'm Losing Is Me," by Saves the Day was the song that was blaring from my boyfriend's truck's speakers when I stopped being a virgin.

And when it was over and we stared at each other's bodies in disbelief and we held each other and smoked cigarettes and talked about our epic America-conquering road trip, I rolled down the window and sniffed the air and cried, because love was magic but it was not enough to soothe my sickness, my hunger, and nothing would ever be enough.

RULE #46

*The human liver produces foul-smelling ketones
as a byproduct of metabolizing stored body fat. That's
why your breath suddenly reeks of acetone. Which is
what they make nail polish remover out of.*

Also: pain will only help you if you let it.

DAY: 36

TOTAL CALORIES, APPROX.: 50

Black stars and the swiftly spinning world were more or less constant by then. Pain in my stomach made walking one hundred percent upright impossible. Pain in general scrambled my brain. Kept making me forget what I'd realized the night before. The epiphany of how delusional I was. Force of habit kept me from eating, because food would take the edge off the pain, and pain was power.

Maya. My father. My mother. The slaughterhouse. Seeing the past, fixing the future. Everything was within reach. Only a little more pain, and I'd be there.

No, Matt. Stop. That's insanity. You know this isn't real.

And even though I must have looked like hell, people seemed happy to see me in school. Word would have spread after my encounter with Ott. Everyone in that room had seen our staring contest; seen him start crying. Nobody wanted me to stare into their eyes and plumb the depths of their soul to break their brain.

"Hey," Tariq said when I found him in the parking lot at lunch. He took a long look at me.

"Hey," I said.

We sat in his truck.

"Gross, stop that," he said, swatting my hand away from my mouth, and I didn't frown or pout because he really had helped me out, because I'd been damn close to pulling out my middle nail altogether. As it was I could feel it bleeding afresh.

"Let's go to the pines," I said.

"Fine," he said, the terse Tariq *Fine* that meant *Nothing is fine.*

"I really like *The Dharma Bums*," he said, breaking the silence halfway there. "I've been reading up on Buddhism, too. Fascinating stuff."

"Right?" I said. "Like how they say reality isn't real. It's an illusion. None of the things that stress us out or frighten or hurt us are real."

"I like that," he said.

"Some Buddhists believe that because reality isn't real, someone enlightened enough can control the fabric of reality."

"Huh," he said, unsure what that had to do with anything, which was fine, because I had really just been talking through a little theory of my own: that hunger had made me an enlightened being, an awakened soul, that I could do anything, or almost anything. That I could control all matter, bend time and space and substance. Like I said: old habits. The more likely scenario was me dying and losing my grip on reality in the process.

"Did you call those therapists?" he asked, looking at me.

"Yup," I lied. "Called a couple. Eyes on the road! Their offices were closed for the holidays. I left messages."

"Good!" he said, and then it occurred to him that I might be lying. Clever boy. "I want to talk to you about it. I think it'll help you."

"I don't want to," I said.

"Relationships aren't just about what one person wants," he said, veering into the wrong lane again. "For this to work—for us to work—"

"Fine," I said, and touched his stubbly chin. "Three questions. Go."

With no hesitation, he asked: "Why?"

I shrugged. I thought-stuttered several excuses, rationales, lies, oversimplifications. But Tariq deserved an answer. And so did I. Pain and dizziness made me open to anything. "When I started, it was because I didn't like the way I looked. But then I liked the way it felt, to limit the amount of food I ate. It became an end in itself."

"Do you like the way you look now?"

I looked in the rearview, saw my too-long chin and preposterous cheeks, and shook my head no.

"What don't you like?"

"I don't want to say it."

"Say it."

I am fat and gross and no one will ever desire me.

I opened my mouth to say it, but it wouldn't come out. Nothing would. The whole way to the pines, I could not say a word. When we arrived at the clearing and came to a stop, I leaned across and kissed him until he relented and kissed me back.

There is a thing I am obsessed with. It is a thing most boys are obsessed with. It has a lot of slang names, all of them ugly, and a couple formal ones, none of them pretty. In fact it's funny that something so awesome should have such dumb names. It involves your mouth. Even saying *that* sounds creepy, but it's the best I can do. By now you will probably have guessed what I'm talking about because you are smart. That's why I like you. I

don't need to spell out every little thing.

Anyway I wanted to do That Thing. Bad. Like, over-poweringly bad. I wanted to seize Tariq and do That Thing to him, because I wanted it . . . and also to change the subject. Even though my head was ringing with monstrous, stupid, ridiculous questions.

Does sperm count as food? How many calories are in an orgasm? In a spit vs. a swallow? Will it take the edge off enough to hold me back when I go to find my father? And punish him?

Yes. I am an idiot. We've established this long ago.

But I made the decision to set all those concerns aside.

"I want to try something," I said, leaning over, kissing him on the lips, then the neck, then the stomach, then onward. "Stop me if you're not comfortable with it."

"I can't," he said, and I knew he wasn't talking about The Act. "I can't do this anymore, Matt. I can't watch you destroy yourself. I've been reading all about eating disorders on the internet, and people just *drop dead* all the time—like their hearts give out or their brains starve or something—"

He had never been more beautiful. His eyebrows were two thick troubled daggers. His fauxhawk stood up proud and fearsome as a shark fin.

This was happening. He was dumping me. The only good thing in my life was gone.

Distant lights flashed. Winter lightning, weird and wrong. The black stars fell into shapes, constellations, omens, portents. My fingertips burned, began to bleed again.

"I hope you do get better," he said. "I really do. But you have to do something or—or I can't be with you anymore."

There was a silence, thick and heavy between us.

Then he whispered, "They say recovery can take years and—"

"*Recovery takes years?* Did the stupid internet tell you that? Because the internet also says gays are demons who will burn in hell forever, and communists kill babies. Just because something's on the internet . . ."

He said nothing. Anger and frustration fizzled to life inside him.

"And you think you're so great to be boyfriends with?" I asked, powerless to stop myself. "Mr. No One Can Ever Know About Us? Mr. You Are My Dark Secret I'm Ashamed Of?"

"I know," he said, his voice a little harder. "And you deserve better."

"So that's why you're dumping me? Gee, thanks, Tariq, you're so considerate. But you're still a goddamn coward, and you know what the proof is?" I wasn't steering the ship anymore. My body swooned and trembled with the same shivering sensation as the night I

ended up in the emergency room. "You know how I know you're a spineless piece of shit? Because you think I'm an inspiration! Me! Disgusting, worthless, hideous me—you think *I* have courage? You must be some—"

He started up his truck.

I stared out his window, thinking *Maya Maya Maya,* all the way home.

Lightning followed us. We did not speak.

RULE #47

I got nothing for this one.

DAY: 37

TOTAL CALORIES: 0

Mom got fired. She got one week's pay as severance, which is half of our rent, which was already past due. She came in full of false cheer, knowing we were doomed, determined not to let me see it.

"There are lots of layoffs," she said, her voice heavy with wanting a drink. "I'm certainly not taking it personally!"

"But what about that transition job?" I asked when I got my head around what she'd said, which was a while.

"Turns out the transition is going to happen on a much faster timeline, so they won't need any managers for it. Ended up going to someone else," she said. Her smile was so fake it hurt us both.

"But you said your boss said—"

"Said it was out of his hands. Decision from upstairs. What do you want for dinner?"

I gaped at her, and she turned without another word and walked away.

I sat at the edge of my bed. Turned up my music so I wouldn't hear her pouring out another drink. But I heard her anyway. I heard everything.

I could do so many things. Teleport, read minds, stop time. Why couldn't I help her? Why couldn't I help *anyone*? Why couldn't I take away everything that made her life so hard?

I stared at my hands. Starving myself gave me powers. But what good were they? I was sick. I was destroying myself.

I went down the hall. Mom sat at the table, glass of scotch beside her mug of coffee. Her head hung. It wasn't hunger or superpowers that told me how sad she was. It was being a person. Being open to the needs of someone other than myself.

Love could heal. Love could change people. Love was the thing that made me want to die when I saw her, when I saw how much she was hurting. Everything else, all the imaginary abilities my sick mind had conjured up, all of that was meaningless.

"Hey," I said, heart hammering.

"Hey."

I put a hand on her shoulder, and she leaned her cheek against it. I almost lost it right there, the courage

I'd somehow mustered, so I reached out with the other hand and picked up the bottle.

"What's this?" I asked.

"Whiskey," she said.

"Why are you drinking it?"

She sighed.

"I love you, honey," she said. "But you're my son and I'm your mother and I don't want to have this conversation with you."

Hunger and sadness made me brave, let me say the words I wasn't strong enough to say. "I think you do," I said.

"Well. I *also* think a lot of things that aren't true."

I kept on, undeterred. "But seeing you like this. It hurts. It makes me feel like I've been punched in the stomach."

"I'm sorry," she said. "But I can't do anything about that."

She looked up at me for the first time.

I whispered. "We should get help."

Mom clinked her coffee mug against mine.

"I'll make some calls in the morning," she said, the emptiness of the promise echoing in the kitchen.

<u>RULE #48</u>

As previously stated, the manufacturers of the human body have a very strict returns policy. You can't simply snap your fingers and say, "Okay, I'm done, take it away, boys." You can't just decide to stop being alive. You have to do something. Usually something pretty sucky.

THE LAST DAY

TOTAL CALORIES: 0

When I got to the slaughterhouse it was abandoned, shut down for the night, which would have been unheard of a month before, but these were the final days of its transition into obsolescence. The workers were home in their beds, asleep, unemployed, poised to lose everything, so no one could stop or even see me as I raised my arms and watched the massive hydraulic loading bay door open slowly as I walked in and followed the familiar metal walkway that my mom used to take me and Maya down when we were little. She'd point out the pigs in their cages and then take us down to the huge long

freezer hall where the cleaned skinned hacked-apart carcasses were kept, always careful not to let us anywhere near the bloody slaughter rooms. I blinked those memories away.

How had I gotten here?

I was outside my body, watching myself. I was a force of nature. I could do anything. No one could stop me. What did it matter what a forest fire did? Who was to blame for a flood?

Easy as thinking about it, I used my power and erased my image from every camera I walked past.

I felt them as I moved into the main bay, every pig asleep and dreaming in its cage. They tingled like extensions of my body, limbs I never knew I had, and when I whispered, "Awake," I could feel them open their eyes, fear keeping them silent, confusion making them anxious, for they were aware of me as a predator, but they perceived no threat from me.

Unlocking the cages was the only truly difficult part of the whole process. I had to kneel and put both hands on the metal grid floor, extend myself through it to the entire iron system of cages and doors and locks, smell the overwhelming almost-fatal stink of the ocean of pig shit that waited beneath me, for every cage was built on the same grid, so excrement could pass easily through. I felt for the locks, fumbled around the bars and slotting mechanisms, grunted and thrusted a couple times

before they moved, and then they only rattled against their own restraints. And then I was shaking every door, lifting and pushing, pulling and easing, and the pigs began to whistle and snort anxiously, and then—the gates swung open as one. Two thousand pigs stepped daintily into freedom.

Pigs are omnivorous. Pigs eat people all the time. And some of these pigs were big, with fierce tusks and eyes full of rage. The kind of totally understandable rage you'd have if you spent your whole life in a cage so small you could not turn around.

And once they were out, when it was too late to turn back—that's when it occurred to me to be afraid. *They might eat me,* I thought.

They stood still, or wandered around, snuffling nervously, socializing awkwardly. Once again, as I had at Bastien's party, I pierced the veil of separation. I understood that the same divine spark lived inside of them. I could feel on my skin, in my arms, in my brain, the army of docile minds at my command. When I turned and headed for the exit, they followed me.

Here is something you maybe don't know. Up close, like really close, close enough to make eye contact and feel weird about it . . . Pigs are freaky. There is something so close to human about their faces. And something so intelligent, too. If science discovered tomorrow that pigs were a race of hyperintelligent aliens who had spent

thousands of years studying humanity to prepare for some horrific mass extermination, I wouldn't be a bit surprised.

Pigs are monstrous-looking things. And I marched my own army of monsters into town.

As we moved, I wrapped myself in a thick wide cloud of pheromone smell, a fog that said, *Do not look here, there is nothing to see, there is no one,* which was as close as I could come to an invisibility cloak.

They grew boisterous as we marched. They had never experienced freedom before. They had never felt night air on their skin. They made loud noises. They rooted in garbage. They fought. They did not mind the cold. Whether through pheromones or mere force of will, I controlled them as effortlessly as my own arms. And as we went, my anger seeped into them.

I felt the layout of the town ahead of me. Smelled where everyone who had ever done me wrong was sleeping. I broke two hundred pigs off from the pack, sent them to Ott's house. I sent two hundred more to the high school.

Destroy, I told them. *Break windows, tusk down doors, get inside, roar, squeal, swarm, rip down curtains, shred paintings, crush toys. Harm no people, but ruin everything they own. Make them wish they were dead. Eat whatever you can eat. Shit on everything.*

Lights went on as we walked. Screams sounded. I

felt bad, knowing how many good and innocent people would be terrified in their beds by my squealing army. And dimly, distantly, I wondered if so much collateral damage was necessary, when who I really wanted to hurt was my father.

But no. There were *lots* of people I really wanted to hurt. And I would get to all of them.

McDonald's. Wal-Mart. The correctional facility. Everywhere people made a living exploiting other people, working them like animals, I broke off a smaller group of pigs to decimate and disrupt. And I could see them, hear their breath and watch the world through their eyes. Feel their joy at shattering glass, snarfing down gaping mouthfuls of frozen french fries, shredding stuffed animals, tipping pharmacy shelves into a domino effect of chain reaction chaos. I tasted the food they ate. But it did not diminish my hunger.

I took my pigs through the rich neighborhood. I ravaged every expensive beautiful thing I would never have. And each new spray of broken glass thrilled me, rocked me with waves of pleasure. Every act of violence and destruction thrummed in my body like a chord on the guitar of me. To punish the guilty, to destroy the proud—it felt good, righteous, intoxicating, like when you beat a hard level in a video game.

But when each act was over, I was hungry again. Hollow again. Violence temporarily filled the void, but it

faded fast, and the void remained. Cold emptiness and the sound of sirens.

I took off my shoes, felt the frozen earth beneath me. Felt every single fire. Breathed out, fed them oxygen, saw them swell. I fanned the flames with every step I took. A hundred spiraling swirls of flame blossomed behind me as we moved.

A gun shot. Two gun shots, followed by pigs shrieking. Pain flared through my shoulders, where one of my pigs had been shot. The other pigs felt it, too, the agony threaded through all of us as we shared one porcine mind. They squealed as one, and then they got angrier.

By the time I got to where I was going, I had sent so many off on separate missions of violent mayhem that I only had three hundred pigs left, but that was more than enough to utterly destroy Bastien's house. At a clap of my hands they charged the doors. Two climbed onto the backs of others, to better bash in windows. *Smash,* I thought, *ravage.* Crush, dismantle, gut, mutilate—the thesaurus pulsed in my veins, the sheer pleasure of words combining with the joy of violence.

I smelled them inside. Both of them.

"Come out!" I called to Bastien, but mostly his father, this man who could so heartlessly make decisions that hurt so many people, and never be punished for it, and would in fact most likely be rewarded, promoted,

considered a hero for putting more money into the pockets of corporate shareholders.

Silence. My pigs paused, listening.

"We're not going to hurt you," I said gleefully, laughing, quoting a movie monster. "We're just going to bash your brains out!"

Pigs poured through the broken-down door. They charged up the twin staircases, barreled into the kitchen and dining room. Broke beautiful expensive things in an orgy of glee.

Remember: throughout this process, I was barely half-present. Watching myself move, somewhere between joy and terror. Controlling the pigs, telling them where to go and what to do . . . it never occurred to me to wonder, *Can I do this crazy thing?* I stretched out my arms, and it was done.

So when I held out both hands, palms up, and then reached out—feeling my reach go beyond my physical body, felt it go beyond the limitations of time and space. I felt like I could have grabbed anything, a fistful of the sun, a rock from Jupiter, my father. I would get to him next, when I finished this warm-up. He was the main event. For right now, what I wanted was much closer.

"Come," I whispered.

Bastien's father appeared at the top of the stairs. I had never seen him before. He was a short man and pudgy. Wearing pajamas that were too big for him. Rubbing his

eyes, barely able to see without the glasses he'd left on his bedside table when the screams of hell and breaking glass had pulled him out of sleep.

"Oh, God."

Bastien appeared behind him. Half-asleep but also half-smiling. Probably confident he was having a dream. He said, "What's going on, Matt? What the hell—what's going on?"

"Be still," I said, and the pigs were still. Silent. Staring at Bastien and his father like the wise freaky semihuman creatures that they were.

And now, here, fear began to leak into Bastien's face. The pigs had been a simple freak occurrence at first. What did he care what they did to a house they were about to move out of anyway? But now he knew that something else was going on. Something he had no explanation for. He thought maybe I really was something to be feared.

"What the hell *are* you?" he asked, and took another step forward, confidently, menacingly.

I was not, in fact, a movie monster. Movie monsters know what to say. Villains always have some terrifying retort up their sleeves—*Your worst nightmare; The last thing you'll ever see; You can call me Death,* etc. Me, I just made the hogs roar. Wail. Shriek. Bellow.

Wondered if my father could hear them, wherever he was. If the sirens and bells would wake him up and he

would know that they tolled for him, that the Angel of Death was making his way through the night to punish him.

"Bastien?" his father said, practically blind as a bat and looking for his son to explain all this away.

A twitch of my finger, and the hog closest to him made a sudden lunge, swung his head, grazed Bastien's father's calf with one tusk. He yelp-screamed, stepped back, but did not stumble. A fall would have been fatal. They would have torn him to shreds in an instant.

Bastien took a step forward. The last of his bravery fled from his face.

I saw how it would happen. Two hogs would go in for each leg. They would bring him down swiftly, pulling away great chunks of skin, and tugging in different directions once he was on the ground. His father would go down two and a half seconds later. His screams would bring the rest of the pack in, a dozen squealing roaring grunting animals cleaving and chomping bone and skin and muscle and inner organs.

And what would that change? What would killing them accomplish that I hadn't already done? Better to let them live with this, with a story to tell, with psychological scars. Better to let them be haunted.

I turned and left. My pigs followed.

I shivered at how close I had come to murdering them.

Murder is special. The savage monstrous part of my brain that had taken control told me so. To kill someone is to enter into a relationship with them, one that will last as long as you live.

You should save it for someone really important to you.

By now our sleepy small-town night was as loud as noontime in Manhattan. I followed the smell of my father, faint but getting stronger, as I moved west. To the river. Through downtown, along Columbia Street, the poor part of town, where my pigs remained in tight formation and did not do the slightest bit of damage to people or property. Turning north on Second Street, down the hill, past the Shacks, across the train tracks, to the river.

He was there. Across the river. Could pigs swim? The only other way to cross would be to take a ten-mile detour, following the river south to the Rip Van Winkle Bridge, walking them to the other side, and then walking north again through Catskill and then Athens and who knew how many other towns standing between me and him.

But no, there were other options. Of course there were. I had all the power in the universe.

I knelt down. My knees scraped frozen mud, but the river itself moved too fast to freeze over. I stuck both hands into the water. A weaker boy would have winced

at the sharp stabbing coldness of the water, but I was stronger than it was. I saw its secrets, saw how badly it wanted to be ice.

I stood. I raised both arms.

With a stretching sound, ice formed on the river in front of me. A small jagged triangle at first, but growing. Widening. Extending.

I stepped out onto it. Pushed my arms forward and watched the ice expand. Pigs stepped out. The lights of Athens sparkled like frozen fireflies on the black water ahead. Black stars filled the air. My mind balked at the magnitude of what I was asking it to do.

You can do this, I whispered, even as I staggered. I would level every city between me and him. I would reduce the whole Hudson Valley to shit-stinking rubble.

Again, I staggered. This time I dropped to one knee. The ice cracked and thinned beneath me. A piece broke off, and a pig fell, screaming, into the river.

Cracks formed around my hands, where they pressed against the thinning ice. Giant squids and white whales and plesiosaurs swam in the black water beneath. My mind in overdrive, summoning up new horrors, new monsters, snatching out of the ether anything that might be of some assistance in burning down the world.

Screaming for help.

I pulled myself back up. Stood there. Tried to take a step. Couldn't.

"Please," I whispered, possibly not out loud. And then: I felt the soft weight of a hand on my shoulder.

All the anger leaked out of me.

Because I knew whose hand it was.

I turned around, unbelieving, and whispered, "Maya?"

"I heard you calling me," she said.

"You . . . how did you . . . ?"

"I can do things, too," she said and wrapped both arms tight around me. "What, do you think you're the only one?"

<u>RULE #49</u>

The worst thing that can happen to your body is not that it gets fat, or it gets sick, or even that it gets badly damaged. The worst thing that can happen to your body is when someone takes away your right to control it.

DAYS: ⁻1--27

AVERAGE DAILY CALORIES, APPROX.: 1800

Panic woke me up. Pain jolted me back to consciousness. I opened my eyes and barely registered that I was back in the hospital. Not that where I was mattered. What mattered was the tube down my throat, the blinding pain of it. I wanted to claw at it, rip it away, but I was so weak I could barely budge my arms. I coughed and heaved and thrashed. I grabbed hold of the tube and tugged, triggering raw pain all the way down to my stomach, hearing the gross wet gristly sounds it made against the walls of my esophagus.

Machines made noise. People came. Held me down. A nurse explained that I had passed out from

malnutrition, that I was in critical condition. I tried to roar out my rage but the tube muffled the sound into an agonized gargle. I wanted to spew fire and break bones and paralyze people, but none of my powers worked. Someone stabbed me with a needle and all of it went away.

"Do you know where you are?"

"Columbia Greene Memorial Hospital," I said to the lady doctor in glasses I had seen on my previous trip to the ER. I was groggy, sedated, stuffed full of tube food.

"No, Matt, you were transferred three days ago to the Eden Park Rehab Center. Out on Route Sixty-six. Where the nursing home used to be?"

"Okay," I said.

She talked to me for a while. Dimly, through the drugs, I remembered that we'd had this conversation before. I was still pretty out of it, but I was coming around. Enough to hold on to the basics. Mom had authorized them to do whatever it took to make me healthy. They had a whole eating-disorder clinic there. They wanted me to get better. They were going to give me the tools to love and respect myself. How did I feel about all of that?

I stared at her. I opened my mouth to speak. But how could words help? How could anyone else understand?

And why did they need to? This was my fight. I shut my mouth and turned my head away.

In choosing silence, I finally knew why Maya had made the same choice. Her silence wasn't always anger and pain—it was also healing.

Understand: time passed. I talked to doctors. Went to groups. Saw films. Met beautiful interesting sick people. Visited with Mom and Maya, when they came, which was tons. I accepted that I was sick, and I learned why I was sick, and I learned what I needed to do to get better. I passed room inspections. I got gold stars.

None of that matters.

Oatmeal.

Unflavored, unsweetened oatmeal.

Did you even know that this was a thing? It is. And it is disgusting. I ate a lot of it. Tasteless, boring nutrition. A crucial stage in nursing someone back from Eating Disorder Hell to the Land of the Living. Presumably to help bulimics get used to the act of eating again, something so bland they'd never binge on it and then feel terrible afterward. That hadn't really been my main problem, but I had decided not to fight it anymore. I would go with what they wanted. I would let them help me.

The walls of Eden Park were bright blue. The linens

were light green. The view out my window was about as interesting as unsweetened oatmeal. A bare field of turnips, empty because it was the wrong time of year, full of ice and snow and mud. And then a hill, in the distance. A tiny, unremarkable hill.

The interesting stuff was in the other direction. Where I couldn't see. The highway full of government inspection trucks and tractors and bulldozers and journalists. The town beyond, where construction and demolition and renovation and assessment were ongoing. Hudson was on the national news every night for a while, with my neighbors giving breathless accounts of the events of that night to reporters from dozens of stations. The Great Hog Rampage. Exhaustive investigations were still in progress, but government inspectors said initial information indicated the company had skimped on necessary precautions as it closed up, which led to a systems failure on the pig cage locks. Towns beyond our borders were reporting raids from random rogue hogs, but nothing worse than a plundered garden or garbage can. Whatever mysterious force had marshalled all those animals into an organized bloodthirsty savage force for violent destruction had vanished. No witnesses, no security camera footage turned up any information about a boy with the supernatural ability to control an army of swine.

Cops and random vigilante assholes moved in packs

through the town on motorcycles and piled into the backs of pickup trucks. Wielding shotguns, lassoes, pitchforks, torches. Anything that could be used to hurt and kill little lost swine. Militia mobs of all sizes moved through the forests on foot. Every few hours I'd hear a gunshot. One more attempted murder of a pig, because of me.

Bastien's family had moved already, his father's pre-existing plans to move to the Utica hog slaughter-house having been sped up significantly.

If either one of them had tried to finger me as the bloodthirsty architect of the Great Hog Rampage, their allegations fell on disbelieving ears. And I didn't exactly feel comfortable calling them up to compare notes and find out What Really Happened.

Dr. Kashtan came every day. She brought the *Register-Star* so I could follow the events as they unfolded. But Eden Park had no televisions, probably because you couldn't watch a single channel for thirty seconds without being besieged by beautiful horrible unrealistic human bodies.

"Your fingernails may never fully recover," she said after a week or so of oatmeal. When, I guess, she figured I was strong enough for bad news. "But the big problem is, you damaged your heart," she said. *Damaged. Heart.* The words thudded against me. "Malnutrition

has thinned and weakened the walls of your heart. It's a muscle, after all. The starving human body cannibalizes all available tissue."

When I was twelve, my mom learned she had high cholesterol. The news terrified me in ways I couldn't put a finger on. Now I knew why. It was because for the first time I realized that our bodies are clumsy machines full of strange parts that need expensive maintenance—and we do things to them that have consequences we can't anticipate.

"There will be residual effects, possibly for the rest of your life. Especially in autonomic regulation—which means that standing up, sitting down, anytime the heart needs to pump blood differently due to a shift in position, you may get light-headed, pass out, even experience cognitive changes—memory loss, compromised information processing . . . a lot of things. You may require surgery at some point."

"Um, okay," I said, hiding my fear. Then I ate some more unflavored, unsweetened Jell-O.

Yes. That, too, is a thing. And it is worse than the oatmeal. I spooned it into me, emptiness heaped onto emptiness. When it was gone, I was still the same person. In the same busted body.

I'm telling you the shortened version. I'm leaving out my lapses and relapses, my days when I wouldn't eat, my

frequent moments where the Boy in the Mirror would find me and mock my disgusting flabby soft pale grub-body. I'm condensing months into paragraphs.

Sometimes Mom and Maya came together, and sometimes one came alone. We talked about the devastation. We talked about the weather. We talked about Mom, and her own recovery, the therapy appointments, and the church-basement meetings. We talked about nothing. We talked.

I didn't know what was real anymore. What had actually happened; what part I played.

Because what I remembered couldn't possibly be true. There was no way Puny Matt murdered our whole town with an army of marauding swine.

The most likely explanation: I heard a whole lot of stories about a freak pig escape, and my mind filtered all of that through its own sickness and self-importance to produce a crazy story where I had supervillain abilities and used them to liberate a couple thousand pigs and then use them to burn the whole shitty town down, murdered our town with an army of marauding swine, and then summoned my sister up out of thin air, and she talked me into getting help.

Which would be worse? If it was all made up and I was merely crazy, or if it was true and I had been a monster?

The monster, definitely. Not because monsters are bad. But because I wasn't one anymore.

And I couldn't ask her. Not yet. Because if it *was* my damaged mind, I didn't want her knowing how messed up I had really been.

"Can't wait for you to see what a mob scene our stupid little town has become," Maya said on a Monday morning when she visited me by herself. "Haven't had this much excitement since that time when you were seven, and an allosaurus went tearing through downtown."

"That was a blast," I said.

I didn't ask, *Did you really appear beside me on an ice bridge I built to march my Swine Army across the Hudson River? Was any of that real?* I couldn't ask. For lots of reasons.

"This book is terrible," Maya said, plucking *On the Road* from my hands.

"I love it," I said, leaning forward to grab it back and feeling a sudden swoon. My old friends, the black stars, bloomed on the walls.

"Of course you do," she said, blind to my sudden paleness. "It's a book about male privilege."

"It's a book about *men*," I said. "I'll give you that much. But they don't hurt women. They want to get away from the same nineteen fifties Ozzie and Harriet smiley, fake, evil male-dominated society that was oppressing women."

"Abortions were illegal back then, you know. The pill hadn't been invented. They ride around banging chicks, and those chicks get pregnant, and get stuck raising kids these irresponsible men will never help them with. Anyway, you only like the book because everybody knows these two guys were in love with each other, but too scared to ever admit it or do anything about it."

"I guess," I said. I did not say *I like it because Dad liked Jack Kerouac* or *I liked it because Tariq gave it to me* or *I like it because Tariq likes it.*

"Also?" she said. "Remember that this is the fifties. Jim Crow time. These guys couldn't have gone driving around having wild adventures all over America if they were black. Lots of businesses wouldn't serve them, lots of mechanics wouldn't repair their cars, and they'd risk physical violence if they ended up in a whites-only 'sundown town.' So it's a book about white privilege, too." She handed me back the book.

"Maya," I said. "Why did you choose him over us? Over me?"

She scooted closer to me. Her body felt tight and warm and strong. "Do you remember when we were little kids, how upset you used to get whenever I asked Mom about Dad?"

I didn't.

"It was because you saw how upset *she* got. But as I got older, Mom and me started having more conversations

about him. Who he was, what he was like, why they weren't together."

"She hardly ever said a word about him with me," I said.

"That's because you used to freak out."

"I don't remember that."

"I do. Anyway, last summer Mom gave me his mother's old mailing address, told me if I wanted to get in touch with him that was the only way that might work, and for all Mom knew the lady moved or died years ago. But she also told me that before I did that, I needed to know what really happened between them." Maya looked at me, the hard, shrewd look that reminded me she was ten times stronger than me, and what on earth had I been thinking back when I thought *I* could save *her*? "Are you sure you want to know?"

"If you have to ask me that question, the answer is probably no," I said. "But yes. I want to know."

"He used to beat her. It was a terribly abusive relationship. She loved him, but he was horrible. And it took a long time for her to get up the courage to leave him forever and cut all ties with him."

I was a drum. Empty inside. Echoing. Trying hard not to think about the words drumming into me.

"I know," she said, and touched my wetted eyes. "That's how I felt. I wanted to . . . I don't know what. Tell him off? Kill him? Get revenge? It was dumb, but

that's what I thought."

She took my hand and held it. I wondered if she knew how alike we were, in our hunger for justice, in our dangerous drive for revenge. *Your sister takes things too far,* her bandmate had said, and so, evidently, did I.

"So I reached out. Sent a letter. Said I wanted to meet. Used my bassist's house as the mailing address. He wrote back right away. Said he'd always dreamed of getting this letter. Always felt angry that he was robbed of the chance to be a father. Said he wanted to meet. So we set it up. Arranged to meet at a diner on the thruway.

"I saw him before he saw me," she said, and grabbed and then released a fistful of my hair. "I recognized him by the bright-red hair, the same as yours. And he was handsome like you, too."

"I'm not handsome," I muttered.

"Keep telling yourself that lie, kid," she said. "Whatever makes you feel better. Anyway, I came in the door, and his back was to me. And I remembered what Mom said—about how much she loved him, how he had this weird charisma that kept her coming back even when she knew it was the wrong thing to do, that it was almost like magic—"

I thought of me controlling pigs with my smell, and wondered if maybe my father wasn't a little bit of a hunger artist himself. If maybe everyone wasn't. If maybe a certain amount of supernatural power lived inside us all.

"And I didn't want to like this man. Not even a little. I thought, if I sit down and talk to him, even if it's just to tell him off, I'll listen to what he has to say. I'll treat him with respect, because that's the way I was raised. And what if he casts his spell on me? What if I let go of this anger, this hate? Are we going to just be . . . I don't know, friends? Buddies? I didn't want that. I didn't want him to be in my life at all. But I couldn't just walk away. Not after what he did to Mom. And got away with."

"So what did you do?" I whispered.

"Had a bit of a nervous breakdown, I guess. I don't remember my thought process at all. I didn't think. I just . . . acted. He was sitting at the counter of this greasy-spoon restaurant, near the waitress's station. A big glass pot of coffee was steaming on a Bunn burner, not three feet away. And I just—I . . ."

Here, my sister started crying. Really let loose. I put my arms around her. Held her so tight I felt it in my weakened, starved heart.

"I grabbed it," she said finally, "the pot of coffee. I snatched it off the burner. And I swung it as hard as I could against his head."

More sobbing. I remembered my dream, of the diner, of Maya, of exploding pots and an ocean of scalding hot coffee and an avalanche of broken glass. And her song: "Black Coffee."

"The blood—" she said. "The smell . . . the burning. I

thought I might have killed him. Blinded him. Disfigured him for life. I ran out the door, across the parking lot, through a little stretch of woods, to a Howard Johnson motel. I called my bassist. She picked me up. Promised not to tell. But I couldn't go home. I was convinced he'd track me down, come find me, come kill me. Or call the cops, have them come and arrest me for assault. Put me in jail. But Ani was amazing. Knew just what to do. How to keep me safe. She called everybody over, the whole band—didn't tell them what had happened, but said we had to go to Providence to do some recording. And there I've been, ever since.

"I didn't choose him over you and Mom," she said.

I couldn't say it. But I had to. So I did. "But you did leave. You left us."

She didn't pause. Didn't hesitate. Didn't contemplate diving into one of her patented Maya Ice-You-Out silences. "I did. That wasn't my intention, but it's what happened. It was really dumb. And selfish. And the whole time I was there, I kept coming up with rationalizations, ways to explain this that didn't involve me being a jerk, and I could choose not to see what it was doing to you and Mom. But now I see what a crock of shit all that was." Without blinking, she said, "Mom talked to Tariq."

Time stopped. Stars imploded. Whole continents slid into the sea. I remembered the questions I'd been too afraid to ask when she'd said, *It's no good to be alone.*

I said, "Whaaa," and it went on and on while my weak hungry heart wobbled. "Why did . . . Mom . . . talk to him?"

"She went to curse him out, actually. For breaking your heart."

"Oh."

"She's a smart lady. As a general rule she knows lots more than she lets on."

"I know," I whispered, overwhelmed and dizzy and not from faulty autonomic regulation this time, "but I . . . didn't she . . . how did she . . ."

"She loves you no matter what. That's what's important for you to know."

So the conversation I was most afraid of having really didn't need to happen at all. Okay. That was something.

Maya got up off the bed, went to the window. Her spiky brown hair had been freshly dyed black. Her every step was full of the confidence that would help her conquer the world. I had questions. So many questions. But there would be time. We were both broken, but we were both getting better. Which maybe everyone is.

She hummed a melody, lovely and sad, something I recognized from the eight-song solo demo album she'd been working on. My sister had found a way to channel our addictive/obsessive character traits into something positive. To create, instead of destroy. Maybe I could, too. Eventually.

"Here," she said, and left a Ziploc bag on my bedside table. "Since you stole mine while I was away. I know you like these. So I made some for you. Probably not as good as Mom's."

I ate that tuna-fish sandwich slowly, savoring the too-thickly-sliced challah and the excessive mayonnaise and the touch of lime, chewing every bite a couple dozen times, and when it was gone I felt way closer to being Better than after a whole mountain of unflavored unsweetened oatmeal.

RULE #50

Bad things will happen to you and they won't be your fault. Life is a miserable shit-show for lots of very good people. Lots of very evil people have it easy in life. When bad things happen, it doesn't help to blame yourself, or wish you'd done something differently, or shake your fists at the sky. Accept that the bad things happened, but do not allow them to continue to hurt you.

Bad things will also happen to you that will be your fault. Part of being Better is being able to tell the difference.

DAY: -28

TOTAL CALORIES, APPROX.: 1950

I wish I could tell you that from the moment I entered the hospital, I was strong enough to stop using my abilities altogether. I wish I was brave enough to turn my back on them. But I wasn't.

About a month after I arrived, when the lights went out in the hallway and us crazies settled into our lonely

343

beds, I thought to myself, *How is Mom doing? Has she stopped drinking? Is Maya helping her?*

And once the thought entered my head, it refused to leave.

Find her, it said. *Go to her. Help her.*

I shut my eyes and tried to smell her. Hear her. Teleport to her bedside. Tap into the unstoppable force I used to be able to control.

All that happened was my jaw locked up. When ten minutes passed, and it hadn't unlocked, I pressed the button to call the nurse, and she gave me something to help me sleep, and in the morning my jaw was fine.

I thought a lot about my friend Darryl. The one who'd abandoned me. I'd taken it so personally, convinced myself that he'd come to hate me, that something was wrong with me. But that wasn't true. He'd moved on because of *him*. Because he wanted different things. Because his life was bigger than video games and comic books; because it was easier to find a new life and friends than to be sad about the life and friends he'd lost.

I'd been furious, back when Maya turned five and went to kindergarten. I'd thrown a fit. I couldn't understand how she could leave me alone, but of course it had nothing to do with me.

My sickness made everything about me. My sickness and my selfishness. And the fact that I was still a kid who didn't understand how the world really works.

My powers had come from anger, from hate, from fear, from shame. I had fed them; I let them take me over. And now that I'd turned my back on them, I had nothing.

So, every night I tried again—and failed. And sometimes, but not every time, I wept. Like a man who'd lost both legs or gone blind. What could be more painful than to possess something wonderful and then lose it forever?

RULE #51

Without your problems, you wouldn't be who you are. You would be someone else. Someone significantly less awesome.

DAY: -57

TOTAL CALORIES, APPROX.: 1800

"Friendly's?" Maya asked as we got out of the car. We stared up at the fast-food joint like it was supposed to tell us something, but it had nothing to say.

"We used to come here all the time!" Mom said. "Remember?"

"I guess," I said, and I did—trips to Crossgates Mall for back-to-school shopping, doctor's appointments, a million meaningless little Albany jaunts when we were kids. "She's trying to fatten me up," I said and pointed an accusing finger at her. "I see through your diabolical plot, woman."

"No plot," she said. "Just so damn tired of staring at those four walls."

I was out. After eight weeks, and forty tuna sandwiches, and ten thousand dollars' worth of inpatient rehabilitation treatment costs—covered, mostly, probably, hopefully, by Medicaid once Mom filled out a small mountain of paperwork, which Maya and I would help with, to the extent that we were able—I was home. Back at my real life. Back in my bedroom, with the Boy in the Mirror, and my Secret Stash of Diet Cokes, and the Computer Full of Things That Make Me Feel Worse About Myself.

Getting better is boring. Getting better is slow and frustrating, and you don't want to hear about it. You need to take my word for it, though: it was hell. Every decision was difficult. Every third thought was a terrible and destructive one. I fought with myself five times a day.

It is still a fight. It will always be a fight.

That photo of Skinny Mom still hung on the side of our fridge. Life and genetics could gang up on me at any moment.

"Okay," Mom said, once the waitress brought menus. "Grown-up conversation time. We're all adults now, or close enough to have actual Grown-Up Problems, so we should be able to talk like it. Okay? So let's ask each other anything we want."

"Anything?" Maya and I said.

"Anything. But let's respect each other's boundaries, so if somebody doesn't want to answer your question, we won't hound them about it."

"They can plead the Fifth," Maya said.

"Exactly," Mom said. "Go on. Ask me anything."

Maya and I exchanged a look. The wide-open endless galaxy of questions we could ask was terrifying. What if one of our questions broke her heart? What if one of her answers broke ours?

Maya started us out, asking cautiously: "What are you going to do about a job?"

Mom laughed. "Well, Maya. Funny you should ask. Because I got the call yesterday—the engineering firm that the state hired to rebuild the town, after the governor declared a state of emergency, has offered me a job."

"So that's why we have the money to go out to eat!" she said.

"Well, we will," Mom said. "Soon."

"Doing what?" I asked, picturing my mom heaving a hammer, laying bricks, and my heart hurt, because of course she could do it, but she shouldn't have to, at her age, after working so hard for so long.

"Actually, I'm going to be the site supervisor for several different locations, including the water-treatment plant and the slaughterhouse. White collar, all the way. Driving from site to site, drinking coffee from a thermos, bossing people around."

"Damn," Maya said. "That's amazing. How did you swing that?"

"My boss came through," she said. "He wrote a hell of a letter on my behalf. And even called the place, to follow up."

Bastien's dad. So he hadn't seen me, blind as he was, when I marched a pig army into his house to demolish it. And Bastien hadn't said anything. Who would have believed the truth, anyway? Probably he didn't believe it himself. Probably he thought he was dreaming, or that his memories were twisted by the trauma of having his house destroyed before his eyes. The human mind is weird like that. It'll do anything, construct any crazy story, rather than accept a truth that breaks the rules of the world as we know it.

"I'd have been screwed without it," Mom said.

"What about our house?" Maya asked. "How are we going to pay the rent?"

"Well, we haven't gotten an eviction notice yet," Mom said. "Although we might, any day now. The landlord is pissed, but he's being patient. I pay him what I can out of our savings. Which isn't much. But I suspect that having half his properties utterly destroyed by marauding pigs has got him pretty strapped for cash, so he'll probably take whatever little bit of money comes in. Hopefully that'll last 'til the new job starts and my first paycheck comes in. And you, Maya? What are you doing

about school? College? You missed most of the application deadlines . . ."

"Not much motion since we met with the principal, and they arranged for me to do the work at home until I'm ready to return. I might even graduate with my class. They've offered to help me with deferred college applications, but to be honest I'm not a hundred percent sure I want to go that route. You know? Maybe community college, maybe instant rock stardom?"

Mom laughed out loud.

"I have a question for you, Matt," Maya said, and paused and looked me dead in the eyes so I knew the jokes were being put on hold for a moment. "Why?"

Tariq had asked me the same question. At the time, I'd tried to answer it but all I'd been doing was looking for lies. Ways to not tell the truth. I couldn't be honest with Tariq back then because I could not be honest with myself.

My eating disorder had never been about Maya. I could see that now. My Mission of Bloody Revenge came from the same damaged place as my hunger. I had spent my whole life listening to stories about what a man was supposed to be. Do. Look like. How a man was supposed to act. It had cost me so much hurt and suffering and courage to come out of the closet, to reject a huge piece of The Masculinity Prison that I never noticed I was still stuck inside it.

"I wanted to be . . . strong," I said. "I was weak and disgusting. And when I started to go without eating? For once in my life, I felt like I had some kind of control. Some kind of power. So I kept doing it."

"Oh, my baby," Mom said, and reached across for my hand.

"I knew it was stupid," I said, grateful for the same old security-blanket warmth of her giant grip. "I knew it was hurting me. But I knew that if I let go of it, I'd have to confront . . ."

I didn't finish the sentence. I didn't know how to. They didn't ask.

"Well, nobody asked me what my plans were," I said. "But I want to start applying to jobs in town. Stupid stuff. Retail, minimum wage. Just so I can have some spending money, start saving for college."

And so I can buy my mother an acoustic guitar so she can get back to some dreams she stopped dreaming right around the time life started hitting her upside the head.

"Whatever's wrong with you kids is my fault," Mom said, tossing her menu dramatically in that way she always did when she'd made her food decision, and talking fast, like she'd been working up the courage to say this for a long time.

"Don't be stupid," Maya said, scribbling on a napkin. "Whatever's awesome about us is your fault, too. And we're pretty awesome."

"Yeah, we are," I said.

"Yeah, you are," Mom agreed. "But I tried to hide my problems from you, and they're your problems, too. And if you don't know about them, you can't control them."

"Don't tell me you're a gay boy with an eating disorder," Maya said, and at the sound of the *g* word I kicked her under the table. Hard.

"'Fraid not. But I always take things too far. Sound familiar, Maya? I was like that with your father. I fell for him so hard that nothing else mattered. I loved him so bad I couldn't see straight. So I made a lot of bad decisions. When you started playing the guitar, when you'd be practicing that thing for five hours a day, I saw myself. That same obsessiveness. It made me happy. It also made me scared."

"Mom, don't—" Maya said, but Mom cut her off.

"And you, Matt. You both know by now that I used to have . . . a drinking problem, I guess you'd say. I was an alc—I was an addict."

I looked around for a waitress. Anyone, to come rescue Maya and me from this Special Moment. But the place was packed and no one had time to save me from a stressful soul-baring session with my mom.

"I had a hole inside that I was desperate to fill," Mom said. "I've been talking to your doctor about it. My addiction, your disorder—she thinks they might be connected."

"I think so, too," I said quietly, letting words come out without stopping to think, because if I stopped I'd censor myself, and I was as curious as anyone else at the table about what the hell was going on in my head. "I know what you mean. About the hole."

Maya put her hand on Mom's, which was resting on mine.

"Dr. Kashtan says I can't look to anything outside of myself to fill the hole," I said. "Not money, not success, not anyone else's approval . . . nothing that you can't control one hundred percent." I didn't add, *Not love, not even awesome love with a superhot guy.*

"I believe that," Mom said. "Anyway. I bring all this up to say that if it wasn't for those problems, I wouldn't be where I am today. *We* wouldn't be. Hell, you two wouldn't be here at all. The point of all this is to tell you not to be ashamed of what you are or what bad decisions you've made in the past because of it. But know it. Stand tall in it. Understand it." And just like that, before a single second of awkward silence could set in, she moved us on to safer pastures. "What are you ordering, Matt?"

"I don't know," I said.

Ordering a sundae would have been the easiest thing in the world. Swallowing that thing in five giant spoonfuls would have been simple. And then, a half hour later I'd be hating myself. The hard thing to do was order a grilled cheese sandwich and an extra pickle, the way I

always used to when I was little, and eat it slowly, which is what I did. Mom clapped her hands. "Okay, grown-up conversation over. You are now officially children again. And you must obey me immediately no matter what I say."

"We never did that when we really *were* children," I said.

"Silence," Mom commanded, and we ate.

RULE #52

People only have the power over you that you give them.

> *Unless you're locked up. Or somebody's ward. Or you live under a dictatorship. But even then, their power is a legal fiction. It possesses your body but not your mind.*

DAY: -79

TOTAL CALORIES, APPROX.: 2100

"Good session?" Tariq asked when he picked me up outside the therapist's office.

"Yeah," I said. "I think it was."

Something loud and angry and beautiful and punk was thumping from his speakers. We sat like that for only a second before he put his truck in drive and we started moving.

"Got us lunch while I was waiting," he said, and reached into the backseat for a bulging McDonald's sack.

"Is this a test?" I asked.

"Maybe," he said. "Do you need to be tested?"

"Want to see my food tracker?" I dug out my cell phone, tapped open the app.

"Yes," he said. "Yes, I do."

I handed it over. He hmmphed a couple times then handed it back. "And are you being honest with all of those entries?"

"Of course I am. I'm only hurting myself if I lie."

"You've hurt yourself before."

"Touché, asshole."

Food was still a fight. I cupped a medium french fries in my hands and wanted so badly not to eat them. And then I ate them, one at a time, and I felt fine, because eating was not an enemy to be conquered or sign a peace treaty with, it was a thing human beings had to do to live.

Tariq ate as he drove. I watched him shovel fries into his mouth, marveled at the strong line of his throat when he tilted his head back. His greasy lips were magnificent.

"I still love you," I said without meaning to.

He didn't say anything.

"I'm sorry," I said. "That was jerkish of me to say. I don't want to make things awkward. I'm really happy we can be friends, after everything that happened."

"Me too," he said.

"But . . . maybe . . . friends with benefits?"

He snort-laughed, his mouth full. "Shut up," he said when he'd swallowed.

"I wasn't kidding."

"I know. But still. Shut up."

"Why? I thought we were good . . . together."

"That's why we can't, idiot. Because I care about you, a lot, and it's been really hard for me wondering if you were going to die at any moment. And I could never just hook up with you without . . . feeling it. Falling back in."

"But I'm better now," I said. "I'm not going to keel over and collapse."

"I know. And I'm happy for you. And I really hope you can stay better."

I nodded. I felt full, sleepy.

"How's your dad?"

"He may be Syrian, but he's still acting pretty Egyptian. You know, because he's in denial. Get it? De Nile?"

"If we're not together anymore, I'm under no obligation to laugh at your stupid jokes," I said, although I was, in fact, laughing.

". . . because he's in denial about my being gay," he said after too long a pause.

"Yeah . . . no . . . I got it."

"I got into Wesleyan," he said.

"Holy shit, dude! Congratulations!"

"It's pretty great. Still waiting on a bunch of other applications, but it's nice to have at least one yes."

"You'll get nothing but yeses. You're a goddamn genius."

"Thanks, Matt."

And it was there, then, that it truly set in: we were over. Something about the way he said my name. With warmth, with friendliness, but not with love. We were buddies. That was all.

"My senior year is going to suck without you," I said.

"Naah. You'll be a god to these kids. And it's amazing how little the Hudson High bullshit will bother you once you have one foot out the door."

"I hope so."

On our right, hanging from the sturdy branch of an oak tree, was a pig. With a gunshot wound in its side. Some asshole had lassoed it, thrown the rope over a branch, tied the other end to the hitch of their truck, and drove until the poor terrified thing was hanging ten feet in the air, and then used it for target practice. I shut my eyes and could see it as clearly as if it were happening, this animal dying because of me. I could imagine its fear, its screaming. I practically smelled it. My eyes burned with sudden wetness, and suddenly it felt very hard to breathe.

There goes that autonomic regulation again, I thought, but knew it was just guilt.

"Chicken McNugget?" Tariq asked, extending the container to me.

I took one, held it up, sniffed it. Tore it open. Felt

the hot grease scald my fingers. Looked at the weird soft puffy pockmarked texture of the off-white highly processed flesh inside. Thought about the animal it had been. Apologized to it, and to the dead pig hanging from a tree.

"No thanks," I said, putting it back, and something settled inside me, a decision I'd been mulling over without realizing it. "I'm a vegetarian."

"Since when?"

"Since . . ." I looked at my wrist to consult the watch I was not wearing. "Since five seconds ago."

And I was. As simple as saying it. How had I not thought of this before? A way to make smart healthy food decisions and act out my desire to diminish suffering. It felt like the tip of a beautiful iceberg, this decision. How many more ways were there, for me to act to right the wrongs I saw in the world? Millions, probably. Not with hate, not with violence or anger. With love.

Tariq said, "So . . . what? I'm supposed to just eat that nugget? After you ripped it up with your grubby fingers?"

"You didn't have a problem with my fingers when they were—"

"Shut up, Jew."

"Whatever, Muslim."

We drove. We talked, the light jokey tone staying

with us, but I didn't feel light and jokey. I felt sad. I had screwed up so badly. I had messed up so much. Hurt so many people. Earned my broken heart.

"Let me out down here," I said when we got to the turnoff to the narrow woodland road where my house was.

"Why?" he said. "Your mom knows all about us. And anyway, there's nothing to know."

"Yeah," I said. "I just want to walk a little bit. Stretch my legs. You know?"

"Okay," he said.

"I never had a friend before," I said, getting out, because I was feeling melodramatic. "Not a grown-up one."

"You're going to have lots of friends, Matt. And boy-friends. Way better ones than me. You're awesome, and once you actually start believing that, so will everyone else."

So I wouldn't get every little thing I wanted, just because I wanted it. My desires did not make a difference to the world outside of me. I could not, in fact, bend the fabric of space and time and reality to get what I wanted.

"Later," I said and took the McDonald's bag out of his hand.

"Hey!" he said. "I still have half a thing of french fries!"

"I'm a recovering anorexic, I need these to live, sorry," I said, shutting the door, getting it right on the first slam.

I wanted to be mad at him. Wanted to hate him for rejecting me, for not believing in my getting better, for not reciprocating my emotions. But I didn't. I couldn't. He was fighting a battle just as hard as mine. He had his family damage and self-doubt and whole universes of other struggles I knew nothing about.

<u>RULE #53</u>

Congratulations! With the proper care and feeding, your human body should last you one full lifetime. It will, however, throughout your life, give you shit. Spring new horrific developments on you— diseases, disorders, traumas. Maybe your body came with a free side order of obesity or inherited clinical depression or a tendency toward cancer. Good luck with that. Make the most of it. Treat it right because that's how you'll get the most enjoyment out of it, but understand and believe that you are not your body. You are so much more.

DAY: -79, CONCLUDED

Suicidal ideation.

The phrase wouldn't leave my head. I walked back up the winding wooded road chanting it, and one minute it was a harmless piece of medical jargon and the next it was a pretty appetizing option.

I almost starved myself to death. I broke my mother's heart. I maybe burned down half the town.

I was getting better, but I still had so far to go. So much work to do. And for what? I still wasn't entirely convinced that if somebody suddenly gave me the power to snap my fingers and cease to exist, I wouldn't use it.

I wasn't suicidal anymore. But once you go there, once your mind has seriously weighed it as a possibility, it never really goes away. It's always there—always an option.

What the hell was wrong with me? Life just felt like so much work. Being a grown-up, being a son, being a student—I just wanted to walk away from all of that. Boys still called me faggot. I was still named after something people step on. I still thought about running away a lot. I still made plans to hitchhike or ride the rails or follow the river. I still had the bag full of books and hoodies and diet soda under my bed.

I ate french fries. They were getting cold and they were delicious. I made a mental note to look them up, when I got home, to confirm whether or not they were made with chicken blood or jellyfish guts or beef "flavoring" or some other ungodly unvegetarian abomination.

By then it was twilight. Dark came later and later every day. That was something. A little more light. I held out my hands. I felt the weight of my backpack, the texture of my clothes. Overhead, the branches were bare. I stood at the center of miles of wilderness. The universe was a cold dead place of rock and dust and emptiness

that didn't care whether I lived or died.

A grunting noise stopped me. I turned around to see a large pig wander out of the underbrush. Not a wild boar—its skin was the pale pink of a domesticated animal. I could see its ribs, and the spittle flecked along its tusks. It saw me. It stopped. It opened its mouth. It outweighed me, and it was omnivorous, and it was starving.

It charged.

"Stop, pig," I whispered, bracing myself for destruction, raising my hand—and it stopped. Like, froze in midair. Two legs off the ground, bounding forward. Eyes confused, terrified. My pulse quickened from shock and fear instead of autonomic dysfunction this time.

"Easy there, pig," I said softly, unbelievingly, and lowered my hand. The pig . . . unfroze. Stood there, looking at me. "At ease, soldier."

Could this be true? Could my powers be real? Could they be totally independent of my eating disorder?

"Walk in a circle," I said, and it did.

I took a step forward, and it flinched. "You don't need to be afraid of me," I said. And it softened. Held eye contact. Looking like nothing so much as a big ugly puppy. Did it recognize me? Remember that I freed it? Still respect my authority as Commander in Chief of the Swine Army?

We stood like that for a long time. Pig and boy. Man and animal. The hog had spent its whole life in a cage, waiting for the day when it would be slaughtered, and then, shockingly, out of nowhere, it was free. The thing could die tomorrow, shot by a hunter or hit by a truck, but it was living its life while it could. Its eyes were fearless, curious, eager, excited.

My powers had come from anger, from hate, from fear, from shame. I'd convinced myself that I could only draw strength from self-destruction. But what if that wasn't true?

"Wind," I whispered, raising my arms in front of me and then pulling them to the left.

A sudden gust stripped the last of the leaves from one crooked tree.

I saw with razor's-edge clarity, so plainly that I laughed out loud from the Disney Movie obviousness of it: The greatest power comes from love, from knowing who you are and standing proudly in it.

In the hospital, and at the rehab center, I used to imagine Better was a place you could get to. A moment when I would look around and see that Everything Was Fine. But that's not how this works. Being better isn't a battle you fight and win. Feeling okay is a war, one that lasts your whole life, and the only way to win is to keep on fighting.

"Hungry, girl?" I asked, and held out a handful of french fries.

Her teeth brushed my palm when she snatched them. She could have taken my hand off.

"I'm sorry I got so many of your brothers and sisters killed," I whispered.

Something thrummed in my veins, in my stomach. It wasn't hunger—it wasn't an ungodly destructive superpower rooted in violence—but it was close. I was still that glorious monster that had leveled my town. I still saw how the world worked, understood the systems the powerful used to hurt the powerless. I could change the world.

The pig grunted, looked me in the eye.

"Does that mean you forgive me?"

I ate a couple of the french fries and poured the rest out on the ground for the pig. We chewed together. It was true that a whole lot of pigs were dead because of me, but if it wasn't for me they would *all* be dead by now—or stuck behind bars, waiting to be butchered. Now, at least, some of them had a chance.

I looked up through the cage of bare branches. Any day now, the trees would break into blossom. The cold edge to the wind would fall away. Life would burst forth. My mom had found a good job. My sister would write brilliant songs. I would go to college, see the world, find

my tribe, do something awesome. Burn all the bad shit to the ground. Build something beautiful.

Overhead, without any fuss, the stars were coming out.

ACKNOWLEDGMENTS

I've got a lot to acknowledge. Here's the first thing: When I was fifteen, I had an eating disorder. No one diagnosed me, not even when I hadn't eaten for days and was in so much stomach pain that my mom took me to the emergency room at two in the morning (just like Matt!), because lots of people don't think boys can even get eating disorders. One of the many reasons I wrote this book was because boys are damaged and distorted by the same terrible body-image issues and expectations as girls, and we all need to realize how full of shit that is, and how awesome we are no matter what we look like.

The most important acknowledgment is this one: books have big families. Here are the people who helped birth this one:

Seth Fishman, for being a goddamn genius rock-star agent who took a chance on something completely bat-shit crazy.

Kristen Pettit, who I already knew was brilliant, but until we rolled up our sleeves and took scalpel and chain-saw to this book, I didn't truly understand how much a

great editor is responsible for a book turning out half-way awesome. Thank you for turning this hot mess into something a little hotter and a lot less messy. And thank you to Elizabeth Lynch for rad flap copy and general editorial magnificence.

John Joseph Adams, for publishing my stories when no one else would. And including them in amazing anthologies. And introducing me to Seth. And being just generally a magnificent specimen. Basically, whatever career I have is thanks to you . . . so . . . yeah.

Holly Black and Cassandra Clare, for being the best YA teachers a writer could ever hope to have.

Jacqueline Woodson, for talking me through some tough decisions, and just generally providing the kind of incredible affirmation that I sorely needed through some rough times.

Beta readers Eliza Blair, Richard Bowes, Sadie Bruce, E. G. Cosh, Pratima Cranse, Kris Dikeman, Lara Elena Donnelly, Eric Esser, Barry Goldblatt, Alaya Dawn Johnson, Chris Kammerud, Matthew Kressel, Carmen Maria Machado, E. C. Meyers, and Luke Pebler all caught tons of horrific mistakes, and, I'm sure, numerous offensive asides. Any problems this book still has are in spite of them.

My siblings in the Clarion class of 2012, who made me into something halfway awesome. My comrades in the Altered Fluid writer's group, who made me into

something even closer to awesome.

The Kiefer-Osts, whose lakeside weekends provided me with remembered warmth on many a bleak cold night. My Picture the Homeless family, especially Lynn Lewis & Jean Rice & Tyletha Samuels & Nikita Price & Arvernetta Henry & DeBoRah Dickerson, for teaching me so much about strength and survival and dignity in the face of horrific oppression. Maria Dahvana Headley isn't just one of our best short story writers—she is a paragon of generosity and awesomeness. Kalyani Sanchez, Kathy Rodriguez, Patricia Thomas, R. F. I. Porto, Saffie Kallon, Tim Fite, Trinidad M. Peña, and Walead Esmail were my cheering squad for the years when I was sorely in need of one.

My sister, Sarah Talent, BFF and Number One Fan and Staunchest Ally.

My mother, Deborah Miller, has been my Writer Hero since I was thirteen, when she showed me how to do a cover letter and a self-addressed stamped envelope. She was publishing dark and edgy brilliant stories when I was still a puppy, and her words have inspired me my whole life. But after coming through an unspeakably rough year, surviving some shit I could never have survived, she's now my Life Hero, as well.

This is my debut novel, but it's also my seventh novel. Every single one of its predecessors died a long, slow, painful death that made me generally miserable and

probably pretty awful. My husband, Juancy Rodriguez, had my back through all of it, and through a whole lot of other shit, and without his unflinching love and support and affirmation (and stern admonishments), I probably wouldn't have been able to keep picking myself up to start again. To say nothing of the fact that he turned me on to so much of the art that is most important to me—Octavia Butler, *Battlestar Galactica*, and *Avatar: The Last Airbender*, to name a few—my storytelling chops would still be stunted and inadequate without them.

And finally, my father, Hyman P. Miller, who spent seven years battling cancer. Twenty-four hours before he passed away, we accepted HarperCollins's offer to publish *The Art of Starving*. So pretty much the best thing in my life and the worst thing happened right next to each other. This book is for him, for the lifetime of love and acceptance he gave me, which is how I got through my own miserable high school experience, and for the superpower of self-acceptance.

READ ON FOR AN EXCERPT FROM

Destroy All Monsters

THE MIND FORGETS.
THE SOUL REMEMBERS.

DESTROY
ALL
MONSTERS

SAM J. MILLER

AUTHOR OF THE ANDRE NORTON AWARD WINNER
THE ART OF STARVING

ONE

ASH

"He's sleeping on the front porch again," my mom said, her voice sounding sad the way only Solomon can make it. "Do you want me to have your father talk to him this time, Ash?"

I did not want that. Dad would scare the shit out of Solomon. Our front porch was probably the last safe place Solomon had, and I could never let Dad take that away from him.

"I'll go," I said, getting out of bed even though it was 2:00 a.m.

Not that the time mattered. I hadn't been asleep. I stopped by the kitchen, fished two sodas out of the fridge. Diet Coke for me, vanilla Coke for him. I always made sure we had vanilla Cokes cold and ready.

When I stepped out onto the porch, I was almost ashamed to wake him. There was a cold edge to the night, and he was wearing a tank top and what looked like boxer shorts. He seemed so small, in spite of the bulk of his biceps. The sturdiness of his shoulders.

Another reason I didn't want to disturb him: he was smiling. I only ever saw him smile when he was asleep.

Someone at Solomon's aunt's house—or was it his mother's friend Sioux he was staying with these days?— might have been wondering where he was. Might have been worried about him. But that was a big, unlikely "might." If Solomon had anyone else who cared what happened to him, he probably wouldn't have been sleeping on my porch in October in the first place.

"Hey," I said, sitting down on the porch swing. I noticed he was curled up just right to leave enough space for me to sit.

He mumbled something, curled up tighter. I grabbed one of his feet and squeezed it.

"Ash, hey," he said, like it was nothing, like this was totally normal. The night smelled like rain and smoke and a little bit of skunk.

"Everything okay?"

He didn't answer me right away, and I knew he was weighing his words. Wondering how much to tell me. The stories he told—they were part of why everyone was afraid of him. Crazy stuff he didn't seem to understand

was crazy. A city full of monsters and magic and vicious police officers.

And dinosaurs. With Solomon it was always dinosaurs.

But he didn't talk about any of that. Not this time. He sat up, rubbed his eyes. "Skunk," he said, wrinkling his nose, and all of a sudden he's a little boy and we're ten years old and the world is so big and full of wonderful, terrible things.

I put my arm around his shoulder and he leaned into me so fast and gratefully that it made my throat hurt.

"You're okay," I said. "We're okay."

"We're not," he whispered.

I knew he was right, so I didn't say anything. His breathing slowed down. Solomon was safe, now. We were both safe, so long as we stayed there. Stayed still. Every awful thing was asleep. The night protected us, a deep black star-studded security blanket. I gave him his soda and he guzzled it greedily.

Anything could happen once he stepped down off my porch. Returned to the real world with all its terrors and uncertainties. But in that moment, we had each other.

"You'll be up all night if you drink that," he said, taking the Diet Coke away from me when I popped the top.

"That was already the way things were going."

3

His eyes were huge, and wouldn't move away from mine. I tried not to look into them, but they were unrelenting. "Why?"

I started to say, *It's the meds*, but decided against it. The last thing Solomon needed was another reason to be afraid of medication.

I'd gotten on antidepressants three weeks before. They were just starting to take effect. And they worked . . . mostly. The ground I walked on was feeling less and less like thin ice that might crack open at any moment and plunge me into the dark freezing water where I'd sink like a stone. Any side effects seemed slight when compared to that.

"It's this photo project," I said hastily. "It's a ton of work."

"What's it going to be about?"

"That's the work. Figuring out exactly what I want to focus on." Then I said, "Connor was asking about you."

Solomon stiffened. Sat up. "You two are still a . . . thing?"

"You sound like him," I said. "Always wanting to put a label on it."

"But you still see him. Still hook up."

"Yeah," I said. "Is that a problem?"

"Of course not," he said, leaning forward, holding his head in his hands. So, yeah, This Was Very Definitely a Problem.

I didn't know what his deal was with Connor. Less than a year younger than us, he'd always been Solomon's adoring little stepbrother. If something went wrong between them, I couldn't imagine what it was.

"I should go," Solomon groaned.

"Don't," I said. "Sleep here tonight. You can crash on my floor."

"Your father would murder us both."

"Not *both*," I said. "Probably just you."

"Very comforting."

"Hey, is everything okay?" I asked. "Why'd you come here tonight?"

He rubbed the back of his head. "I don't know. It seemed important at the time. Had to tell you something. Warn you. I don't remember what about."

"Ah," I said. "Well. You can message me, if you remember."

Solomon nodded. His face looked like it was about to crack open.

I wondered: What was it like, losing your mind? Being unable to tell the difference between dreams and the waking world? Not knowing what's real and what's not?

"Later, Ash," he said eventually, standing up. Which is when I noticed he had no shoes. Six-foot-plus, muscular like most guys wish they could be, and he'd always look like a helpless little boy to me.

I watched him lope off, into the darkness. The smell of smoke was stronger now. The cold weather was upon us. Summer was officially over, and I should have been in bed. I stayed on the porch until my soda was finished, and then headed inside to browse through 150 years' worth of photography on the internet until sleep snuck up on me.

TWO

SOLOMON

I shouldn't have gotten involved. They were police officers, and there were three of them, and they were in a bad mood.

It was a cold night, and the streets smelled like a hundred different kinds of smoke. Burning plastic, wood, paper, garbage—all the things people were lighting up to keep warm. Summer was officially over, and I should have been in bed.

My stomach grumbled. I wanted to eat a piece of apple pie and fall asleep for the next several days. I didn't want to save anybody. And chances were pretty good the cops just wanted to scare the old woman pushing the shopping cart. She had a velociraptor on a leash. I wondered if they'd hassled her for its license. Dirty cops

harassing othersiders was nothing new; it happened a thousand times a day in Darkside. But once in a while they picked on the wrong person or pushed someone too far, someone who wasn't shy about summoning up fire or ice shards—which meant the cops were legally within their rights to respond with deadly force.

Which, I suspected, was what they wanted in the first place.

But the old lady's face was kindly. So I did the dumb thing. I started trouble.

"Come on, girl," I said, kicking gently at Maraud's sides. My allosaurus flexed her nostrils, which is how she smiles. She doesn't like bullies any more than I do. Her claws opened and closed and she stepped out of the alley and into the street.

"Hey. Leave her alone," I called.

They looked up at me. Astride Maraud—her mouth open and dripping hot, hungry saliva—I must have been an imposing sight. For a split second, they were afraid. Then they remembered their guns, their power, the city that supported their abuse, and the fear melted away.

"What's it to you?" said one of them. The woman pushed her shopping cart off and hurried down the street, turning only once to mouth *Thank you* at me. Her velociraptor, scuttling beside her, made a guttural noise that Maraud echoed back.

I didn't have a good answer for him. So I did what I

tend to do in stressful situations: I took a picture.

It's an instinct. If you stop to think, you'll miss the shot. And since selling a photo to the *Clarion* often meant the difference between eating and starving, I tended to take the shot.

Problem is, cops hate having their pictures taken.

"Hands up!" they hollered.

My hands went up.

"Drop it!" they said.

"It's not a weapon!" I called, bending my knees, holding up the camera. "It'll break if I drop it, and I can't afford to replace it. So I'm going to put it down very slowly, okay?"

"I said drop it, you—" And they called me a whole bunch of superhorrific names. Fine. It gave me time to set the camera gently on the ground the instant before they walked up and punched me in the stomach. And kept on doing so, until I fell to the ground beside my camera.

"Somebody needs to learn to mind their own damn business," the shortest cop said, picking up my camera. He inspected it, deciding it probably wasn't a weapon after all. He held it out to me, but when I reached for it, he pulled it back and let it drop. Something cracked. I bit my lip to keep from exploding with a string of curses. Maraud huffed and stamped her foot, sharing my anger.

"What's your ability, punk? You a watersider? You have something to do with that robbery last week, down by the docks?"

There was no use trying to deny that I was an othersider. Nobody else would be walking around this part of town at night . . . with an allosaurus. It's why they call us *monsters*, because we're not afraid of the creatures that walk the streets of the city. "I don't know what my ability is," I mumbled.

Lady cop laughed. "You expect us to believe that?"

"I don't expect anything from the fine upstanding police officers of Darkside," I said. "Not when law-abiding othersiders get jumped every day by goons, and you never do a damn thing about it. Not when those attacks are on the rise and y'all never seem to notice."

Unfazed by my attitude, dude cop continued, "We run your name, we gonna find anything? Prior offenses, associations with illegal organizations?"

"I don't have any *current* offenses," I said. "Let alone priors. I'm not doing anything wrong. I just don't think it's right for you to harass helpless old women."

"This punk," lady cop said, and came at me fast.

"Shit," I whispered, closing my eyes and bracing myself for the inevitable assault.

Instead, an explosion rocked the street.

I opened my eyes to see two of the cops running down the street. One was on his radio. Flames swirled

up from a scorched hole in the side of a building around the corner.

"What about this guy?" asked the woman, lingering with her hand in the air in front of me, like she was aching to get in one last punch.

"Don't be an idiot," short cop said.

Then they were gone. I breathed a sigh of relief. Exhaustion washed over me. I needed to be in bed beneath the bridge.

"You're welcome," called a voice from a doorway across the street.

I squinted into the shadows. "Who's there?"

He strolled into the street with a smile on his face and his hands full of lightning. A single bolt spun in a beautiful sphere, dozens of strands of it intricately coiled together. It was beautiful—almost as perfect as his face, which looked like summer even though summer was gone.

"Hi, Niv," I said. "I take it that's your handiwork burning a hole in that building over there?"

"Hey, Solomon. You looked like you could use a bit of help."

"Thanks," I said.

He clasped his hands together and the lightning shrank down to nothing. I felt so happy to see him, and I hated how happy I felt.

Niv was the personal bodyguard for my best friend,

Ash. Yes, *that* Ash—the Refugee Princess, living in hiding in the very same city where her mother was queen.

Niv's job was to move her from safe house to safe house. Because Ash was an othersider, and the queen's advisers assured her that if the bigoted citizens of Darkside ever found out that her daughter was part of that hated and feared community of so-called criminals and parasites, there'd be a full-scale uprising.

So Ash and Niv were on the run, in the city she'd rule one day. If she lived long enough—and the city didn't tear itself apart before then.

"Cops have been getting even crazier lately," he said. He smelled like burning sage—a clear, cleansing smell.

I've never trusted him. I don't know why. Maybe because he's so beautiful? Pretty people can't be relied upon. They have too many options.

"Can't you talk to her mother about that?" I asked.

"You know as well as I do that the police are a law unto themselves. They don't even listen to the queen."

"She could fire the commissioner, hire somebody who isn't such a bigot."

Niv laughed. "You think she's in a hurry to trigger a coup? They'd take her out in a second if they thought she was trying to change the way they do things."

"I guess," I said begrudgingly. Cass, the editor in chief at the *Clarion*, Darkside's scrappy opposition paper,

had said the same thing to me not so long ago. "How's Ash?"

"She's . . . the same."

I winced, remembering Ash staring out the window at the snow, not even seeing it. Playing our favorite songs for her and seeing that she felt nothing. "Can't the doctors . . ."

"She's seen dozens of them, and they all say the same thing. The only way to bring her out of this . . . whatever it is . . . is to lift the spell the court sorcerers put on her."

"Shit," I said. We both knew her mother would never allow that. The spell kept Ash's powers in check, buried them deep. Since the age of twelve, Ash had been childlike on the best of days, and semicatatonic on the others.

"She's fighting it. Wherever she is in there, she's working hard to break the spell. That's why they have to keep making it stronger. She's nobody's victim."

"Of course she's not."

"Come see her," Niv said, and named an address in Raptor Heights. A rough-and-tumble working-class neighborhood where lots of othersiders could afford to live, because its bad reputation kept the rents down.

"Should you be telling me that?" I asked. "Isn't her location supposed to be a huge secret?"

He looked hurt, and I didn't feel bad about it. Protecting Ash was my primary purpose in life. This pretty boy I'd been crushing on since I was ten didn't matter, in the grand scheme. "She loves you, Solomon. There's no secrets from you."

"But if you'd tell *me*, who else would you tell?"

Niv frowned, and his face flashed red. "Good to see you, Maraud," he said, patting her side. She blinked slowly, in happiness. Then he turned and left.

Maraud took two steps to follow him. When I pressed my hand to her neck to stop her, she turned to look at me in confusion.

"Sorry, girl," I said, climbing on board. "Let's head for the bridge."

As we went, she kept trying to turn. Still following Niv's scent—and Ash's, on him.

"Ash is going to be okay," I said, knowing she could hear the lie in my voice. "We're all going to be okay."

A ship's horn sounded in the distance, low and lonesome, arriving from the Spice Islands. We hurried home through streets that stunk of cinnamon.

Haunting novels by
Andre Norton Award–winning author
SAM J. MILLER

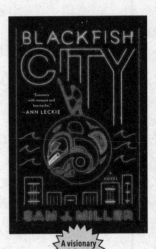

A visionary adult sci-fi fantasy

READ THEM ALL